D1449573

More Praise for Jay Lake

"Jay Lake is one of the few writers who can take the dumb things words are for most of us — with their everyday meanings and their everyday forms — and weave transcendence and meaning out of them."
> —Sarah A. Hoyt, author of *Any Man So Daring*

"Don't try to label him. Just read him!"
> —Andy Duncan

"What good fiction is all about."
> —*Chronicle*

"I was astonished and delighted by the range of this fine new writer, and you will be too. Discover Jay Lake now — he won't be a secret much longer."
> —James Patrick Kelly, author of *Think Like a Dinosaur*

"Jay brings a radically varied palette of life experience and a scary brilliance to his work. This stuff is weird. Enjoy."
> —Nina Kiriki Hoffman

"You can always count on a kind of gutsy vitality [from] Jay Lake. This is fiction that isn't afraid to get its hands dirty."
> —Ray Vukcevich

ROCKET
SCIENCE

JAY LAKE

FAIRWOOD PRESS
Auburn • Seattle

ROCKET SCIENCE

A Fairwood Press Book
August 2005
Copyright © 2005 by Joseph E. Lake, Jr.

Fairwood Press
5203 Quincy Ave SE
Auburn, WA   98092
www.fairwoodpress.com

Cover image © Getty Images
Cover and Book Design by Patrick Swenson
Introduction © 2005 by Deborah Layne

ISBN: 0-9746573-6-0
First Fairwood Press Edition: August 2005
Printed in the United States of America

For Floyd and Lois Bryant, whose secret history this almost isn't, and Uncle Paul, a tiny piece of whose real history this is, and everyone else in my family who hopes no one notices them in this book.

INTRODUCTION

DEBORAH LAYNE

Who Needs the Yellow Brick Road?

Oz has got nothing on Kansas. At least it's got nothing on Kansas Jay Lake Style. You don't need to travel a yellow brick road to get to the Weird Stuff. You've just taken the first step on a path to a strange and wonderful — well maybe wonderful isn't the right word, but strange definitely comes in here — place.

In this Kansas, you won't find good-natured farm-hands dispensing life wisdom. No cute little dogs either. Instead, you'll find a recently returned WWII vet with a somewhat variable moral compass, a gang of elderly enforcers, the local police, the state police, Army CID, Nazis, Reds, and just wait until you meet Pegasus.

Rocket Science is Jay Lake's first full length novel and it more than delivers on the vast promise of his short fiction. Nearly all the obsessions that drive Jay's short fiction are on display in *Rocket Science*. He loves gadgets, and the gadget at the center of this story is one of his best. Jay's fascination with United States history is on full display here as well. Jay is fascinated by conspiracy theories (and theorists), secret identities, spies, and gadgets. Did I already mention the gadgets?

I've known Jay as a short-story writer since late 2000. Indeed, I published his first two collections, *Greetings From Lake Wu* and *American Sorrows*. In 2004, he won the John W. Campbell Award for Best New Writer on the strength of his short fiction. Here, in *Rocket Science*, Jay has a chance to engage his vast imagination and follow the trails of "what ifs" that drive his storytelling.

If you've read much of Jay's work, you can probably guess that his background is...well...diverse. His father's career in the foreign service took Jay and his sister all over the world. He's lived in Taiwan, Nigeria, and even Texas. He survived high school at a New England prep school (Choate) and college at the University of Texas.

These early experiences inform much of Jay's work. He writes about people who are not exactly in their natural element. He writes about the weirdness that underlies the ordinary. And yes, there is weirdness everywhere. Even in Kansas. *Rocket Science* is your ticket to glimpse a little of it. Enjoy.

Deborah Layne
Portland, Oregon
May, 2005

CHAPTER ONE

When my best friend Floyd Bellamy came home from the war in Europe, Augusta, Kansas had a parade for him. The city meant to honor all the returning veterans, but the parade happened just as Floyd got off the troop train at the Santa Fe depot on the east side of town. There he was — healthy, tanned, fit, blond hair and white teeth gleaming in the Kansas summer sun, turned out in his best khakis with a chest full of medals and a jaunty scar on one cheek.

Floyd's Nazi bayonet instantly won the loyalty of every boy in town, while his casual good looks won the heart of every girl. Mary Ann Dinwiddy had a prior claim that she quickly enforced with a long, slow kiss in front of Mayor Cooper, Bertha Shore from the *Augusta Daily Gazette*, and various assembled dignitaries on the reviewing stand.

So Floyd stood there in front of the reviewing stand on the bricks of State Street with Mary Ann, prom queen of 1940, hanging on his arm in her best silk stockings and a polka dot dress. He waved at the high school band, smiled at the Masons and the Shriners, saluted the VFW. Half of Butler County was out to watch the parade, and Floyd took center stage in their minds.

Later, we sat in Lehr's having coffee and cherry pie, on the house for Floyd. The whole restaurant bustled around us, dishes and steam and the smell of fryer grease conspiring to leave a little zone of respect and quiet for the war veteran and his friends. My bad leg bothered me more than usual, the ghost of childhood polio, and I felt crabby from the heat. Floyd and Mary Ann looked as if they had stepped out of a Hollywood poster. He'd picked up a couple of female admirers, who managed to ignore me completely — even Lois, who I'd taken out from time to time over the years.

The way it had always been with Floyd.

He was telling us about the Battle of the Bulge, him trapped in burnt-out tank while half the German army marched by in one direction, then marched back the other two days later. "You should have been there, Vernon. Half the gosh darned Wehrmacht — oh, golly girls, I'm sorry. Pardon my French." Floyd actually blushed. I remembered him in junior high school, practicing that blush in a mirror. He could wiggle his ears, too. Anything for the girls.

Sometimes I hated my best friend.

"I'm trapped in this tank with these two poor Gusses who got it when our tank took a shell, and —"

"Floyd," I interrupted. I'd had enough. "You were in the Air Corps. What were you doing inside a tank?"

Floyd gave me one of his patented double-edged looks, the kind that had promised Indian burns or wedgies when we were kids. "I was on detached duty. Intelligence work, you know." He winked at the girls. "They had a picked crew of us flyboys on the ground looking for secret German aeronautical stuff OSS thought was hidden in Belgium. Hush-hush, can't discuss."

Floyd was no pilot, I knew that for sure. He had shipped over as a mechanic, maintaining those big Pratt & Whitney engines on the B-24. But I wasn't going to bother my best friend with facts again. He had a story to tell, and he was going to tell it come hell or high water.

Floyd cleared his throat. "*As I was saying*, I'm trapped in this burnt out tin can with two dead GI's — God rest their souls." He paused to bow his head in a brief moment of respect. "There I am peering out through the driver's periscope, watching the Jerries beat a retreat from our boys, when something really unusual went by."

"What did you see?" asked Lois, on cue. Floyd was getting her best face for free, the look that I had to pop for a dozen roses and dinner in Wichita to see. I loved Floyd like I loved my brother Ricky, but right then I could have blackened both his eyes for him. Of course, my brother broke my arm once, before the big creep went off and got killed under MacArthur on some jungle trail in the Philippines.

"It was a cargo convoy, pretty small — just three vehicles. But there were SS troopers escorting it, and the troops were letting it by. That was kind of unusual, you see. By that time in the war the Germans were having a rough time of it, so combat units always got top priority. The SS had better things to do than ride herd on supplies."

"What was on the trucks?" asked Mary Ann.

Floyd winked again. "I can't rightly tell you. That's a matter of national security and I've been sworn to secrecy. But you can bet I followed those trucks and snooped a look at their cargo that night."

As a matter of fact, I *did* have a security clearance, because of my work in the aircraft industry. I knew perfectly well that people involved in security matters never talked about it. All through the latter part of the war, since I graduated from Kansas State, Lois thought I was a parts manager at the Boeing plant in Wichita. I really did that job, part-time, but I had actually been working with a combined team from Boeing and North American on improving ordnance deployment from bomb bays. Still, there wasn't much point in stopping Floyd when he got going. I could tell from the soft, shiny look in Mary Ann's eyes that Floyd was going to get whatever he wanted tonight.

Floyd settled back in at his parents' farm out east of town, about halfway between Augusta and El Dorado on Haverhill Road. His dad's health had broken while Floyd was away, so like the good son Floyd pitched in with fixing the run-down farm equipment that was all Mr. Bellamy could afford. Harvest time wasn't far off, even in August, and Floyd was needed.

I was proud of him. Whatever Floyd had or hadn't done in the war, even if he was the biggest liar God ever placed on His green Earth, Floyd loved his folks and did every dirty, nasty or just plain dumb job that had to be done on a small farm. All of it without a word of complaint, not even to me in private. Every Saturday night he would come into town in his dad's Willys pickup truck. He and Mary Ann and me — and sometimes even Lois — would drag State Street, just like we were back in high school again. If we were feeling flush, we'd pile into my '39 Hudson 112 and head to Wichita for steaks and beer.

Fall came and brought the end of the Pacific War with it, along with the harvest. Ever since I went off to college, I had managed to avoid working the fields. First there was school, then the war work. But V-J Day had come and gone, with Harry S Truman's atomic gamble paying off handsomely. Being from Missouri, Harry S was almost a Kansas boy, so we were as proud of him as if he were truly one of our own.

Now, with the war over, things were slowing down. I managed to keep my job at the plant, working full-time as a parts buyer now, but I had evenings and weekends free for the first time in years and a chance to use up some vacation time. So I took two weeks off to help the Bellamys with their corn harvest, bad leg and all. Heck, they'd done so much for me over the years it was the least I could offer.

"Hey, Vernon," Floyd puffed from the top of the silo. Poor or not, the Bellamys had a lot of corn. "Guess what?"

I killed the clattering engine of the battered Farm-All tractor, leaned on the steering wheel and wiped my forehead. "What?"

"Remember that German convoy I told you kids about?"

Floyd had never mentioned the Battle of the Bulge again, so I figured the whole story had been bravado, the returning hero showing off for his hometown chums. "Yeah..." I said cautiously.

Floyd had his exasperating I've-got-a-secret grin. "Borrow one of your old man's trucks tomorrow. I've got something coming on the Kansas City train."

My dad ran an on-again, off-again cartage business and had a couple of old medium-duty Mack trucks — a 1932 AC model and a 1929 off-highway AP model — which more or less worked. If you were lucky and it hadn't rained lately. "What — a panzer tank?"

"Nah," said Floyd, still smirking. "Something much better. Trust me, you'll love it."

I drove the grumbling old AC stakebed up to the freight platform at the Santa Fe depot. Though my bad leg was on the gas pedal side, I never was much for the pressure of a clutch, but Dad's old monsters speed-shifted anyway. Kansas weather is unpredictable in late September, and Wednesday's warm fall day had turned into a damp, windy Thursday. If it started raining, the Mack might well decide to develop one of its innumerable electrical shorts and refuse to run until Thanksgiving. The weather bothered my game leg as well, tugging at the muscle and joints like a pair of harsh hands until simply bouncing along in the cab was sheer torture.

Floyd was already at the station, sitting on hood of the rusted Willys pickup rolling a cigarette. "Hey, Vern," he called, waving his handiwork. "Smoke?"

"No, thanks. Trying to quit." Truth be told, I had never enjoyed cigarettes much. Floyd didn't drink or smoke before he went off to Europe, but nearly four years in the Army Air Corps had turned him into a connoisseur of bad habits.

"Train's late," Floyd said. He cupped his cigarette to light it in the damp wind.

"I can see that." I stretched my back and studied the ragged gray sky. How soon would it rain?

Floyd finally got his cigarette lit and took a deep drag. "You didn't tell your old man what you were doing with the truck, did you?"

I laughed, trying to disguise the bitterness. "He was sleeping."

Floyd smirked. "Drunk again?"

"Yeah, drunk." I didn't like to talk about that. Dad's drinking was one reason I took a room in Mrs. Swenson's boarding house on Broadway Street. I hadn't liked stepping over him on the hall floor, or under the kitchen table, or on the porch steps — wherever he was when his drinking finally overcame his muscle control. My polio had disturbed him enough — Dad always called it "the disease that ruined my son." But Dad had given up and crawled inside his bottles since Mom died.

Floyd studied the railroad tracks. "What are you gonna do now?"

"About Dad? Not much I can do." *Except clean his side of their joint cemetery plot*, I thought.

"No, no," Floyd waved a hand. "I mean, the war's over, America's getting back on its feet, all that stuff. Everybody will go off rationing soon, the service is discharging a million guys just like me, jobs are tough to get. What are you gonna do?"

Floyd knew I had a good job at Boeing, and a college degree and pilot's license to go with it. I figured he was really talking about himself. Floyd didn't much like to ask for help, or even advice. I spoke carefully. "Well...I figure I'll marry the right gal, maybe buy a house here in town. Keep working in Wichita." *Watch my Dad die from drinking.* "What about yourself? Got plans with Mary Ann yet?" Plans more complicated than condoms and a mattress in the back of the Willys, at any rate. He kept both in the barn at home when he wasn't planning to use them.

"Yeah, we've talked." Floyd flashed me his million-dollar smile. He really ought to move to California and go into movies. "She wants kids, dogs, a flower garden. I don't know..."

Floyd was rarely uncertain of anything. It was almost charming to watch him wonder. Every now and then I could still see the rough-edged farm boy who'd carried me around school and town on his back, that first year after the polio got me. "So, what's on your mind?"

"Well, you know...take you, Vern."

I hated being called Vern. He knew that.

"While I was off getting my gourd shot at in Europe, fellows like you were safe back here going to college and getting swank jobs you could keep after the war. A poor Gus like me, never even finished high school, I don't have a chance unless I want to run my father's farm. Any fool can see that's a losing game these days."

I was too surprised at Floyd's comment about high school to be angry for what he said about me. We'd get back to that later. "Floyd, you finished school. I remember. You were sick for graduation, but so what?"

Floyd shook his head, then took a deep drag off his cigarette. "No. That was just a story. I failed senior English and American History that spring. I was ashamed, so I didn't tell no one. Then I went off in the service the week after everybody graduated. It never came up again."

I didn't know what to say to that, but I tried. "Still, a guy like you — you've got a clean service record, you know aircraft engines. You could get on at Boeing or Beech Aircraft in Wichita real easy. I can put in a word for you in personnel if you'd like. Maybe get you on my team, even." I tried to sound enthusiastic. He might be the nearest thing I had to a brother these days, but Floyd working under me was not high on my list.

"Yeah, well, about that service record..." Floyd broke off and stared down the tracks. He looked like he might bust into tears right there. Then we both glanced up at the scream of a train whistle, coming in from the east.

"What happened?" I asked gently.

"Nothing." Floyd wiped some dust from his eyes. He gave me another million-dollar smile. "I'll tell you sometime when we've got nothing better to do. There's plenty of work coming for both of us on that train."

The Santa Fe Baldwin 4-8-4 oil-burner sat just past the platform, chuffing and wheezing. It was a big steam engine, fairly new, black as Tojo's heart with white and gold lettering. Even though my life was about aircraft, I appreciated the design compromises and manufacturing know-how that had gone into that magnificent beast belonging to the previous century. This was the age of flight, and my heart always wanted to soar.

Odus Milliken the railway agent, a cadaverous veteran of the Spanish-American War who seemed likely to live forever, had told us that this route would be getting the new diesels soon, so we'd better say goodbye to the steam trains. As much as I admired the old machines, I could live without the noise.

Odus and Bertie the switchman had conspired to drop two flat cars off onto the depot's freight siding. One was loaded with an enormous crate, the other had something bulky secured under a tarp. Floyd and some of the old guys from the Otasko Club strained with the swing-arm block and tackle on my Dad's stakebed truck to shift the massive crate from the first flat car. With my bad leg and all I stayed out of the way. The crate was almost too big for the truck — easily large enough to contain a small omnibus. I couldn't imagine what something so massive and heavy could actually be. Had he shipped home artillery? I wouldn't put it past Floyd.

Odus stood with me, shaking his head and laughing in his creaky old-man voice. "Those boys are idiots," he said. "They ought to trot over to the lumberyard and borrow a forklift. It's gonna take them all day to get that crate off. Plus he's got that other load, too."

I hadn't realized that both flat cars were for Floyd. Where had he gotten the money for the freight charges? "What else does he have?"

"Come on," Odus said. "Let's have look."

Odus and I walked around the flat cars, staying out of the way of Floyd's work party. Odus untied the lashing that held one corner of the tarp to the second flat car. We lifted the canvas and saw a massive rubber tire. I peered up. "It's a truck."

"Really?" asked Odus. "I never would have guessed."

I eyed the four-foot drop off from the flat car to the rails below. "How are we going to get this onto the ground?"

"Well, if they'd listed this correctly on the manifest, I would have had it off already," said Odus sharply. "I've got a ramp we can drop at the end of the car. You just drive it off. Why don't you pull the tarp off it while I go set it up?" He trotted away.

I tugged and pulled to get the tarp off the truck. The tarp was huge, heavy and damp, and nearly smothered me when it finally slid off. That was when I discovered it wasn't a truck. It was a halftrack. Definitely German — field gray with the big black cross on the doors. Floyd had shipped himself a German army vehicle complete with bumper numbers and swastika. But it was the weirdest halftrack I'd ever seen — nothing like those newsreels of troops riding in an armored box over muddy, cratered landscapes.

The front looked just like any truck built in the last fifteen years — I didn't recognize the make, of course, but it had to be German. The tracks in back looked a whole lot like an old Caterpillar 60 with extra wheels in the middle to extend the tread length. But the body on top was planed and angled like it was meant to fly away. There wasn't a vertical surface anywhere on the back of the halftrack. I cocked my head, studied the thing. It really did look streamlined, or perhaps as if it had been meant to deflect explosion.

"Oh, Floyd, what have you done?" I whispered to the halftrack.

It started raining as soon as we left the depot and headed out of town, and it poured all the way back to the farm. I kept praying that the creaky old Mack would make it without sputtering to a halt. I didn't look forward to dragging the truck and Floyd's monstrous crate down muddy dirt roads with Mr. Bellamy's ancient Farm-All. Lucky for me the spirits that moved the old truck smiled, and it kept turning over in spite of the dampness.

Somehow we got the vehicles all the way to Floyd's place without attracting attention from the Butler County Sheriff. We parked both Dad's truck and the German halftrack in Mr.

Bellamy's ramshackle barn. All but a few of the cattle had been sold over the summer, because large animals had become too difficult for the Bellamys to manage. In addition to a whole gallery of rusted plows and spreaders, generations of rotting hay and Floyd's recreational mattress, the barn now sheltered an inbred tribe of resentful cats, three blank-eyed heifers, a single goat, and some stray bantam hens with one nasty little rooster. That left plenty of space for us.

Floyd got out of that weird halftrack and leaned on the fender, flashing his million-dollar grin. He patted the Nazi vehicle. "What do you think, Vernon? Hometown boy makes good."

"Smuggling back a Wehrmacht halftrack hardly counts as the crime of the century," I snapped.

"Hey," Floyd said. "It's not just a halftrack. It's a *Feuerleitpanzerfahrzeug auf Zugkraftwagen.*" He rattled off the German tongue-twister like he'd been speaking the language all his life. "Adapted from the Jerries' V2 control post."

That explained the shape. It really *was* a blast deflector.

"Cheer up," Floyd continued. "The f-panzer's just a souvenir. What's inside it, and inside the crate — those are the real prizes." He paused, mock serious. "And *they* may well be the crime of the century."

"Really." I couldn't decide if he was crazy, stupid or pulling my leg in a very big way. Maybe all three. The war addled people.

"Come on, take a look." He walked to the back of the halftrack and stepped up onto the ladder that hung from the hatch at the rear of the strangely-angled cargo box. A huge stainless steel padlock secured it, with an eagle engraved on the lock body. The bird was so large I could see it from ten feet away. Floyd took a key ring from his pocket and fit one in.

"That lock looks like it's worth a fortune all by itself," I said.

"Oh, probably." Floyd shrugged. "Some kind of special SS lock. You want it?" He turned to face me, open lock in his hand.

"Nah, keep it. It's yours." His words about wartime stay-at-homes like me taking all the good jobs still stung, in part because there was a measure of truth to them. I figured Floyd was going to need all the valuables he could get in life. Unless the truck was full of diamonds. Or something worse.

Floyd pulled open the latch and swung the door wide. He stepped up inside, calling, "Get in here."

I stepped up the ladder to peer in. There was a profusion of radio and electronic gear in the truck, much of it obviously installed in haste. Loose wires trailed everywhere, and a box of stray vacuum tubes was jammed under an operator's console. A hooded glass screen was bolted to one side of the van, while racks of gear lined the other. It looked like a radio operator's idea of heaven.

Or maybe hell. I wasn't sure which.

"What does it all do?" I finally asked. He'd mentioned the halftrack was an adapted V2 launch controller, but as far as I knew they were ballistic rockets — nothing that would require all this radioelectronics.

"I got no idea," said Floyd cheerfully. "That's why you're here."

"Floyd, I am a materials science engineer specializing in aeronautics. I know how to refine aluminum, how to machine wires and struts. I can find my way along the parts list of a B-29 in the dark. I don't know *anything* about electronics, past winding a radio crystal." I waved my hands around the van. "This might be a television studio for all I can tell."

Floyd didn't seem perturbed. "Vern, you'll do fine. The boffins I...well, got this from...they said the German word for this thing translated as 'telescanner' or 'farseer.'"

I knew about radar, from my work at Boeing, but it wasn't common knowledge in the fall of 1945, so I didn't say anything. But this truck certainly seemed as if it could have been used to control a German radar installation, perhaps out in the field.

Floyd looked at me, waiting for me to answer. I just stared at the electronics and wondered how long we would both spend in the stockade at Fort Leavenworth for this. After a few moments, Floyd spoke again. "You haven't seen the best part yet, old buddy. This f-panzer is just a sideshow. Let's open my crate."

I followed Floyd back out of the control center, whatever it was. I carefully shut the door behind me. Floyd had removed the shiny German lock. I looked around for him, but he had disappeared, only to return a moment later with two long-handled crowbars and an axe.

"We've got to tear this baby down," he said, handing me one of the crowbars.

"Uh, Floyd, let's talk this over first."

"Sure, sure, Vernon. What's on your mind?" Floyd was obviously feeling expansive. I might too, if I'd swiped a German secret weapon.

"Look, I don't know how to say this, but...I don't want to look in that crate."

Floyd's eyes crinkled as his mouth turned down. It was like he was acting out his emotions. "I thought you'd love this stuff."

"Oh, I could love it, believe me. Only, what's in that telescanner truck of yours is enough to get us both put away for a long, long time. That's a military secret Floyd. I don't know where you got it, I don't know how you got it, and I certainly have no idea how you got it all the way from Germany to Kansas, but it's—"

"Belgium, actually," Floyd interrupted.

"Gosh darn it," I yelled. "I don't care if you bought it in the camel market in Timbuktu! That thing is trouble, great big heaping buckets of trouble. Either you go and drop it in a quarry, or we call the authorities in Wichita and hand it over to someone in a position of responsibility. I don't want to know anything more about it. Ever." I turned my back on him.

Floyd made me so furious, sometimes. For years, he had gotten everything he wanted on charm, good looks and athletic ability. But the war was over, we weren't in high school any more, and Floyd's thoughtlessness was really starting to show through. I couldn't even begin to imagine how Floyd had thought stealing some Nazi secret weapon and shipping it back to Kansas would be a good idea. Not even he could be that dumb.

"Vernon." Floyd spoke in his small voice. I was about to hear the I'm-so-sorry-it's-all-my-fault-it-will-never-happen-again speech. I could recite that one from memory. "I'm not going to apologize for what I've done," he said.

He surprised me. Floyd really did. Maybe he was growing up after all. "What are you going to do?" I asked, turning to face him.

"I'm going to ask you to do me one more favor. Then, if you don't want any part of this, walk out of the barn and go home. Just forget the whole thing. I'll never say another word, you'll never be involved again. If there's any trouble your name won't come into it. Promise. Honest injun."

I knew from long experience what Floyd's promises were worth. He was sincere — he was always sincere — but somehow things never quite worked out. Now he was taking a whole new approach to conning me into something he knew I didn't want to do. That made me curious. The scam was obviously huge. Being an idiot, I took the bait. "Maybe. What's the favor?"

Floyd smiled again, flashing that million-dollar grin. He played lousy poker because you could always tell when he knew he had won. "Just take a look in the crate. One peek, I promise. After that, either you'll be in or you'll be out. And I guarantee you'll know what you want the second we open that crate."

I shook my head, but I couldn't stop from cracking a smile. "Floyd, I've got to hand it to you," I said. "You could sell ice makers to Eskimos."

He handed me one of the crowbars. "Take that end of the crate," he ordered, "and I'll work the other. We can pull this face off all at once."

We dropped the wooden stakes off the right side of my Dad's old Mack truck. With a strain on my gimpy right leg I got up on back of the bed where I pulled and tugged with the crow bar on my end of the crate. It had been nailed shut by an expert, that was for sure. The wood groaned and splintered before the first nails loosened. As I worked, I noticed that the crate had the words "Scrap Metal — Sharp Edges" stenciled on the side. I wondered if that was a sample of Floyd's sense of humor.

With a mighty grunt, Floyd heaved at his end of the crate. The wooden wall came swinging down. I jumped back out of the way, falling off the truck onto my butt on the littered floor of the old barn. That hurt like blazes, and it was a miracle I didn't get punctured by some old nails or worse. There was a resounding crash as the wood hit the floor, sending loose straw and dust clouds flying and bringing outraged squawks from the bantam hens. It darn near nailed me, too.

As the dust settled I stood up off the floor on my shaky legs and craned my neck to look into the crate. After a moment, I knew two things.

First, even though I couldn't properly see the oddly twisted and curved lines of the thing, I knew I was looking at the most gorgeous aircraft I had ever seen. It looked as if it had been milled out of solid titanium, so smooth I couldn't even see the joins.

Second, I was going to find a way to fly it or die trying.

CHAPTER TWO

"The Cuban War! *There* was a war!" Mr. Bellamy promptly fell into a coughing fit. He had become so ill so fast, it was strange.

The Bellamys' dining room was a claustrophobic landscape dominated by a claw-footed dark oak table with matching chairs upholstered in a faded blue floral print. An orphaned breakfront that wasn't related to any of the rest of the furniture hulked along one wall, while the remaining open space was littered with strangely-carved end tables and stained glass floor lamps from back East somewhere. Doilies were scattered on every flat surface like white crows in a cornfield. Everything was sandwiched between carpets the color of my gums and a pressed-tin ceiling corroded to a splotchy black.

Mrs. Bellamy patted Mr. Bellamy on the back. They were of a feather, those two, old as the hills and tough as nails, at least before Mr. Bellamy's latest illness. Mrs. Bellamy looked like everyone's grandmother, pale with curly white hair and thick around the waist. Mr. Bellamy was an old shoe — wrinkled, brown and tough.

"Now Daddy, what have I told you about yelling?" Mrs. Bellamy turned to face me and Floyd, her pinched face flushed with anger. "What is the matter with you boys? You know not to excite him."

"I, we —" I started to say, then stopped at a look from Floyd. Mrs. Bellamy was already ignoring me again, patting Mr. Bellamy's back as if he was a colicky baby.

"Don't bother," whispered Floyd. "You'll just cause a fight.

He comes out of nowhere with this stuff, and Mama always blames me. At least you're here as a diversion."

I picked at my baked chicken. One of the yard hens had met an untimely demise to give us a fresh, farm-cooked dinner. The feral bantams in the barn were too small to bother with.

"Now Archie, there was a hero," announced Mr. Bellamy as he got his breath back. He resumed his oration as if he had never been interrupted. I was fascinated by the way he blindly waved his carving knife to punctuate his monologue. "Archie rode up San Juan Hill with Teddy Roosevelt, you know."

He stabbed the knife at me. "Did you serve in the Spanish-American War, Veldon?"

"Ah, no sir." I wasn't even born during that war. I was certain that the question was rhetorical anyway. Mr. Bellamy wasn't interested in my biography.

"He was a hell raiser, that Archie," said Mr. Bellamy with the great sigh of old man who'd wrested satisfaction from his life.

"Alonzo, don't you use those words in my house," warned Mrs. Bellamy. "Besides, poor Archie died of the influenza down there in Florida along with all them other boys."

"He was serving his country," grumbled Mr. Bellamy. He set down his knife and glared at me. "Which is more than I could say for some people at this table. Your parents never did have a candle in their window for you, did they Varney?"

I flushed a deep, hot red. My brother Ricky may have died in the Philippines, but all the bombers built in America would never make up for the fact that I wasn't allowed to serve. Not to people like Mr. Bellamy. Never mind that Mom was gone too.

Mrs. Bellamy came to my rescue. "Alonzo Hartwig Bellamy, you apologize to poor Vernon right now. He did his best for our boys in the war, with his bad leg and all, which is more than you did when poor Archie went off to die, or during the Great War, either."

"I served my country!" bellowed Mr. Bellamy, picking up his carving knife. He started off into another coughing fit and collapsed into the tureen of gravy next to his plate.

"Vernon, I'm so sorry," fluttered Mrs. Bellamy as she helped her husband up, dabbing at him with a napkin.

He seemed disoriented as they walked slowly out of the dining room. I could hear him muttering, "Never know what Floyd sees in that Volney boy anyway..."

Floyd shrugged and smiled at me. "Hey, Vern, I'm sorry, too. I guess I shouldn't have asked you to stay for dinner, but I was excited."

I felt distant, sad. I understood how hard it was to be Floyd, beneath the bluster and the charm. "Is he always like this now?"

This wasn't the Mr. Bellamy I remembered from my childhood, who taught me how to drive when Dad was busy and Mom wouldn't get in the car with me. I realized how out-of-touch I'd been with Floyd's folks while he was fighting overseas. I was preoccupied with Mom's death and Dad's drinking, but that was no excuse.

"Yeah." Floyd toyed with his chicken, using his fork to shove it around. "Uncle Archie died of the flu in a camp in Florida. Daddy never got over it, I guess."

"Archie was your Daddy's brother?"

"Yeah," said Floyd. "They were twins. There's a picture of the two of them at the 1896 Kansas State Fair in the upstairs hall."

"I always wondered who those boys were."

"Hey," said Floyd. "He didn't mean that stuff — about not being in the service and no candle in the window. Mama knows about your brother and everything. And Daddy's just old and confused. Some days he's fine, some days he thinks he's Woodrow Wilson."

"I know. I'm used to it, Floyd. The worst thing that could happen to a fellow in the war was to get killed. Back home, we just went on living and living, and the young guys like me that couldn't go...well, it wasn't much of a life."

He laughed. "You're crazy. You had the jalopies, the jills, the jobs. Heck, I'll bet you got three squares a day all through the war. You should see what we ate over there."

"Yeah, maybe I had a job, but half the town thought I was a coward and the other half thought I was a fool." I slammed a fist into the table, setting the plates to rattle. "I can't even walk straight up a flight of stairs. There's people said I should have lied about the polio. Like I could have hid my game leg from an Army doc? And none of the girls wanted anything but a soldier to date. No action here."

Floyd smirked. "Not like the action we saw in Europe, that's for sure."

I knew exactly what he meant — Belgian girls and French wine. I don't think Floyd ever saw a bullet in Europe. Not even with his Battle of the Bulge story. Floyd worked on bomber engines, and they park those nice, expensive airplanes a long way from the front lines. Nevertheless, he was over there while I was safe at home in Kansas.

"Besides," Floyd continued, "without you fellows home building tanks and planes, I'd still be hip deep in a trench somewhere in France, I'm just sure of it."

"I know. They also serve who stay home and listen to the radio." I pushed my plate away. "Let's clean up for your Mama. I'll bet she's got her hands full with Mr. Bellamy acting up."

"Now that's the Vernon I know," laughed Floyd. "Always ready to do someone else's chores." He followed me into the kitchen with an armload of plates.

And yet, underneath the pain of his snippy words, I could still remember Floyd carrying me through summer fields, laughing at the crows and singing campfire songs.

We went back into town late that afternoon, driving the Farm-All because we couldn't bring Dad's truck or the halftrack, and Floyd had left the Willys down at the station.

"I can't believe we're riding fifteen miles on a tractor to go back and get your dad's truck," I said, shouting over the clatter of the engine. Mr. Bellamy needed to give this thing a valve job, really bad. A new muffler wouldn't hurt, either.

"It's a longer walk," Floyd yelled back. "Especially with your leg. I'll bring the tractor back tonight. You come over tomorrow in Daddy's truck."

By the time we got to the depot, my ears were ringing. Odus Milliken was just locking up for supper.

"Boys," he said as we shut off the tractor and got down to stretch. "Pretty strange shipment you got in today."

Floyd smiled at me like he'd been expecting the question — which made me wonder if he'd planned to leave the pickup here for this exact purpose.

"Odus," he said, taking the railway agent's arm. "As one veteran to another, let me buy you a beer. The State Street Lounge good enough for you?"

"Well, I was heading home for—"

"Nope. Dinner's on me, too." Floyd cocked his head at me. "Come on, Vernon. We'll let you sit in. But Dutch treat for you, mister stay-at-home."

I was glad for lengthening shadows. They hid my renewed blush as I limped after Floyd and Odus.

The State Street Lounge was crowded with roughnecks from the Mobil refinery over on the southwest side of town. The war might be over, but America's appetite for petroleum didn't seem to be. The workers seeped in with their greasy overalls and their steel hardhats and took over the place. A lot of the guys were vets like Floyd — the women and kids and oldsters that had run the refinery during the war were dumped for men who needed the jobs as soon as those men had come home, despite Floyd's fears about employment.

We wound up in a booth at the back, me, Floyd and Odus, not too close to the radio speakers. Everything was dark red, almost the color of wine, except the plywood floor which was covered with peanut husks. The whole place reeked of stale cigarettes and old beer — that bar smell you probably find everywhere in the world. Floyd flagged down a waitress, who surprised me by laying a big, wet kiss on Floyd's cheek. I wondered what Mary Ann would have thought about that.

"Hey, Midge," Floyd said. "You know Odus Milliken, from the station." She winked at him. "And my buddy Vern, works over in Wichita." I didn't get a wink. "Beer all around."

You couldn't get liquor by the glass in Augusta. A fellow had to drive to Wichita for that privilege.

Even though Floyd was being free with my Dutch treat money, I wasn't going to argue about the order — I'd just sip around the edges. It was Floyd's show, and I wanted to see how he would manage Odus. My buddy could be a real artist when it came to handling people.

"I thank you kindly, Corporal Bellamy," said Odus, "but what's the real story here? You've never stood an old man a drink before. Why start now?"

Floyd leaned over the table with a look on his face like he was going to share the Secret of Life. "Business confidentiality, Mr. Milliken. Commerce in all its glory, bringing jobs and money to Augusta."

Odus drummed his fingers on the table for a moment. "Floyd, it's none of my business what people do or don't bring in here from Kansas City or Chicago or Baltimore. Heck, London or Hong Kong don't make me no never mind. But I saw you drive a Nazi war machine off that flat car Floyd Bellamy, me and half the town. That ain't business, that's plum *weird*. What the hell are you up to?"

I was pretty interested in Floyd's answer to the question.

"Business, Odus, is about getting ahead of the other guy. Santa Fe Railroad's going diesel, right? Tell me, why is that?"

Odus shrugged. "Don't know the details, ain't my job, but it's about cost I reckon. Steam locomotive's expensive to operate and maintain. I hear one man can run two, three diesels together. Try that trick with steam, you're like to wind up in the ditch with thirty tons of scrap metal parked on your forehead, right quick."

"Cost." Floyd ticked his points off on his fingers. "Efficiency. Quality. Same reasons we won the war. We could do it better, faster and cheaper than anyone else."

He glanced around the room, made a show of checking for eavesdroppers. The conversation paused while Midge brought our suds. Floyd got another wink. She never even looked at me. "I'd never be one to give aid and comfort to an enemy, but Odus, you've got to know the Jerries had some great technology. German optics, chemicals, color dyes, fertilizers, machine tools — best in the world before the war. Heck, they'd still be the best at that kind of stuff today if those bombers Vern built hadn't flattened them."

My B-29s only flew in the Pacific theater, which Floyd knew perfectly well, but this was his spiel.

"Maybe you have that right," Odus answered grudgingly, "but it feels darned weird to be talking up the enemy."

"They're not the enemy any more," Floyd whispered fiercely. "Those are our boys now. If General Patton had had his way, we'd be fighting side by side with the Jerries against the Red Menace already." He sat back in his seat and took a long pull off his mug. "No reason in the world some hard-working American boys can't make money off some of Jerry's good ideas."

"I ain't giving you no money," said Odus automatically.

Floyd waved his hands, as if pushing Odus away. "No, no, Odus, you misunderstand me. I don't want your money. I just want to keep a lid on things for a while — maybe four, six months."

"Lid?" Odus sipped his drink. I toyed with mine, then shucked a couple of peanuts from the little ceramic bowl.

Floyd gave Odus a narrow-eyed stare. "You see that halftrack I pulled off the train?"

Odus chuckled. "Of course."

"It wasn't no halftrack."

Odus' chuckle turned into a laugh. "Floyd Bellamy, if you're going to flim-flam me, you're going to have to do a lot better than that."

"No, Odus, it had wheels and treads. That's not what I mean. But that funny little housing on the back? It was a mobile fertilizer plant. High-yield fertilizer straight from bunker-grade crude. Nazis had to develop that stuff to survive near the end of the war when we had 'em cut off from overseas shipments and on the run."

Odus gave a low whistle. I was pretty impressed myself — Floyd must have worked on that routine for a while.

"Anyway," Floyd continued, "Vernon here's an engineer. Me and him are going to break down that equipment, reproduce the process, and make Augusta, Kansas the fertilizer capital of the world. And we only need one thing to do it."

"What?" After that last bout of resistance, Odus was completely under Floyd's spell. I figured Floyd could get money from him now if he had a mind to.

Floyd reached across the table to touch Odus' lips. "Your silence," he said.

Odus sipped from his beer and thought that over. He glanced around the bar at the oil-stained roughnecks. I could almost see him thinking about all the wells in eastern Kansas, the business it would bring to the railroad, wondering where the plant would be built. I've got to give Odus credit — he held back.

"I'll make sure the boys keep their mouths shut," Odus finally said. "I'll put out the word it was European farm machinery."

Floyd clapped him on the shoulder. "Odus, we'll all be famous someday, because of the wisdom of men like you."

If I had half Floyd's gift of gab, I'd be a wealthy man. Somehow on the way out the door, he convinced me to keep the tractor and drive it back to the farm the next day.

Early that morning — it was a Friday — I drove my Hudson the thirty mile round trip into Wichita and borrowed some tools from work, including a magnifying glass and a set of measuring calipers. I was extremely curious about the manufacturing history of the airplane we had hidden in Floyd's barn. When I got back to Augusta, I parked down by the railroad depot and got on the Farm-All. My knees would be sore by the time I got to the Bellamy place, but Floyd could darn well give me a ride home in his dad's pickup.

When I came sputtering up their drive into the yard of the farmhouse, Floyd and Mrs. Bellamy were sitting on the front porch in the deep shade of the giant wisteria that grew on the front of their house. From the parlor, you couldn't even see outside, just a dark jumble of sticks and leaves. I killed the Farm-All out by the oak tree and walked up to join them. I was covered with mud and sweat.

"Vernon, you really should take more care of yourself," Floyd's mother said.

"Good morning, Mrs. Bellamy."

"I'll fetch you some apple cider." She swished inside, under way with the same slow determination as a Mississippi barge.

Floyd stretched his arms upward, rolling his neck to clear a crick. "Have a nice night?"

"Went home, listened to the radio."

"I really appreciate you taking care of the tractor. I had to catch up with Mary Ann."

"Without your mattress in the truck?"

"Vern," Floyd hissed. "Mama's right in the house." He grinned. "Besides, there's other places and ways."

And women, I thought, remembering the waitress laying that big old kiss on Floyd in the State Street Lounge. I'd never know, at least not until I was married. If.

Mrs. Bellamy came back on to the porch, rescuing me from my thoughts. "Floyd tells me you boys have a special project going in the barn."

I glanced at Floyd. "I was wondering when he was going to let you in on our little efforts."

She handed me an apple cider, then sat on the glider. It hung on rusted chains from the wasp-blue porch ceiling, which was why I had taken one of the shell-back metal chairs. I was too much the engineer to trust those old chains and their hidden mounting.

"I don't hold with airplanes, Vernon Dunham," she said. "I know its what you do for a living and all, but they are the work of Satan."

"I'm sorry you feel that way, ma'am." I'd gotten this lecture when she found out what I was studying in college, and gotten it again when I went to work at Boeing. I'd never had the heart to tell Mrs. Bellamy that I was a licensed pilot.

"If God had meant man to fly," she went on, "he'd have given us brains like the birds."

"Uh, yes, ma'am." I couldn't work out if that meant only the stupid should fly, or the fearless, or the natural aviators. It didn't matter — the general tone of her opinions was quite clear.

She shook a finger at me. "Rest assured, Vernon Dunham, Daddy and I will stay out of that barn. But you know what that means?"

I shook my head, eyes wide. I glanced at Floyd for a signal. He just covered his mouth and laughed with his eyes. "No, ma'am, what does that mean?"

"You have to help Floyd with his chores."

Of course.

In the barn, we set about stripping the rest of the crate off the aircraft. That took some doing to accomplish safely — Floyd had to rig a block and tackle in the rafters so we didn't have any more incidents like yesterday's near-accident with the first panel. I spent the whole time focusing on the wood, cursing and picking splinters out of my fingernails. Every time I looked at that damned airplane I'd stop working and just stare, until Floyd yelled at me to get back to work.

Several hours' work with the crowbars and the ropes exposed the airplane, sitting on aluminum landing skids on the crate base, still on the bed of Dad's truck. I didn't want to move it off the truck until I knew what I was doing — we didn't know the simplest things, like the attachment points for a safe lift. Besides, Dad wouldn't miss his equipment for weeks, even if he somehow managed to sober up in the mean time. Nobody else would even care where the truck had gotten to.

"That is just about the smallest airplane I've ever seen," I told Floyd. We were on a break, sitting on the stacked crate panels and drinking root beer from bottles Floyd had brought in a little bucket of cold water from the spring house.

"Not as small as it looks." Floyd took a deep swig of his beer. "It sort of folds in on itself."

I stood up and walked around the back of the truck, inspecting the aircraft from various angles. "It is sort of...*folded*," I told him. "You're right. Crumpled, almost...but not like a wreck." God knew I'd seen plenty of those along the way.

"What are those planes they flew on aircraft carriers?" Floyd asked.

"You mean the F-4U?" The Chance-Vought fighter had folding wings so it could be stored efficiently in the below-deck hangars. "It does look folded. But why bother? This wasn't carrier-based, was it?"

"Arctic duty," Floyd said, "but I don't get all the details. That's why you're here."

I shot him a look. "I understand you were spinning a line with Odus about the fertilizer. Hell, it was a great grift you did on him. What's your line with me? Where is this thing going when we crack it open and work it out?"

Floyd smiled. "Blue sky, Vernon. You and me and that thing heading for the open air."

I snorted. "You never did anything just for pleasure."

"Well," Floyd said, glancing at the mattress in the corner behind a rotary plow, "a few things."

"Cripes," I muttered. He never would change, my buddy Floyd. In a way, I had to admire that. I struggled back onto the bed of the truck and pulled out the magnifying glass and the calipers.

Up close, it still looked seamless, like a milled block of metal. I decided it wasn't titanium, but I was hard pressed to put a name to it. I resolved to take some shavings into work for analysis —

Jay Lake

I'd be going back next week to my regular schedule. Regardless, this aircraft was easily the most finely machined piece of equipment I had ever seen in my life.

It took me almost ten minutes to identify an actual joint in the body segments. The folds and crumples in the airframe that were visible from a distance seemed to vanish into smooth convolutions up close. Sort of like looking at the ground from a thousand feet up — the abrupt lines of the watersheds so obvious from the air are impossible to find on foot.

Using the magnifying glass and the calipers, I tried to measure the manufacturing tolerance in the joint. The metalwork was too finely machined for the scale my calipers could manage. "Damnation," I hissed.

"What?" Floyd had been watching me without comment from a perch on the corner of the truck bed.

"I'm going to have to find a micrometer to measure this join."

"Why do you care?"

I sighed. "It's not obvious to me what this is made of. Or how it was built. Most aircraft are lightweight deathtraps — wood or aluminum bolted to a skeleton, cables and wires running through. There's a hundred ways to cut into one, a thousand ways to shoot one down. This thing...the Germans have a great reputation for quality metalwork, and some of the best machine tools in the world. But this, it's way beyond anything I thought possible." I tore my eyes from the rounded edge I was fondling to glance at Floyd again. "Which of their aircraft designers did this? Do you have any idea how?"

"No. Like I said, why do you care? Here it is."

"I don't mean to sound goofy, but it makes things a lot easier if I know what it was for, who built it, why. Floyd, it doesn't even *look* like an airplane. It's obviously meant to fly — I'm guessing that when all the folds straighten out into their proper positions it'll be a lot bigger than it is now. It's basically just a great big wing. That's damned hard to do."

Floyd shrugged. "It was a secret project. They wanted to use this thing to challenge our air superiority late in the war. I don't know a whole lot more — most of the documentation was destroyed."

I didn't want to ask why the Army hadn't taken this thing to Wright Field. I knew perfectly well Floyd had somehow stolen an entire airplane and its ground support. I was a willing accessory after-the-fact to his crime just for the privilege of being around such a glorious machine. But I really wanted to know where it came from. I really wanted to be in the mind of whoever built it.

I turned around to ask Floyd the question again, but he was gone. Fine. I would study my airplane, understand it, and be very careful of whatever scam Floyd was running on me. He might be my best friend, but I knew him too well to trust him completely — with my life, yes, but not with my honor.

He wasn't going to tell me everything he knew, I didn't have to tell him everything I discovered.

CHAPTER THREE

fter lunch, we were back in the barn. I wanted to make the most of my last few days before getting back to work. "You know what I really hate?" I said to Floyd.

"What?" Floyd was measuring distances to rig a block-and-tackle to get the airplane off the flatbed.

"I'm going to go in to work on Monday, sit around all day talking about fasteners — you know, clips and rivets and bolt shear and tensile strength. If I'm lucky. Sometimes I have to go count the damned things, when the guys down on the floor find extras they shouldn't have after attaching a wing or something."

Floyd snorted back a laugh. "Yeah, I'd hate that, too."

"That's not what I hate." I set my hands on my hips and just stared up at the collapsed beauty of that aircraft. "It's just my job. What I *hate* is that I'll be there instead of here, and I won't be able to talk about it. Not one little syllable."

"Oh, Vernon." Floyd shook his head. "We can't talk about this to nobody."

"Do you think I want a permanent vacation in Leavenworth?"

He laughed at that, his smile pulling a reluctant chuckle from me in turn.

I was up on the trailer with the aircraft again, while Floyd crawled around in the rafters making sure the rigging points for our eventual lift were secure.

"How did it fly?" I called up to him.

"That's your problem."

"No, I want to know what you saw. Or were told by those 'boffins' you spoke with. It doesn't have any propellers, or even engine cowlings. Heck, the darned thing doesn't even have a cockpit windscreen." Lindbergh had crossed the Atlantic without one, but I wouldn't care to fly in combat that way. Did the pilot use periscopes?

"Ever heard of a *Schwalbe*?"

Schwalbe. I vaguely remembered vocabulary lists from college. "German for 'swallow,' I think."

"Right. It was this Nazi secret weapon. The Jerries called it *Turbo*."

"Oh, the Messerschmitt 262." I knew what jets were. We'd seen some of the classified research at the plant, mostly on the know-your-enemy line, because the Japs had been rumored to be building an Me-262 knockoff, the Nakajima Kikka, or "Orange Blossom." Not that I'd ever seen a jet airplane, or even so much as a jet engine.

And Floyd was right — this had to be a jet — no air screws, no place for them, and the smooth, curved lines that I had seen discussed in literature and had hashed over in late night engineering bull sessions. But this couldn't be an Me-262. I had no idea how the Germans had manufactured this thing, but it didn't come off any normal aircraft assembly line.

Even more than the fabrication techniques, the metal itself bothered me. The thing had obviously taken damage, because there were fairly crude aluminum patches on the bottom. Also, some of the tubing in the landing skids looked freshly milled and much less carefully finished than the fuselage work. But the rest of the ship was as smooth as a peach, and almost warm to the touch.

Climbing carefully down off the Mack flatbed, I went over to the f-panzer and stepped up into the cramped control box. I wanted to look around, to see if there were any more clues to the strange nature of my aircraft.

The f-panzer was just as crowded as I had thought, looking inside it past Floyd the previous day. There were no vertical surfaces, and the only horizontal area was the floor — everything else sloped like a pup tent. And it was all Nazi gray, hard-edged and sharp. The inside smelled of old metal and sweaty socks. Floyd's Battle of the Bulge tank story was on my mind, though it didn't look like anyone had died in there.

I'm not especially tall, but even I had to hunch to get into one of the operator's seats. The sloped rear armor above them had embedded glass vision blocks that yielded a blurry, dark view of the inside of the barn.

Passing over the control panel for a moment, I swiveled one of the chairs to look over the glass screen console. It looked just like the few American-built cathode ray tubes I'd seen — slightly bulbous with rounded corners, set in a grounded metal frame. There weren't a lot of uses for such a thing, which confirmed my suspicion that this was a part of a German radar rig. The rack-mounted equipment on the other side was more confusing. It had obviously been hastily installed, apparently as an afterthought to the radar screens.

I studied the racks carefully. Most of the gear was electronic test equipment — a heterodyne tone generator, test probes, similar things I didn't recognize in detail. Next to the electronics kit there was a set of shockproof braces holding a small metal box. I unlatched the braces and opened the box.

Inside the box was a twisted piece of metal that looked for all the world like flowing quicksilver frozen in place. I knew perfectly well mercury didn't have a solid state under room-temperature conditions, but the glossy, gritty sheen of the thing was hard to classify. It was about six inches long by half an inch wide, with three prominent buttons. It fit snugly in the palm of my hand, the eye-bending shape as comfortable as if it had been made from a cast of me.

I stepped to the open hatch to get better light and studied the metal piece more carefully with my magnifying glass. It was made of a similar material as the aircraft — another smooth, unclassifiable metal. And the workmanship obviously didn't match anything else inside the radar truck. I decided to try again to get some history on the aircraft from Floyd. He'd been unhelpful before, but I couldn't tell if he was being stupid on purpose, catty or just not paying attention.

Then maybe I could know whether it was a good idea to do some laboratory testing.

"Floyd," I called, climbing with care out of the halftrack. I set the twisted metal piece on the deck just inside the open door. Floyd was still in the rafters, checking bolts. I was prepared to buy the new block-and-tackle we needed with some of my meager savings as I didn't want to trust our prize to Mr. Bellamy's aging hardware. It made me nervous enough to have to rely on the beams of the old barn's roof to support the weight of the aircraft.

"Yeah?"

"We need to discuss this aircraft."

He looked down at me for a moment, then carefully set down his measuring tape and tools before crawling back to the hayloft. A minute later he was standing in front of me, picking straw out of his hair. "We've already been over all this. What's so important now that I had to climb all the way down here?"

"Where exactly did this thing come from? Germany?"

Floyd scuffed his shoes. "Belgium."

"No, Floyd." He was being stupid on purpose, I decided. "You may have found this in Belgium, but this was not built by Belgians. Belgians make French fries and wine and wool, but they do not make precision aircraft. Certainly not during a Nazi occupation."

"Well, it *is* German." Floyd looked at me, almost pleading.

That was the nub of the problem. I couldn't see the angle yet, but this was the finest piece of technology ever produced by the hand of man. Who but the Germans could do it? Besides the United States of America, of course, but it wouldn't have been sitting around in a Nazi convoy in Belgium if we'd built it. "How do you know that?"

He looked at me like I was crazy. "I found it on a German truck behind German lines."

"Where was it made, Floyd? Where did it come from?"

"I don't know. Why does that matter so much?" Floyd was starting to whine, which with him meant he was about to get belligerent. "We want to use it ourselves, not return to sender."

"Look, I don't want to know where or how you swiped the thing. We're past that — I've bought into your deal. It's just that the metalwork in that aircraft is the most unusual stuff I've ever seen. I should be able to recognize it. Aircraft materials are my profession."

"Well..." said Floyd. "There's a big pouch of documents on the back of the f-panzer's hatch. If you can read German, they might tell you something."

This was more like it. "Why didn't you show me those in the first place?"

Floyd shrugged. "Slipped my mind."

"Fine, fine. Let me have a look."

I pulled myself up onto the edge of the truck bed, in the shadow of our mysterious airplane. I really needed to drag a normal chair into the barn, before I hurt my leg even more. Floyd jumped up past me, stepped into the f-panzer for a moment, then brought me a fat manila envelope from inside. I opened it to have a look at my new toy's pedigree.

The envelope had a cover letter and a large bound report. The whole thing was typed on SS stationery — original ribbon, not carbon, which was interesting. That meant the Nazi officers in charge had intended for very few, if any, copies to be distributed. There were also all kinds of attachments and appendices, charts, graphs and photos, along with a folder full of flimsy carbon copies of what had to be operational orders. All in all, it looked like manuals and field orders for the aircraft. The fact that I even held these documents in my hand at all confirmed that Floyd had pulled an enormous con on the Army — no military intelligence officer who could still draw breath would have left a trove like this loose inside captured enemy equipment.

Despite my college classes, I didn't read German very well. Lack of practice, for one thing. I knew a few technical words, newspaper terms like *blitzkreig*, but the grammar defeated me, as well as those incredible compound words that just balloon into monstrous collections of meaningless letters. German and English are pretty close in some ways, though, so I could puzzle out words such as *Nordeuropa* and *Arktischer*. By and large the meaning of the documents escaped me. It was apparent that I would need some translation assistance. And just as apparent that I didn't dare show these papers to anyone.

"Floyd," I called. "I'm going to the library."

"Okay," he shouted from somewhere above me.

"And I am not driving that infernal tractor back into town."

I could hear him laughing almost all the way back to the parked Willys.

Augusta is like any other rural town with high hopes and a small budget — two- and three-story commercial buildings downtown, railway depot a little bit bigger than it really needed, public school a little bit too small. It was nice to see business booming now that rationing was going away and the boys were home. There had been more weddings in the past few months than in the whole year before. That meant more people spending money at Lungford's Furniture, that meant the land office kept busy. The war had been kind to Kansas, at least after the fact.

I went by my boarding house and dropped off the Bellamys' truck for my Hudson. I was tired of the Willys' shuddering, bouncy ride, and the truck's balky shifter. Driving downtown, I parked on State Street and headed around the corner for the library. The car wallowed a little bit. I'd have to remember to check the air in the tires.

The public library was about what you might expect in a town like Augusta. It was upstairs from the police and fire stations in the city building, which also held City Hall and the Municipal Court. Three rooms plus an office, brick-walled with oak wainscoting and big oak shelves and some fairly nice Middle Eastern carpets on the floor. Part of the collection had pride of place in glass-doored cabinets near the circulation desk, while a few wingback chairs and set of study carrels stood along the north wall by the tall double-hung windows. Old gas lighting still hung on the ceiling, electric wires wrapped around the fixtures from the flickering bulbs.

The library was stocked with a few magazine subscriptions, an *Encyclopedia Britannica* from the turn of the century, and a couple thousand books in the stacks, mostly classics and general literature. It made me miss the Hale Library at Kansas State, but it really wasn't a bad little place.

I didn't have a library card, of course. You had to be a property owner to have a library card in Augusta, and I rented. I guess I could have asked Dad to get me a card, but then he would have expected something in return. That wasn't worth the trouble. So when I needed to use the library, I just did my reading inside the building.

The small reference section actually had a German-English dictionary. It was printed in 1892, so I didn't figure on getting much in the way of aeronautical vocabulary. But it might help me puzzle out the sense of what I had. The technical stuff I could probably pick up from cognate words and borrowings — I was well aware that the United States shared an academic and research tradition with Germany.

I grabbed one of the study carrels by the window and spread my papers out. The cover letter from the envelope looked like an ordinary business letter — I could probably translate it without the dictionary. Instead I went to work on the table of contents of the bound report.

The title translated as something like "Report on the Arctic Expedition for Secret Contact." It was pretty weird. Some of the section headings had titles like "Science and the Supernatural" and "The Hollow Earth." Puzzling through this stuff in my bad translation was like reading Charles Fort. Backwards. In a mirror.

Taking a break from the dictionary and the headache it was inducing, I looked at the foldout map bound into the main report. It showed a dotted line, which I assumed to be the route of the "Arctic Expedition for Secret Contact." The path left Tromso, Norway, headed up to Nord Kap, over the frozen seas to Svalbard, an ice-locked island in the Arctic Ocean, then described a circular path across the Arctic ice cap before returning to Svalbard. There were circles with citation numbers marking two points on the ice cap and a spot on the north coast of Svalbard. Dates and times noted along the path indicated that the expedition had taken place in the spring and early summer of 1943.

I flipped through the report, looking at photographs and diagrams. I had an uncomfortable suspicion about what I was going to find. First, there were smiling men in Arctic survival gear waving at the camera. Then there was a picture of a convoy of half-tracks and dog sleds, obviously the expedition's main body, with a zeppelin hanging distant in the bright sky. There were several pictures of camp sites. There were pictures of bone fragments being dug out of the ice, with a whole chapter devoted to discussing them. I kept looking.

The kicker was the first picture I found of the aircraft, my aircraft. It was in the ice, at the bottom of a freshly-dug hole. Part of the machine was still embedded in the ice beneath it, surrounded by a dark stain. Two smiling Germans leaned against the side of the aircraft, waving at the camera. It looked like nothing so much as a rounded-off flying wing, something the Germans had been developing since the 1930s. I'd seen pictures in a Dutch aviation magazine called *Vliegwereld*.

How long would it take for an airplane to become embedded in ice, I wondered? If you landed a DC-3 on the Greenland ice cap and just walked away, how many years before it lay ten or fifteen feet below the surface? Ten years? A hundred? A thousand? I got queasy just asking myself the question. I was afraid of how the answer would make me feel.

Something that old was impossible.

Inhuman.

Impossible.

Trying to put that *last* thought out of my mind, I walked back into the reference section, wondering where I was going to find information about the rate of deposition of ice caps in the Arctic region. I might have to call a friend from my time at Kansas State who now did graduate meteorology work back East. I didn't know what I would say when Freddie asked me why I was interested in such a strange topic.

The assistant librarian, Marion Weeks according to the nameplate I had seen on her desk when I first came in, approached me. "Mr. Dunham?" she whispered. She was young, but not pretty. "Are you Vernon Dunham?"

I froze, skin prickling. How had she known my name? The library didn't have a sign-in policy.

"Yes," I whispered back after that brief moment of panic. "Why are we whispering?"

She gave me a look that would freeze diesel fuel. "It's a *library* Mr. Dunham." Even in low and quiet, her voice was finicky, the words over-enunciated. "People *whisper* in libraries."

I felt foolish, so I smiled at her. I was no Floyd, but I could be charming enough when the need arose. "Sorry. I was trying to be funny."

"Yes, well," she sniffed. "You have a telephone call." Her look made it clear to me that this was most irregular. I thought it was too — outside of work, I didn't get three or four telephone calls a year. Mrs. Swenson charged her boarders a dime a call, which tended to discourage conversation.

I followed her through the oak door with the frosted glass panel into the office behind the circulation desk. It was cramped, with no pictures on the brick walls, and oddly, no books either. It looked more like the examining room of a doctor who had fallen on hard times — just the desk, one chair behind it, and a hat stand. Another, vaguely familiar older woman in a natty muslin dress was installed at the desk behind a nameplate reading "Mrs. Sigurdsen: Chief Librarian." She held the black telephone handset as if it were a snake that might bite her. "Are you Vern Dunham?" she snapped. No whispering in here.

It was just like being on the carpet in Principal Miller's office back in junior high. "Yes, ma'am," I said in my politest voice. Who would think to call me at the library? It would have taken a lot of trouble to track me down here. Only Floyd knew where I was, and he would hardly bother me at the library even if his parents had a telephone in the first place.

"Deputy Morgan is on the line for you." Mrs. Sigurdsen: Chief Librarian offered me the handset with a glare that was clearly the model for Miss Marion Weeks' apprentice attempt at a chilling stare.

"Vernon Dunham here," I said as I took the telephone.

Oddly, there was no operator on the line. "Mr. Dunham?" Deputy Morgan sounded like he was inside a wind tunnel. The connection was terrible, considering he was probably down-stairs from me.

"Yes?" I'd already identified myself.

"Deputy Bobby Ray Morgan of the Butler County Sheriff's Department speaking, sir. We've got your father downstairs here at the Augusta police station. Could you please come get him?"

"What's happened to Dad?" I could easily imagine all kinds of disasters occurring to my father, but none that would put him the hands of the Sheriff's Department. If he was driving around drunk again, they would have just locked him up in the county jail in El Dorado to sleep it off. There wasn't any particular reason why the Sheriff's Department would have brought him into Augusta.

Even over the lousy telephone line, I could hear Deputy Morgan shuffling papers. "The U.S. Army Criminal Investigation Division brought him in." The cadence of his voice changed as he read from a report. "They were interviewing him about the disposition of one of his trucks. He had an episode of de-lirium tremens and attacked the investigators with a wrought-iron floor lamp."

That sounded like Dad, alright. He never got over the idea that he'd killed Mom with his drinking, and that just fed his anger and kept him stuffed further inside the bottle. I hadn't gotten over blaming him either, come to think of it, but that was both uncharitable and untrue, at least strictly speaking. More to the point at the moment, I could easily imagine which of Dad's trucks Army CID would be interested in. It was parked in a barn fifteen miles away from here with a secret Nazi weapon still loaded on the back. "Is Dad all right?" I asked, visions of Fort Leavenworth's penitentiary walls dancing in my head.

"He's fine, except for a couple of bumps to the head," said Deputy Morgan. "There's a very unhappy Captain Markowicz here with a broken arm, however. I believe he is keen to speak with you in person."

"I'll be down in a minute," I said. "Thank you for your time." *And for not locking Dad up*, I thought. Not to mention the courtesy of the telephone call, instead of simply storming up the stairs with handcuffs and a truncheon. I handed the telephone back to Mrs. Sigurdsen: Chief Librarian. "I appreciate the assistance with that important call, ma'am." I winked. "Government matter." If I was going down, I would go down in style.

I walked out of the office right past assistant librarian Weeks' desk, heading for the carrel where I had been doing my research.

It was absolutely clean.

No German-English dictionary. No Encyclopedia Britannica volumes spread around. And no envelope of Nazi papers. "For the love of Christ," I hissed under my breath. I couldn't believe I had been foolish enough to turn my back on the materials.

I turned away, my face hot and sweaty, and stepped back to the circulation desk. "Ah, Miss Weeks?"

She looked up at me, distaste obvious in the set of her lips and her narrowed eyes. "Yes, Mr. Dunham?"

"I left some research materials in the study carrel over there when I took my telephone call."

"Yes. I reshelved them. Reference books are not to be left lying about, Mr. Dunham."

"I don't care about the darned books." Miss Weeks' glare intensified, as if she could deliver me a black eye through sheer nerve. Her boss maybe, but not her. And that was definitely the wrong thing to say. I shook my head. "That's not what I meant. I'm sorry. What I'm very concerned about is the packet of materials I left at the study carrel when I took the telephone call. Some technical reports to be specific."

"Nothing like that was there when I cleared the carrel," she said primly.

"What do you mean they weren't there?" My voice rose sharply. "I left them spread out with the dictionary when I went back to the reference section. From there, I followed you into the office."

"Lower your voice, please, Mr. Dunham, or I shall be forced to ask you to leave and bar you from the premises. You must have taken them with you when you received your telephone call. Perhaps they are in your pocket."

Which was ridiculous as I was wearing canvas work pants and a denim shirt. No pockets big enough. I was certain the papers were not in the office, but I pushed past her desk and walked into the office without knocking. The old bat who roosted there was talking on the telephone. It didn't sound like English, but I didn't catch enough of what she was saying. She covered the handset when I walked in. "May I help you, sir?" she asked in a tone that could have frosted glass.

"I need to find a manila envelope with some documents. Miss Weeks thinks I may have left the materials in here."

"I have no such envelope in here."

"Are you sure?" That hot, angry feeling was building in me, matching my sweaty face and racing pulse. My game leg started to ache, too, a sure sign I was in deep trouble.

"I suggest that you leave this library, Mr. Dunham," she said. "Your presence here is disruptive and no longer welcome."

"But my envelope —"

"There is no envelope here, Mr. Dunham. I am sure you have done something else with it. Now I believe that you have business with the Deputy Sheriff?" It was clear she would find some business for me with Deputy Morgan if I didn't exit gracefully.

The Chief Librarian stared me out of her office. I backed out, shutting her door, and looked around for Marion Weeks. She was nowhere to be seen, vanished just like my envelope of documents. I slowly turned and walked out the front door of the library and down the old flight of wooden stairs bolted to the outside wall of the city building.

There had to be a connection between Army CID talking to Dad and someone stealing my documents out of the library. Taking the envelope wasn't Floyd's kind of prank. He wouldn't be willing to compromise our little project, not even in the name of scaring the pee out of me. Nobody else in Augusta, Kansas could possibly have wanted anything from those Nazi documents. They wouldn't mean anything to anyone here except me. Or a military intelligence officer. CID wasn't M.I., but the broken-armed Captain Markowicz could be playing a double role. I would if I was him.

I wondered why the CID man wasn't bringing criminal charges against Dad for assault and battery. I would.

CHAPTER FOUR

Ollie Wannamaker, newly minted Augusta police officer, sat at the desk in the police department's cramped waiting room. Two benches flanked the desk, war bond and ration posters on the wall. The sandstone floor was blotched with odd stains, and someone was snoring inside the barred cell barely visible through a cracked open door behind Ollie's desk. It sure sounded like Dad's rattling breath, music to an entire childhood's worth of sleepless nights.

"Oh, hey, Vernon. How ya' doin'?"

Before the war, Ollie had been a moon-faced, big-boned kid with an unfortunate tendency to sprout blackheads. He'd gone through high school with me and Floyd. He even dated Mary Anne for a while, when we were all juniors and she was mad at Floyd for two months running. After graduation, Ollie went into the Army. Uncle Sam made him a military policeman in Hawaii, dragging drunks off beaches and patrolling nightclubs. At the end of the war, Ollie came home to Kansas — thin, tough, and tanned right out of his skin condition. He became a police officer — the natural thing to do given his service as a military policeman. I knew his Seventh Day Adventist parents weren't too pleased about the career choice, but Ollie was a good cop who cared about the folks he had sworn to serve.

"I'm here for my dad, Ollie."

Somewhere behind Ollie, the old man snored. Ollie scratched his head. "Your dad?"

"Yes, Ollie. My *dad*. Remember him? Grady Dunham, town drunk?" I stuck my hand out about the level of my eyebrows, about five foot six. "Maybe yea so high."

"Hey, hey." Ollie actually waggled his finger at me. "No need to be sharp about it. Matter of fact, I haven't seen your dad in weeks."

This was very odd. "I just got a call from Deputy Morgan that my dad was being held down here. Isn't that him back there?"

"No," said Ollie. "It's old Johann Strait. What would I be holding your dad for anyway?"

"Assault." If Ollie didn't know whose arm Dad had broken, I wasn't going to tell him.

"Now why would a Sheriff's Deputy bring someone into the city police station on an assault charge? They would have taken him to El Dorado to see the judge, or at least dumped him in the county lock-up there." El Dorado was the county seat, a tender subject as Augusta was the original seat of Butler County. "You been drinking, Vernon?"

"Ah, no. But why would Deputy Morgan tell me he was being held here?" My stomach dropped to somewhere around my knees, as I suddenly felt dizzy. It was the missing envelope. Could the whole telephone call have been a set up? My gosh, was I a prize stooge.

"How do you know he was with the Sheriff's Department?" asked Ollie. "I don't know of any Deputy Morgan over there."

"Well, he told me on the telephone he was a Deputy." That sounded stupid as soon as I said it. But it wasn't like I could have asked him to hold his badge up close to the handset.

"Hey," said Ollie reasonably, "Anybody can use the telephone. It's a free country. I could call you up and say I'm the governor. How would you know the difference?"

"Yeah, yeah, I get the picture," I muttered glumly. I mulled things over. I should go over to the house and see if Dad was home. I didn't really want to talk with him, but I needed to know where he was and what, if anything, had happened to him. Nobody but me cared about Dad anymore. I was all he had — a sad comment on both me and the old man.

One more thing occurred to me. "Ollie, you ever hear of an Army captain named...ah...Marcus. No, Markowicz. Yeah, Markowicz. Know anything about him?"

Ollie got a funny look on his face, and glanced around the little office as if to see if anyone was listening from behind the file cabinet. "He was in here today asking questions about your buddy, Floyd Bellamy."

That couldn't possibly be good news, no matter how I tried to stretch it. "What kind of questions?"

Ollie looked even more uncomfortable. "I can't rightly say. Military stuff. You know." His tone of voice reminded me that he and Floyd had served our country, brothers-in-arms even while they were across the world from each other. I, the town gimp, had stayed home safe and warm with all the girls.

I tried again. "Tell me this. Is Floyd in trouble? Or is this something else, maybe a background investigation?" Floyd or no Floyd, my aircraft was in danger. I could smell it coming.

Ollie scratched his head again and stared down at the gum wrappers on his desk. "Take some advice, Vernon. Stay away from Floyd Bellamy for a few days. I know you've been palling around with him more than usual lately." Still not meeting my eye, he raised his hand as if to stop traffic, or maybe wave me off. "I didn't say nothing to the Army investigators, but your name is gonna come up if they keep asking around. I don't know, you might ought to take a business trip to Kansas City or something. Augusta probably isn't the best place for you right now."

Ollie folded his arms and finally met my eye, giving me his best cop stare. The interview was over. I'd probably already learned more than I was really supposed to know.

"Thanks, Ollie," I said. "I appreciate it." I made an effort to sound like I meant that, covering my anger and confusion.

I turned and walked out to 5th Street. I didn't really feel like calling Dad's neighbors from the telephone on Ollie's desk. The Johansens were as sick of him as I was, with the late night screaming and the shotgun blasts and the knocked-down mail-boxes. But Mr. Johansen would have gone and checked if I'd asked him to. Besides, I wasn't sure who might be listening. It would have been bad enough to have the conversation in front of Ollie.

Most of all, I hated the fact that I was starting to think this way. The war was over, we were all supposed to be going back to our normal lives.

My car was parked around the corner and down the block on State Street. Walking toward it, I morosely studied the Hudson. She wasn't that old, just barely pre-war, and was a good car — had seen me through college and the war. I had been looking at brochures for new Studebakers at a dealership over in Wichita, but the money was more than I could spend. My faded black sedan had served me well. She was cheap, loyal and dependable, and I loved her lines. If I squinted in a bad light, I could almost convince myself I was driving a Hudson Terraplane, just like the Negro bluesman Robert Johnson.

I laughed. Being an engineer didn't exempt me from wax-ing emotional about the machines that served me. I was al-ready in love with the German airplane in the Bellamys' barn, no matter who — or what — had buried her in that deep ice. I would come to understand her. I patted the Hudson's fender and opened the door.

The crank telephone call really had me wondering if I should go over to Dad's place. I drummed my fingers on the Hudson's cracked bakelite steering wheel and stared out at the street. To-day was Saturday. He would be drunk as a lord until Monday or Tuesday, then dry up just far enough to wander into town.

Dad had been a weekend alcoholic for years. But he'd slid further away, losing the habit of working after Mom died in that wreck while he slept off a bender in the back seat, and he'd pissed away months after in the rehabilitation hospital. Dad's weekends stretched out to encompass most of the week. He usually managed to do something on Wednesdays and Thursdays, hauling junk or doing odd jobs to earn enough to stay alive and get drunk for another weekend. I should let him be, stop by on my way back from work next Tuesday.

On the other hand, if something really had happened to Dad, if the telephone call had not been a complete ruse...who had made it? I tried to imagine any other reason for the call other than distracting me to effect the theft of my German files. Nobody cared about Dad. Then I tried to imagine how I would feel if I didn't go by until Tuesday and he had been missing for three days. I didn't need that kind of responsibility.

I pressed the starter on the Hudson, and checked my mirrors before pulling out. I noticed a police car parked three or four spaces back down the street from me. That was odd — the station was around the corner. The police department had plenty of parking there.

Ollie, keeping an eye me.

Avoiding eye contact with Ollie, I pulled out and headed up State Street. The car still lagged just a little, as if I was carrying extra weight. I figured I'd go ahead and stop at the service station and check the air in my tires, then drive out to Dad's house on the north side of town, near the lake, and try to make it back to my boarding house for the supper seating.

Mrs. Swenson had strong opinions about people who came late to meals.

A siren interrupted my thoughts. I looked in the rearview mirror to see the police car right up on my bumper, its revolving light flashing. That was when I realized it was a Sheriff's patrol car. Not Ollie following me at all. I pulled over to let him pass. He pulled over behind me.

"Wonderful," I shouted at my windshield, fist curling and uncurling on the steering wheel. My head started to pound — blood pressure rising, which was bad for my game leg. I wondered if CID had arranged to have me arrested so they could pull me in without being obvious about it.

I turned off the Hudson and rolled down my window. The deputy walked up to the car. It was Deputy Truefield, from El

Dorado. He had turned Dad over to me a few times rather than driving him all the way back to the county seat to lock him up. Deputy Truefield was okay, if a little stiff.

"Taillight's busted out, Vernon," he said as he leaned in my window. His peaked cap brushed the head liner in my Hudson. Deputy Truefield had razor stubble that would have scared a porcupine, which he kept long in an unsuccessful attempt to cover a chin that receded like the tide.

My taillight? "I'm sorry, sir. It was fine the last time I looked at it." I glanced over my shoulder, out the back window. As if that would tell me anything. "You want my license?" I asked, hoping this was just a routine traffic stop.

"Nope," he said. "I know you're clean. No warrants, never had any trouble from you. But I'd be much obliged if you stepped out of your automobile."

I resisted the urge to ask why, knowing that would only irritate him. Truefield looked sufficiently nervous and annoyed as it was. I opened the door of the Hudson and got out, trying my hardest to look like a good citizen. Truefield motioned me around to the rear of the car. His right hand kept brushing his service revolver.

"See there?" he asked. The taillight was indeed broken. The license plate was bent up on its mounting bracket as well.

I had no idea how that had happened. "That's odd."

"Thought so myself," said Truefield. "You mind opening the trunk?"

"Why?" I asked before I could stop myself. Me and my big mouth.

"Because I have reliable information that causes me to want to inspect your trunk," he said flatly, his eyes narrowing. Truefield's hand closed on the grip of the revolver. "Now look Vernon, you and I, we ain't best buddies or nothing, but I've done you a few favors regarding your dad in the past few years, on account of your mama dying that way and all. I know it's been hard on both of you." His face relaxed at the memories and the hand wandered away from the revolver. "Do me a favor, open the trunk. If I have to call Judge Abernathy, you and I are both gonna wish you'd just opened the trunk when I asked in the first place."

There was nothing in the trunk I could think of except a badly patched spare tire, a few tools and my laundry for McVay's Cleaners. Nothing about Floyd's aircraft, I was certain. I popped the latch and pulled the trunk open.

I was wrong about the contents of my trunk. Dad was in there, dressed in his underwear, curled up so tight he seemed as if his knees and elbows had been broken. And from all the blood on my grubby office shirts, Dad wasn't doing too well.

"Vern," said Truefield slowly. He had drawn his revolver, but kept it pointed at the street. "We should discuss this."

It could have been worse. I suppose if Dad hadn't still been breathing Deputy Truefield would have arrested me then and there. On the other hand, dragging Dad's bloody, unconscious body out of my trunk and settling him into the back seat of Truefield's patrol car on a Saturday afternoon on State Street pretty much ensured that all of Augusta would know by supper time that something bad had happened to my father, and that I had something to do with it.

Truefield didn't say much, just grunted, as we folded Dad into the patrol car. He waved me into the front as he got in on his side. Truefield started up the lights and siren.

"I've got to say, Dunham," he yelled over wailing and clicking, "you'd better have a mighty good explanation for all of this."

I twisted around and looked at Dad. It was like looking in a funhouse mirror, one that made me older and shorter and worn out, like a weathered stump on a river bank. He appeared relaxed, stretched out in the seat as if he was taking an afternoon nap. The nervous guilt that always haunted his face was absent. Bloody, unconscious, maybe breathing his last for all I knew, Dad still looked happier than he ever had since Mom died.

I wondered what that said about me.

"Where are we going?" I asked Truefield as he ran the blinking red light at the Wichita Highway.

"Doc Milliken ought to be home this time of a Saturday," he answered. "Otherwise we have to go on to either El Dorado or Wichita. Don't rightly know if your dad could make that trip right now."

"Okay." I was a little short of choices myself.

Truefield pulled onto Broadway, the patrol car sliding across the paving bricks as it lunged for a skid that Truefield steered right out of again. Kids scattered as we swept down the road. Doctor Milliken, Odus Milliken's brother, had a large house about two blocks down from Mrs. Swenson's where I boarded. More neighbors to watch and wonder about me. I was pretty sure my brief career as an upstanding citizen of Augusta was on its last legs.

Truefield pulled into Doc Milliken's driveway, knocking over the old hitching post in the process. "Let's get him up onto the porch," he said as he jumped out of the car. I climbed out more carefully and came around to Truefield's side. The Deputy already had his hands under Dad's arms, tugging him out of the back seat. Dad groaned, his face crumpling into pained wrinkles even in his sleep.

My eyes began to fill with hot tears. This was Dad, my daddy who carried me across icy winter creeks on his shoulders and fed me water with a spoon all through the frightening, stunning heat of my polio. Dad, who had been dying in the trunk of my car with blood all over his face while I sat in the library reading German reports about some crazy Arctic expedition for some worthless airplane I'd cared too much about.

"Damn it, Dad, don't leave me," I whispered. I grabbed Dad's legs as Truefield pulled him out of the back of the patrol car and staggered off after the Deputy.

Mrs. Milliken came out onto the porch, screeched once with her hands on her cheeks, then ran back inside. I hoped she'd gone to fetch Doc Milliken. His blue Cadillac convertible was parked in the driveway, so I figured he was home.

Truefield dragged Dad bodily up onto the porch with me swinging along behind. Tears ran down my face as my nose flooded hot and prickly. I had lost Mom for no better reason than a jackrabbit and a bald tire one night when Dad had a little much and was sleeping it off in the back seat instead of driving them home like he usually did. Now Dad was going to die because I'd gotten involved with Floyd Bellamy's secret Nazi airplane. To heck with the documents, to heck with the mysteries of the ice. I decided to burn down Mr. Bellamy's barn as soon as I could, and be shut of the whole mess for good and all.

Doc Milliken came out in a dressing gown and pajamas. He had a pipe in one pocket and a newspaper in the other, with little half-moon glasses and a grouchy expression. He didn't look much like his brother the railroad agent, except for the weight of age on both their faces.

Doc helped Deputy Truefield and me get Dad into his examination room where he laid Dad out on the table. "Ruthie," Doc shouted, "get me sterile rags, and prepare a suture kit."

"Is he going to die?" I asked. Someone asked that question in everyone's life. I hated that it was me, now, standing next to Dad as he bled his life away.

"Just hold on a minute, son," snapped Doc Milliken. "Help me get his shirt off."

As Doc Milliken cut with a pair of short-bladed steel scissors, Truefield and I pulled Dad's shirt away. I could see fresh red marks along his ribs. Dad groaned and twisted as we tugged at the cloth.

"Be careful," Doc said. "It looks like someone broke his ribs for him."

Mrs. Milliken came in with some clean white rags. She smiled at me a moment, then went to work on Dad's face, wiping the blood off. I fought back my tears, but my sinuses had filled up and were driving more out and I couldn't blink away the pain inside me.

Doc Milliken grasped Dad's face between his hands and thumbed back the eyelids. "Take it easy, Vernon," he said softly over his shoulder as he shut the lids again. "Grady's a tough old buzzard. He isn't going to check out today." He began to examine Dad's scalp.

I looked around for Deputy Truefield. He was in the front room, talking on the telephone. I'd had enough law enforcement shenanigans for one day, and didn't really want to know what he was discussing. Instead I took Dad's hand and held it. The rough, callused fingers were familiar, their hard textures reminding me of my boyhood. I looked down and realized that he was still wearing his wedding band.

I had no idea he'd never taken it off. Not even knowing that much about Dad made me sad all over again.

Doc Milliken, Deputy Truefield and I stood on the front porch. Mrs. Milliken had brought out a tray with some frosty bottles of grape pop, then gone to sit in the front hall, listening through the screen door. The ceiling above me was painted blue to keep the wasps off it, and I found myself studying the knobby gingerbread along the edge of the porch roof.

Truefield cleared his throat. "Sorry about the hitching post, Doc."

"I expect that young Vernon will make good on it." Doc Milliken winked at me. "It was historic, you know." I smiled weakly as Truefield glared at me.

"Sheriff's on his way over from El Dorado," Truefield said conversationally. "There's going to be some hard questions asked."

I opened my mouth to protest, but no words came out. I didn't have anything to say. Doc Milliken patted me on the shoulder. "Don't you think that the Augusta police should handle this, Peter?" he asked Deputy Truefield.

"Normally, yes, but I'm already involved. There's reports to fill out, and where there's reports, there's questions." Truefield shrugged and looked uncomfortable. His expression reminded me of the way Ollie had looked at me back at the police station.

"He's going to be fine, you know," said Doc Milliken. "There's been no murder done here."

"No, but we have attempted murder for sure."

Milliken caught Truefield's gaze and stared him down. "Vernon didn't do it."

I was glad to hear that. I knew I hadn't done anything to Dad, but I wasn't sure I could convince anybody else of that. Having him in the trunk of my car would be pretty convincing to a judge and jury. It wouldn't be hard to construct a motive for me, either. God damn Floyd Bellamy and his magic Nazi airplane.

"How do you know?" demanded Truefield.

"Three ribs cracked, several more bruised. I'd like to send him on to Wichita for X-rays, just in case I missed some."

"So?" Truefield's tone was belligerent, his hand straying toward the revolver. I really wished he would stop that.

"Do I have to spell it out?" snapped Doc Milliken. "Vernon Dunham's been lame from polio since he was eight years old. I know. I treated him through it and damned near lost him. It's a miracle he can walk at all. Grady Dunham's ribs were kicked, very hard, by someone. Now, do you suppose Vernon stood on his good leg and kicked his dad's ribs in with his lame leg? Or did he stand on his lame leg and kick them in with his good one?"

"Oh," said Truefield. "I see,"

I felt miserable, but I had to point something out. "I could have had an accomplice."

"Whose side are you on?" asked Doc Milliken. "Besides, whoever hit your father in the head didn't know him well. That knock would have killed almost anyone else, but they got him right in his metal plate. He'll be weak from blood loss and have a heck of a headache when he wakes up, but that's about it. You would have done a better job."

The metal plate. Dad's reward for surviving the accident that had killed Mom. The jackrabbit in the middle of the road had lived for a while, but Mom had her head torn off by a fence post. Sleeping like a baby in the back seat, Dad's head just got bashed in. The nice metal plate that the surgeons at St. Francis hospital in Wichita had implanted in his skull put him back together just like new — a medical advance courtesy of the war. Dad was as good as ever, except for his endless capacity for gin, draining through the Mom-shaped hole in his heart.

"Yeah," I mumbled. "I know all about the plate." Mom's surgical steel tombstone, stuck in Dad's skull.

"That might let you off the hook," said Truefield sternly, "but it still doesn't look too good. County attorney will want to talk with you for sure." Then, in a weird echo of Ollie's advice, "I wouldn't take any trips if I were you."

I shook my head. "I'm not going anywhere." Never again.

Who would have wanted to kill Dad? He made it to services at the First Christian Church downtown once or twice a month, he did a little hauling and light chores. He was harmless. Dad was the town drunk, but everybody knew why. Most folks looked past it and treated him well enough. There were even a few widows with designs on him, although Dad was pretty adroit at avoiding that kind of attention. He hadn't been very adroit at avoiding someone else's attention, though.

Something occurred to me. "Doc, you see anybody in here in the last day or so with a broken arm? Maybe an Army captain named Markowicz?"

Truefield's head snapped towards me so hard I could hear his neck crack. His eyes narrowed and his hand went firmly to the butt of his revolver. Doc Milliken gave me a narrow-eyed look and said, "Now what would you know about that, Vernon?"

"I heard a rumor that Dad might have broken the Captain's arm for him. Maybe he did this to Dad." I waved back vaguely into the house behind us where Dad still rested.

"I think maybe we shouldn't discuss this," said Deputy Truefield in a low, tight voice.

That finally broke through my blues to make me angry. I tolled the litany of my complaints. My dad had been dying in the trunk of my car. Some strong-legged bastard had kicked a harmless old rummy in the ribs, whacked him upside the head, not caring whether he killed or not. Truefield kept trying to pull his gun on me, like I was John Dillinger or something.

I thought about my missing Nazi envelope, about Floyd's stupid stunt of stealing the aircraft in the first place. I thought about how out of control my life was getting and how fast that had happened.

"You big...big...*goober*!" I screamed at Truefield. I could feel my lips stretch back, spit flying as I yelled. My leg throbbed in time to the angry cadences of my speech. "You talk about arresting me for trying to kill my own father, but when someone with a real reason to do it comes up, you don't want to discuss it. This isn't Germany, by God, this is Kansas. We don't think that way around here."

Doc Milliken put a hand on my shoulder, his fingers firm and warm. "Vernon, calm down."

He turned to Truefield, who had his revolver pointed at my chest. "Now Peter," said Doc Milliken, "put that gun away. Young Vernon's just upset because something terrible has happened to his father. I suggest you go wait in your patrol car for the Sheriff to arrive. We won't say any more about broken arms, none of us, until the time is right."

"You be careful, Vernon Dunham," said Truefield to me, sticking his left index finger in my face like a little pink gun even as he holstered the pistol. "There's some pretty big stuff going on. You're likely to be swept away by it." He paused, catching his breath. "I want things back to normal here in Butler County. That includes you and your dad, Vernon. So just you take it easy."

He turned and stomped off the porch, heading back to his patrol car. I watched Truefield open the trunk and get out some rags. He began to clean Dad's blood out of the back seat. If I wasn't so angry, I would have gone to help him. I wondered when I was going to get to clean out the trunk of my Hudson.

"Come inside, watch your dad sleep, and wait for the Sheriff," said Doc Milliken gently. "Or you can go help Peter clean his car. I know what I would do."

I turned to look at the doctor. He held out another rag and a little glass bottle with a sprayer screwed into the top. Disinfectant.

I thought about Truefield dragging Dad up the stairs. He hadn't busted my head, he hadn't taken me in. He'd done right by Dad, regardless of his suspicions about me.

I took Doc Milliken's rag and headed for the patrol car. As I bent to work beside the Deputy, neither of us willing to speak the other, I wondered what reliable information Truefield had been given about me and my car.

Where he had gotten it?

From whom?

CHAPTER FIVE

We were in the Millikens' living room. It was a tasteful version of what Mrs. Bellamy had aimed for out at the farmhouse, wingback chairs and a horsehair couch, with doilies everywhere and a water clock on the hand-carved mantelpiece, where dolphins chased bare-chested mermaids through walnut-grained waves.

"I'm going to have Deputy Truefield take your father into Wichita to Saint Francis Hospital," said Sheriff Hauptmann, leaning forward in one of the dining room chairs reversed under him, his hands clutching the chair back to his chest. Hauptmann was a big man, creased skin and folded muscles like a ham out of the can, all crammed into his green uniform. The Sheriff had a tiny little voice for his size, like a kid whispering in church. "That ambulance over at Dunsford Funeral Home won't be available until tomorrow afternoon at the earliest."

"It's getting on to evening, Vernon," said Doc Milliken from the wingback chair next to Hauptmann's precarious perch. The doc was being gentle with me, as if I was the one who was sick. I had thrown up in the lilac bush after helping clean Dad's blood out of Truefield's patrol car, but that was just nausea. Mrs. Milliken was cooking pork roast in the kitchen, and the smell was making me sick all over again even as my mouth watered from hunger. Seated on the couch, I kept an embroidered pillow pressed to my lap to hide the trembling of my bad leg inside my work pants.

Doc gave me a sidelong stare. "We don't know how long he was out in the trunk of your car. He might have a concussion, and I still want those X-rays."

"We won't find much out else until he wakes up," squeaked the Sheriff.

There was a knock on Doc Milliken's front door. "Come in," called the Doc.

Ollie Wannamaker walked into the room, rubbing his hands together, followed by Truefield who had been outside smoking. With night falling, it was getting a little chilly, even for late September. "Well," he said. "I've been over to the Dunham house."

"And...?" asked Sheriff Hauptmann pointedly.

Ollie glanced at me. He didn't work for the Sheriff, but Hauptmann outranked him every way there was. He didn't like being pushed around. The town cop shrugged. "Place is a wreck." I smiled sadly and shook my head. "More so than usual," he added.

"What do you mean?" asked Hauptmann.

"Furniture's turned over, couple of busted picture frames, that kind of thing. Not like a search, or a burglary. Looks more like there was a knock-down, drag-out fight. Found some fresh boot prints in the yard that didn't look like Grady's size nines, either."

I wondered briefly how Ollie would know my Dad's shoe size, then realized he'd been looking in closets.

"Your Dad know how to fight?" Hauptmann asked me.

"Yes sir," I replied. "He bayoneted three Germans in the Somme during the Great War. That was in one afternoon." I'd seen the stains on that big old knife. It scared the heck out of me, even now, that Dad had kept some German's heart blood in the tool shed for all these years. He always said it reminded him what he was supposed to do.

"Good thing he's a quiet drunk now," laughed Truefield. I wanted to pop him one, but held my ground.

Sheriff Hauptmann looked calmly at Truefield until the Deputy blushed. "Deputy Truefield, why don't you get started taking Mr. Dunham to Wichita? It's a long drive. Stay at the hospital with him until they can tell you something useful, then call it in to me."

"I'll get my hat," said Truefield, stepping toward the coat tree by the front door. "Can someone please help me bring Mr.

Dunham out to the car?" He was a lot more polite with Sheriff Hauptmann around than he had been before.

"I'll help," volunteered Ollie.

"Get some blankets from Mrs. Milliken," Doc Milliken said. "Can't have him getting chills in his shape."

The two policemen clattered and huffed around the house, finding blankets at the direction of Doc's wife, then fetched Dad from the examining room. I watched from my chair as they carried him out. He didn't look peaceful now, just pale and ill. Old, he was, that funhouse mirror of who I would be. It made me want to gather him in my arms and weep as if he had been my son instead of I his.

A moment later, I was left alone in the room with Sheriff Hauptmann and Doc Milliken.

The Sheriff and the Doc looked one another in the eye for a long moment. Something that I couldn't follow passed between them, words unspoken lingering in the air just out of my earshot. Hauptmann cleared his throat.

"Vernon," he began. "We don't know each other, but the Doctor here speaks highly of you."

"Yes sir," I said noncommittally. I was worried about Dad, sick of Floyd's airplane, and now Hauptmann's tone made me feel like I was about to be pitched at like a farmwife facing off with a brush salesman.

"I understand that you and your father don't get along, and I believe I understand why."

Now Mom's ghost was in the room, hanging over me as if she were waiting for Dad. I nodded, not trusting myself to speak right at that moment.

The Sheriff kept talking, his eyes narrowing as the lightly-built dining room chair rocked on its back legs under his weight. "Doc Milliken says there's no way you felt strongly enough to attack him, let alone try to kill him. The medical evidence points pretty clearly away from you." He glanced at my legs.

"Yes sir." I wondered where he was heading — it was time for him to give me the proposition, whatever it was going to be.

Sheriff Hauptmann cleared his throat again. I suddenly realized that unlike Deputy Truefield, he didn't even carry a gun. Confidence? Power? "Now, this doesn't release you as a suspect, you realize, but unofficially I'm confident that you didn't have anything directly to do with the assault on your father."

I thought about that. "What do you mean, *directly*?" I asked.

The Sheriff leaned his chair perilously far forward. "You have a government clearance from your work at the Boeing plant over in Wichita, is that correct?"

We weren't supposed to talk about that stuff outside the plant, but the war was over, and the Sheriff seemed to have something important on his mind. He wanted to say something that hung on this point. I decided for Dad's sake to go along with him. "Yes sir, I do have a clearance."

"Then I am going to tell you something I wouldn't normally reveal to an outsider. But in return for my confidence, I need your full cooperation."

I thought about Floyd Bellamy, and the penitentiary at Fort Leavenworth. I was already deeper than I had ever wanted to go into a bad situation, but there seemed to be nothing for it. Dad was on his way to the hospital in Wichita, somehow because of Floyd's secret. His beating was connected with the papers, with the airplane. I needed to hear whatever the Sheriff had to say to me. "Yes sir. You have my full cooperation."

The Sheriff exchanged another significant glance with Doc Milliken. "The United States Army Criminal Investigation Division is here in Butler County, pursuing a highly sensitive matter."

"I know," I said cautiously.

"How, boy?" Hauptmann leaned forward in the dining chair he was using, Doc inching forward in his own flowered wingback. "Who told you that?"

"Someone calling himself Deputy Morgan called me on the telephone about Dad, said that Dad had beaten up an Army captain."

Hauptmann frowned. "I don't have a Deputy Morgan, son."

"That's what Ollie told me."

"Did he tell you what the CID was looking for?" asked Doc Milliken.

"No, but I think they're after Floyd Bellamy." I was a rat, betraying my best friend, not to mention myself, to the Sheriff. But after what happened to Dad, I would much rather deal with Sheriff Hauptmann than the mysterious Captain Markowicz. I still felt miserable about the whole business.

"Floyd Bellamy?" Sheriff Hauptmann looked puzzled.

"Alonzo Bellamy's boy," said Doc Milliken. "They have that place out there off Haverhill Road, as you head toward Leon."

"Oh, yeah," said Sheriff Hauptmann. "The Bellamys." He laughed. "Why would the CID want him?" He looked at me sternly. "Is Floyd Bellamy a Nazi sympathizer?"

I was quite surprised by the question, and it must have showed on my face. "No, no."

I couldn't even imagine such a thing. Floyd had been an easy, confident liar most of his life, in the name of popularity, convenience and heavy petting back in high school. At least once he had been thief, because there was no legitimate way he could have gotten that Nazi equipment back home. But Floyd was no Fascist, I was sure of that. He loved his good old American freedom way too much.

"Floyd is a ne'er do well, a liar, and most probably a petty thief at opportunity," said Doc Milliken, echoing my thoughts. "I also understand he is a good Christian, a Kansas Republican, an Army veteran and, sadly, not much different from half the other men in Butler County. He is most certainly not a Nazi."

Doc Milliken sure knew a lot of what went on around Augusta. More than I might have thought. I wondered what he knew about Floyd's freight delivery on last Thursday's Kansas City train. His brother was the railway clerk, but there hadn't been anything specific on the manifest. Floyd had fed Odus a good line about agricultural equipment. Were these two looking for a cut of that business?

"That's my friend," I said with a sigh of relief. "So why is CID here?"

"The CID is in Butler County because there was a cell from a Nazi spy ring based here in Augusta during the war. The cell was responsible for watching the aircraft industry in Wichita. Your kind of work, Vernon." Sheriff Hauptmann cleared his throat again. "Army counter-intelligence was able to control what they learned and manage the cell's activities."

"Why didn't they just shut it down?"

To my surprise, Doc Milliken answered. "Because the operation would have just started up somewhere else, and it might have taken too long to track it down all over again."

"Right," added Sheriff Hauptmann. "Better to manage it and minimize the damage where they could, than let the spy ring get away and set up somewhere else completely unopposed."

I wondered which of my friends, which of my neighbors, might have been recording my comings and goings during the war. I worked at Boeing, I was an engineer. I observed good security, as far as I knew, but what could a trained spy have ferreted out of me?

"The war is over. Why is Army CID here now?" I asked. "Cleaning things up?"

Sheriff Hauptmann shook his head. "We don't even know who all the individuals were. And really, that doesn't matter now. Justice should be served, but like you said, the war is over. No, the problem is the activity level is higher now in Butler County than it ever was during the war. The Army has become directly involved, because it's a matter of military secrecy."

I blurted out my questions. "What do you mean, 'higher than ever?' Am I suspected of being a German spy?"

"No, no, son. You're off the hook. Common sense tells me that, and I'm confident the County Attorney will agree with me. For one thing, if you were a spy, you wouldn't have beaten your own father, hidden him in the trunk of your car, then tipped off Deputy Truefield to come pick you up for it."

"So what is going on?"

"Remember that Captain Markowicz you asked about?" asked Doc Milliken. "I did set his broken arm yesterday. He showed me identification that proved to my satisfaction that he was Captain Markowicz of Army CID He asked me to keep his visit confidential."

"So it's confidential." They were talking, but they weren't telling much. Who had broken Markowicz's arm? Dad could have, but I couldn't see why he would have bothered.

Sheriff Hauptmann stepped away from his dining chair and walked across the room to the mantel. Running his fingers along the carvings, Hauptmann turned to face me. "Captain Abraham Markowicz was found beaten to death in Kansas City, Missouri three days ago. I received a telegram from the Missouri State Police this afternoon advising me to be on the lookout for someone using his identification. His papers were presumed stolen at the occasion of his assault."

"And the Sheriff happened to mention it to me," said Doc Milliken. "So I told him I had seen a Captain Markowicz yesterday."

"So this Captain Markowicz, you think he's a Nazi?" I asked.

"Quite possibly," answered Sheriff Hauptmann. "He or a confederate doubtless posed as Deputy Morgan on the telephone to you. Interestingly, the tip that Deputy Truefield got about you came from a man identifying himself as Morgan. The question that we can't readily answer is what interest they would possibly have in you or your dad. You've got some value through your work at Boeing, but with all respect, nobody here thinks you're a big fish there."

"I'm not," I said. "I buy parts. Fasteners, rivets, screws." *Big deal*, I thought, but someone had to do it.

But I knew perfectly well why the bad guys were interested in me and Dad. It was Dad's truck that Floyd Bellamy and I had used to haul that special cargo away from the train station this past Thursday. That was the interest right there. The German agents had not yet made the connection to Floyd, maybe because they hadn't yet managed to look at Odus Milliken's freight records. Obviously some German agent had seen me driving Dad's truck with the stolen cargo.

It all came back to my beautiful aircraft. Should I just give Floyd and his stolen German equipment up to the Sheriff now, or should I try to get out there tonight and warn him and his parents?

"Vernon?" prompted Doc Milliken gently.

I lied to two honest men who were trying to help both me and their country. I prayed the ghost of the real Captain Markowicz would forgive me. "No, sir, I can't imagine what they would want with me or Dad."

Perhaps the unpleasant Mrs. Sigurdsen in the library was a Nazi agent. That would certainly explain where my envelope went.

I talked with Sheriff Hauptmann and Doc Milliken a while longer, about the weather and football at Kansas State — the things people say to each other when they have run out of purpose but don't know how to walk away. Every word was a struggle.

Generally, I tried not to lie to people. For one, I wasn't very good at it. Every time I opened my mouth to those two, the whole story threatened to pop out, about Floyd and the Battle of the Bulge, about the Nazi "Report on the Arctic Expedition for Secret Contact," and airplanes frozen into the Arctic ice, and the unbelievable machine sitting in Mr. Bellamy's barn on top of Dad's old Mack stake bed. The truth strained to escape my grasp and soar upward into the world.

I couldn't afford to tell them, not yet. I was worried about the Bellamys. Even though Mr. Bellamy didn't like me very much any more, I still liked him. I've always had a soft spot for old people. They've tried so hard in life, and for their reward they get ground back into dust. The world owed old people better than most of them ever get.

I owed my father better than I gave him.

I begged out of our conversation after a few minutes.

"Gentlemen," I finally said, "I need to be getting along. It's been a terrible day for me."

"Of course, son," said Sheriff Hauptmann. "You're worried sick about your dad, I'm sure."

"Doc, can I borrow your car?"

"Why?" he asked. "You only live two blocks from here."

This was a reasonable question. "I want to go out to Dad's place and check on things," I said. "It's dark, and that's a long walk. The Augusta police are holding my Hudson as evidence in the assault on Dad." I suspected that Chief Davis had seized the car as minor local protest against Sheriff Hauptmann getting involved in business in town, but either way just as inconvenient for me.

I still had no car.

Doc Milliken smiled. "The keys are in the Cadillac. I can drive Ruthie's Dodge tomorrow if I need to go anywhere. Just get the car back to me by Monday morning. Without any dents, if you please, Vernon."

"Thank you, sir."

We all shook hands as if we were friends and neighbors instead of conspirators working at cross-purposes — for certainly that's what I was. I bid Mrs. Milliken good night and walked outside.

The night air smelled of wood smoke and leaf mold. People joke about Kansas being like an ironing board, but eastern Kansas has rolling hills and lots of hardwood stands. West of Wichita, it's what the movies show you. Around here, you could be in Missouri or Arkansas. It's the edge of the Ozarks. Even with the lights in town, I could see plenty of stars in the cold sky, and voices rose and fell as a distant mutter.

Not a lot went on in Augusta, Kansas on a Saturday night. A few people scurried in and out of the Augusta Theatre, and Lehr's restaurant had late hours for the highway traffic trying to make it on to Wichita. Otherwise people stayed home and listened to the radio. Or whatever it was that normal people did at home on Saturday nights.

I stopped and breathed in the smells and sounds of my town, pleased to be at rest for a moment, back in control of myself after a day of being pushed, pulled and frightened nearly out of my wits. Mom, Dad, the airplane, Floyd — they all receded into the peace of the night.

After a few minutes of communing with nature, I was ready to get on with my evening. For one thing, I was cold, still only in my work shirt and khakis.

The Cadillac was the first car I had ever driven with a radio in it. It was also the nicest car I had ever driven. It was 1941 Series 62 convertible, factory painted blue, from the last production year before the war. Doc Milliken had kept it up like showroom new, even gotten fresh tires somewhere. My poor Hudson still had the wartime civilian-issue bald tires almost everyone else had.

Doc Milliken had left the top on the Cadillac down, and I didn't bother to put it up even though the night air was chilly. Nothing wrong with the heater, and I really enjoyed convertibles. I could just imagine cruising with a girl — maybe Lois if she decided to talk to me again — top down, the wind in our faces, sitting close to stay warm. A fellow could get a lot of going steady done with a fine ragtop like this.

I drove through quiet streets of Augusta and listened to radio talk about the United Nations — a new League of Nations that was being ratified into existence from the charter signed last summer in San Francisco. Overseas, Italians squabbled over their first post-war elections, while all the sections of occupied Germany were restless.

It was a wartime habit, obsessively listening to news.

As I headed east, towards El Dorado and the Bellamys' place, I turned the radio back off and pretended that the Cadillac was mine, and Lois and I were driving to California on vacation. The muddy Kansas roads out near the Bellamys' farm became the parkways of sunny southern California, lined with orange trees and eucalyptus. I had never seen a parkway, but I sure could imagine one, smelling like cough drops and drenched in endless sunlight.

* * *

The Bellamy house was dark as I drove up. The Willys pickup was back at my boarding house, while the Farm-All was parked out front near Mr. Bellamy's old Ford coupe — which to the best of my knowledge hadn't moved in years. The barn was closed up.

I parked Doc Milliken's Cadillac. The night was clouding up and we had a new moon. I found a flashlight in the glove box, so I borrowed it and went into the house.

The old frame farmhouse was quiet. It was about ten in the evening, long after Floyd's parents normally retired, but I had expected to find Floyd around. Not wanting to wake anyone up by lighting a fire or the oil lamps, I flicked on the flashlight and looked around the living room. I knew the place like I knew my own bed — spent a lot of nights out here over the years — but tonight was different. I don't know what I thought I was looking for, but I imagined Nazis under every piece of furniture. Here in the quiet dark, the old house creaking in the cool night air, Sheriff Hauptmann's descriptions of spy rings and the murder of Captain Markowicz made me nervous all over again. The calm I had felt in the car vanished like smoke in the wind.

Despite my newfound case of nerves, the living room seemed normal. I moved on into the dining room. A loose board by the door creaked under my weight and I froze. All I could hear besides the rough hiss of my own tight breathing was the wind rattling in the eaves of the house.

The flashlight deepened the sharp shadows around its bright cone of light. It was hard for me to tell what I was seeing. Mrs. Bellamy's massive breakfront startled me, looming the darkness like a *kommando* on the prowl. I banged into an unseen side table, barking the shin on my lame leg. I sucked in my breath at the pain, stifling a yelp.

Darn it, I'd spent years of my life in this house, now I was stumbling like a burglar.

Covering the flashlight with my hand, I walked to the kitchen door, which was shut. I put my ear against it, listening for any kind of noise. I heard a slow creaking.

What the heck was it? It sounded like a door being opened, only the noise went on and on, as if the door were infinitely large. After a moment I realized that it was the noise of a rope bearing a heavy load.

I looked down at my feet, dimly visible in the glow of the hooded flashlight. There was a dark stain between them. I spread my fingers a little.

Blood.

My skin crawled, and I swear my hair stood up on end. I thought of old Mr. Bellamy and his dead twin Archie, and what the Nazi pretending to be Captain Markowicz had done to my Dad. The rope creaked again, and I realized that I had to go into the kitchen. I reached up a hand to push the door open.

There was a loud clack, the sound of a shotgun being pumped. I felt cold metal right behind my right ear as barrel pressed into my skin.

"Yah!" I spun to the left, favoring my bad leg and swung my flashlight like a club. There was a deafening roar as the shotgun went off, then the back of my head stung like fire. I must have taken some birdshot. My flashlight hit the barrel of the shotgun, knocking it out of Mr. Bellamy's hands.

"Vidal!" he shouted, "What in the name of God Almighty are you doing sneaking around in my house at night?"

"You could have killed me!" I screamed back. Blood sheeted down my neck from the scalp wound.

"It would have served you right, you idiot delinquent." Behind him, Floyd ran into the dining room brandishing a baseball bat.

"What's going on down here? Daddy, you okay?"

"Yeah, I'm fine," grumbled Mr. Bellamy in a more normal tone of voice, rubbing his hand. "Just tried to top off young Victor here, that's all." He glared at me, demonic in the light of my dropped flashlight. "Should have finished the job when I got the chance."

Floyd peered at me. "What's the matter with you, Vernon? Sneaking into people's houses like a crook. Daddy could have killed you."

I remembered the blood on the floor. It didn't make sense — Nazis hadn't slaughtered Floyd's family in their beds like I had feared. What was it doing there? "Where's Mrs. Bellamy?"

Floyd coughed, looked nervous. "Mama's at her sister's tonight. My Aunt Perneta over in Leon."

"Then whose blood is that?" I asked, pointing at the floor.

Floyd bent down and looked at it, while Mr. Bellamy picked up his shotgun to inspect it for damage. Floyd laughed, his voice thin. "We slaughtered one of the hogs this evening. Cats must have knocked over the drip pan."

"You slaughter pigs in your kitchen?"

"No, we slaughter 'em in the yard," said Mr. Bellamy. He tested the action on his shotgun. "We slaughter burglars in the kitchen."

"We cut down the joints in there," Floyd said. He looked at the shattered woodwork of the door and its frame. "And Mama's gonna slaughter you, Vern, when she finds out about her kitchen door. You'd better fix this in the morning."

Great, I thought. *What a day. Dad's in the hospital in Wichita and I'm down one Hudson, one historic hitching post and a kitchen door. Not a Nazi in sight here at the Bellamys.*

"Virgil," said Mr. Bellamy, "why don't you just stay here tonight? It's late, and you and Floyd will need an early start to fix that door before Mrs. Bellamy gets back from her sister's."

"Thanks, sir. I think I will." I picked up Doc Milliken's flashlight and shut it off. Mr. Bellamy was already going back upstairs with the shotgun under his arm.

"He knew it was you all along," said Floyd quietly.

"What do you mean? We surprised each other."

Floyd laughed. "Daddy can shoot a tomato off the vine from fifty feet and not touch a leaf. There's no way he missed you unless it was on purpose."

I realized that I had knocked the shotgun out of Mr. Bellamy's hands after he fired. "Why would he do such a thing?"

I asked, incredulous, as I wiped blood from my collar. I was accumulating far too many bloody shirts.

"He just wanted to scare you," said Floyd, shaking his head. "Let's go to bed."

"What about the pig's blood?"

"Oh, you can clean that up in the morning when you fix the door. If you're lucky, I'll even help you." Floyd flashed me his million-dollar grin. He had his nerve back, now that the gunfire was over. War will do funny things to a guy.

We trudged up the stairs. Floyd called out, "Good night, Daddy!"

"Good night boys," wheezed Mr. Bellamy from down the hall. A cackling laugh followed, disintegrating slowly into a cough.

It was a darn good thing I liked Mr. Bellamy, I thought, as I wiped more blood off my collar. "Floyd," I said, "I need a bandage, please."

CHAPTER SIX

The land rose behind the Bellamys' house, making a long back yard with a little stand of peach trees where wrens flitted back and forth. The bright morning sun glinted on the dew-soaked grass as I went to the tool shed that sat at the edge of the small orchard. There was a small stock of trim and molding in there, according to Floyd.

It was still early in the day when I started cutting pieces to patch the frame of Mrs. Bellamy's kitchen door. I hauled out a pair of old sawhorses, their two-by-fours weathered to the sandy gray of granite. I set my vises and measured, then began cutting with the hacksaw, all the while thinking about Nazis and their airplanes, buried in the Arctic ice for far too many years. I felt like Lewis Carroll's White Queen, trying to believe six impossible things before breakfast.

After getting my longest piece of molding sawn down, with the mortis cut at the top, I took a break. I went over to the barn to fetch the twisted silvery thing I had found in the f-panzer. Inside, with the bantams clucking and the straw-smell so overwhelming, the airplane loomed over me like the sculpture that it was. I stood and stared up at the mysterious lines, somehow crumpled and folded, yet obviously a deliberate design of intelligence and skill. The same intelligence and skill that had allowed it to lie buried in the ice above Norway.

Somehow the truth was too strange. Had I really meant to come and burn this thing out? It was too powerful, to great a machine, to succumb to such a simple exorcism.

I shook off the spell and stepped into the f-panzer to find

the little device. I left the barn without looking back at the airplane, and headed back for the tool shed. I drove a couple of nails into the tool shed wall to prop the thing on so I could keep looking at it as I worked, trying to puzzle out the shape, the materials, the metallurgy. It was a tiny reflection of the miracle that was Floyd's airplane.

My airplane.

"Hey, Vernon!" Floyd called, coming out from the house with a cup of coffee in his hand. It looked like his mom's good china.

"I hope that's for me," I said hopefully.

Floyd looked genuinely puzzled. "No. Should it be?"

Typical. I had to laugh. "Never mind. What do you want?"

"I want you to tell me that you're gonna fly that plane today."

"No. Not anywhere near ready to do that." I realized that last night I had been too tired to explain anything to Floyd. I took a deep breath. "Besides, I don't think I'm going to fly it at all."

"You can't be serious." Floyd looked puzzled and sly at the same time, as if he thought I was pulling his leg and he was pretty sure he was in on the joke.

"Maybe you noticed the blue Cadillac parked in front of the house this morning?"

"Oh yeah." Floyd slurped his coffee with a satisfied smile. "I just figured you were moving up in the world."

"Sadly, no. I had car problems. Nearly fatal, in fact. A funny thing happened on the way to the library yesterday."

"No kidding?"

I sighed. Where to begin? "My Dad was almost beaten to death. Whoever did it stuffed his body in the trunk of my car, then called in a tip on me to the Sheriff's Department. A frame job. Thank goodness it was badly done."

Floyd slammed his coffee cup down on one of my sawhorses, nearly cracking Mrs. Bellamy's china. "Jesus Christ, Vern, I am so sorry. Who did it? We'll get the sons of bitches, you and me. I got friends, you know."

"This is crazy stuff, Floyd. Nazi agents, apparently, right here in good old Kansas. They've already killed an Army CID officer who was on to them. One of them pretended to be him on the telephone with me. At any rate, that's what I was told, *after* Sheriff Hauptmann decided not to arrest me for the crime." I jerked my head toward the barn. "They're hunting our airplane, Floyd."

I was mildly surprised to hear myself use the word "our airplane." I'd almost said "my airplane." Last night I had been full of resolve to burn the thing to ash, today I was ready to defend it to the death.

Floyd didn't even blink at the mention of Nazis. I guess a few years in Europe could do that to a guy, too — gun shy at night, brave as a rock in daylight. "Why your Dad?"

"The only thing I can figure is someone saw us using his truck when we hauled everything home from the railroad depot the other day. I didn't mention that to the Sheriff. But it gets worse anyway."

"For your Dad?" Floyd seemed genuinely concerned, and I silently blessed him for the question. Some days it was easy to remember why we had been such great friends all these years.

"No, Doc Milliken says Dad's going to be okay. He didn't come to, so Hauptmann and the doc sent him on to Wichita for X-rays in case he has a concussion. The it-gets-worse part is that the paperwork from the f-panzer was stolen while I was at the library. The fake CID man pulled a con on me, got me away my desk at the library with a telephone call. When I went back, the papers were gone."

"Crud," Floyd said. His brow furrowed for a moment, then he grinned. "We don't need any paperwork, Vern. That's why we've got you."

"There was a lot of critical information in those papers, Floyd. For one thing, now I know where the airplane came from."

Floyd gave me a strange look. "Belgium."

I remembered the men down in the hole in the ice, the

airplane with the dark stain beneath it. "A lot further than that," I said. "Above the Arctic circle, deep in the ice."

"Huh." Floyd didn't seem impressed. "So after you found out about your dad and these roving killer Nazis, you borrowed Doc Milliken's car and came all the way out here late at night to check up on us. Wow, chum, that's some dedication."

"I didn't know if those lunatics who tried to kill my Dad would have come here looking for you. Lots of people saw us at the train depot. It won't be hard for them to put it together."

Floyd sucked his lower lip under his teeth and shook his head. "Vernon, there's nothing you could have done if there were Nazis here at the farm. Hit them over the head with your flashlight, maybe."

I realized what Floyd was politely telling me. "I guess that was pretty stupid of me."

"They tried to kill your dad, who is, pardon me, a lot tougher than you." God bless him, he didn't even look at my legs when he said that. "They capped off this CID guy, and he was a trained soldier. What do you think they would have done to you?"

Floyd's concern was touching, but a bit misplaced. "What about you and your parents?" I asked. "I almost spilled the whole story last night, but I wanted to catch up on my sleep, talk it over with you at length, and have one last look at the aircraft before we turned ourselves in."

"Turn ourselves in? For what?" Floyd seemed genuinely shocked. "You're crazy."

"Floyd, there are Nazi killers right here in Butler County, looking for something. There is a Nazi secret weapon in your barn. Put two and two together. What else could they possibly want in Kansas? It ain't wheat or pork bellies, I promise you that. As for me, I would much rather be answering uncomfortable questions from Sheriff Hauptmann and the U.S. Army CID than wondering where the next bullet was going to come from. They almost killed my dad. I don't need any more warnings." Even as I spoke, in my heart the airplane soared, giving the lie to my noble sense of self-preservation.

"Bullets aren't that bad," muttered Floyd. "A lucky man can dodge them. But I guess you have a point." His face brightened as he snapped his fingers. "What if we just get that thing out of here? It's still on your dad's truck. We could drive it away. Mary Ann has cousins in Ponca City. We could take it down there, get it right out of Kansas altogether."

"Floyd, the Nazis are looking for a truck from Dunham's Cartage. They'll be swarming all over the county soon enough. Besides, I'm not taking that thing to Ponca City. That's across the state line in Oklahoma, and that makes whatever trouble we're already in a problem for the FBI." Which might be on the case already, for all I knew. A dead CID captain was bound to attract a lot of attention in Washington, and the trail lead from Missouri right here to Augusta. "Finally, if we move the aircraft and the f-panzer, we're just moving the problem. These maniacs will tear up Butler County until they find it, and if they don't, they'll tear up the rest of Kansas. We're safest with our own authorities."

"No, no, that's not how it works," said Floyd. "I seen it plenty of times in Europe. A guy stumbles across something big, a busted bank vault or the treasury under some old chateau. He turns it over to the MPs or the Judge Advocate General, next thing he knows, he's peeling potatoes on bivouac in Libya while some officers cut themselves in for a percentage and maybe take a few extra medals for the poor guy's trouble. We need to keep this between us two. See, the way out is, we catch the Nazis and turn 'em over to the authorities ourselves. The war is over, how many of them can there be around here?"

I thought about the inimical Mrs. Sigurdsen from the library. Maybe we could work an angle with her, rat her right into Leavenworth. It was a pleasant if passing fantasy.

I shook my head violently. "Floyd, now you have me thinking like an idiot. We are *not* going Nazi hunting. The farther away we stay from these people, the safer we will all be. You, me, your parents, my dad. Everybody."

Floyd opened his mouth to say something else when the fire siren went off in Augusta. We were more than ten miles away from town, but when the wind was out of the west, you could hear it. That siren was loud.

"Oh, crud," said Floyd, turning to run back into the house. "I hope that's not a refinery fire."

The Mobil refinery was Augusta's biggest employer. If anything bad happened there, the town was in deep trouble.

I dropped the molding I had been cutting and trotted after him. As an afterthought, I stopped, turned to grab the silvery thing, and jammed it into my pocket. It didn't seem like something to leave lying around outside, not even in the Bellamys' yard. Especially not there, perhaps.

I can't run like Floyd, because of my bad leg, but I can walk pretty fast when the need arises. I made it through the kitchen just as Floyd clattered up the stairs. I followed him up to find him standing outside his bedroom window out on the porch roof. From down the hall, Mr. Bellamy was yelling something about fire axes.

"What is it?" I asked. I knew Floyd could see part of Augusta from the porch roof if he stood on his toes and strained. The Bellamys' farm was pretty high up on a ridge east of town, off Haverhill Road.

"Smoke," said Floyd.

"Is it the refinery?"

"No, looks like a building fire. Let's get into town."

"I'll drive," I said. I wasn't letting him touch the wheel of Doc Milliken's Cadillac, and his truck was at my boarding house.

I limped downstairs and started the convertible. Floyd came running out of the house, carrying an axe and a shovel, followed by Mr. Bellamy moving more slowly, carrying another axe. They threw the tools in the back seat. Floyd jumped in after the tools, while Mr. Bellamy opened the passenger door and got in the front.

"Let's go, Varian," rasped Mr. Bellamy over the rumble of the Cadillac's V-8 engine. As we pulled away, he began to cough.

* * *

We roared into town in the middle of an impromptu caravan of volunteer firefighters — everything from rattletrap hay wagons to a cut-down bus. As we drove up Highway 54 towards State Street, I had a sinking feeling about where the smoke was coming from. Reverend Little was at the head of our little caravan in his flatbed Chevy, and as he turned north onto State Street, I was sure the fire would be on Broadway.

It was. Mrs. Swenson's boarding house was in flames. My heart seized with that moment of cold terror you experience when you fly over the neck of a horse, or try to land an airplane solo for the first time. The thick, tarry smell of a burning house filled my nose. It was hot to be near it, hotter than a summer's day in the hay fields. Even the willow tree in the yard was burning, which in some illogical fashion struck me as a greater tragedy. The house was dying a terrible death. I prayed no one was dying with it.

Augusta's lone fire truck pumped valiantly as men rushed around the house with buckets, blankets and axes, but there looked to be no hope for the building. Mrs. Swenson stood in the front yard crying into Ruthie Milliken's arms, her dressing gown dotted black with ember burns. I looked up toward the window of my room on the second floor. It was a roaring inferno.

There wasn't much I had that I really cared about. My childhood things and most of my college books were still at Dad's house. Mr. Bellamy's pickup was far enough down the street to be out of danger. All I was really losing were my clothes and some notes and keepsakes. But the sheer effrontery of it really angered me.

I was sure the fire was deliberate, and that it was aimed at me. Small towns in Kansas were supposed to be safe, not crawling with Nazis and Army investigators, arsonists and father-beaters.

"Well, I guess there ain't much call for these axes." Mr. Bellamy leaned on the front fender of the Cadillac, watching the house burn and fighting his hacking cough.

"I'm going to check with the hose crew, see what help they need," said Floyd. He ran off toward the fire truck.

I walked around the yard, looking for Ollie or another Augusta cop. Instead, almost immediately I found Sheriff Hauptmann, flipping through a notebook. I tapped him on the shoulder. "Hey, Sheriff, what are you doing in town this early?"

The Sheriff turned. His eyebrows rose as if he was surprised to see me, but then he smiled. "Vernon, how are you? I was afraid you might still be inside."

He didn't look very afraid. I glanced at his notebook. I recognized it as one of my engineering workbooks. "Where did you get that?"

He looked down at the book as if he had never seen it before. "This? It was on the lawn. I was trying to figure out whose it was."

"My name is written on the cover," I pointed out. "How did it get on the lawn?"

"You do remember our conversation of last night? I think the fire was deliberately set, by someone searching your room. They could have thrown this out the window." Sheriff Hauptmann looked concerned, as if Nazis were going to leap from the lawn and drag me away.

I glanced back toward the burning house. There was certainly plenty of junk scattered around it, thrown out of windows or dropped as the residents fled. Now it was all getting soaked by hoses and trampled by eager firefighters. "Anybody hurt?"

"You were the only one unaccounted for. Where were you, by the way? I didn't see how you got here."

I looked at Sheriff Hauptmann holding my notebook, and I wondered what I could tell him. The same instinct that made me hold back the night before kept me quiet again. I just wasn't ready to squeal on the Bellamys yet. I looked him straight in the eye and lied. "I was at my dad's place, sir."

If he caught me out by hearing from someone else that I had just driven up from east of town with Mr. Bellamy and Floyd in the car, so be it. With any luck, I'd be away from him before that happened.

Sheriff Hauptmann smacked his forehead. "Son, son, I completely forgot. It's this house fire — it put me off. Your dad, we don't know where he is."

My sense of terrified dread from yesterday returned as if it had never left me. "What do you mean? Deputy Truefield took him to Wichita. How lost can he get?" It was all of a fifteen mile straight shot into the city from Augusta.

Hauptmann shook his head. "Truefield was tired, so he stopped for coffee just outside Wichita. When he got back to the cruiser, your dad was gone. He must have wandered off. We have the Wichita police and the Sedgwick County Sheriff's Department out looking for him."

I could barely contain my anger. "Coffee? I can't believe Truefield stopped for coffee with an injured man in his car. What the heck is the matter with that idiot?"

Hauptmann frowned. "Vernon, I know you're upset, but you'll have to take it easy. I've already reprimanded Deputy Truefield for negligence, and we'll find your dad. No one's dropped him down a well."

"You don't know that. The fake Markowicz might have followed your precious Deputy and kidnapped Dad while Truefield was having his little cup of joe. Dad literally *could* be down a well right now. They already tried to kill him once. Abandoning a man whose life is clearly in danger isn't negligence, it's dereliction of duty."

"Vern, son, you'd better go sit down. I know you're under quite a strain what with your dad being attacked, then your house burning down, but you're starting to say things you might come to regret. I'm doing the best I can, as are all my men, and I'll thank you not to push me further on it. Now go get some rest. I will find you if I need you, or when we have news of your dad."

Hauptmann shoved past me and walked toward the fire truck. As I watched him go I could see Floyd dragging a new hose across the street for the fire crew. Hauptmann stopped walking and stared at Floyd, then turned and looked back at me. I just stared the Sheriff down, keeping my face noncommittal.

There was something odd about the way he was handling all this. He wasn't acting as I would have expected a cop to act — more defensive and secretive than anything else. The CID people must be making him keep a tight lid on things. I suddenly realized that Hauptmann had kept my notebook.

I walked back to the Cadillac, fishing in my pocket for the keys. I found the twisted silvery thing from the f-panzer instead. Even standing near the angry heat of the huge house fire, it still felt warm to my touch. I pulled it out as I sat down in the driver's seat, and turned it over in my hands.

I pressed the buttons, one after another. The first two had no effect, but the third one made the thing tingle in my hands. It felt like a mild electric shock. I realized that I shouldn't be fooling with the device out here in public, so I put the twisted thing back in my pocket, leaned on the steering wheel and watched the fire complete the destruction of my home.

The passenger door of the car opened, and the Cadillac shifted slightly on its springs. Without turning, I said "Hello, Mr. Bellamy." I wondered what name he would call me now. Since he'd started getting sick, he had gone the past year without calling me "Vernon" once.

Then he kissed my ear.

"Yikes!" I jumped, then looked to my right. Lois smiled at me, pearly teeth like kernels of corn between her fresh, full lips.

I hadn't seen her in weeks, not even to say "hi" to on the street.

"Hey, Vernon. How are you?" She glanced toward the fire then back at me, her eyes big and soft with determined compassion that melted my heart.

Lois wore one of her Sunday-go-to-church dresses, a green shirtwaist number with a pink sweater over it. She looked gorgeous. I'm a sucker for girls with dark hair in pink sweaters.

"Yeah, I'm fine. I wasn't here when the fire started or anything, so I was never in any danger."

"You look pretty upset," she said. "You should be."

I wondered what she wanted, but I wasn't going to turn down the attention.

"It's not good," I sighed. I thought about telling her about Dad getting beaten half to death by the Nazis, while the CID chased them, and maybe me, around, but that didn't seem to be a good idea. The less said about that stuff, the better. "Dad's missing," I finally said.

"Missing?" Her eyes were soft, drowning pools of memory. "Oh, Vernon, you know how he is. He's just sleeping it off somewhere stupid, where nobody can find him."

"No, I wish that was all there was to it. He was injured yesterday, took a bang on the head." I edited down the real events — no need to tell Lois how angry I was at Sheriff Hauptmann and his Deputy, any more than talking about Nazis hiding in the Augusta library. "He wandered off when the person taking him to the hospital in Wichita stopped for an errand."

"A head injury," she said. "That's the last thing he needed."

"I know that, too." I suddenly wished I had been a lot nicer to him all along. He needed me at least as much as I needed him. His leaving me for a bottle was no excuse for me to run away in turn. The smoke from the fire stung my eyes as I thought about him.

Lois touched my shoulder. "Does it have anything to do with that plate in his head?"

"He got hit right on the plate, actually. Doc Milliken sent him on to Wichita for X-rays. That's when he disappeared, on that trip."

"Oh, Vernon, this is so terrible." Lois hugged me, tight. I could feel her bosoms pressing into my side. She wasn't a very demonstrative girl, and we'd never been that close, so I must have been very obvious about needing a hug.

Heck, I hadn't even told her about Doc Milliken's hitching post and Mrs. Bellamy's kitchen door.

After a minute Lois leaned over to whisper in my ear. That about made me jump out of the car, startled with a ticklish pleasure. "What are you doing in Doc Milliken's car?"

"He loaned it to me," I said. "I had a problem with the Hudson yesterday."

"Think we could go for a ride?" She ran her hand across my shoulder. "I want to let you know *in person* how I glad I am that you're safe and sound. And you had such a *rough* day yesterday."

It was just liked I'd imagined. The convertible had an effect on Lois that my ratty, faded-black Hudson sedan had never managed. I looked at the fire. Sheriff Hauptmann was nowhere to be seen. Mr. Bellamy was chopping down a tree near the flames, looking quite spry for a man with a near-fatal chest condition. Amazing what stress could do. Floyd pulled yet another hose from somewhere down the street.

There was nothing for me except to be miserable and worry about Dad. Except go for a ride with Lois.

"Sure thing," I said, starting the Cadillac. It was early enough in the day that I even if we did a little mugging I might get her back in time for church. Though probably not Sunday School. I drove down Broadway, away from the fire, a smile stealing across my face despite my woes.

A voice spoke in my ear. "*Wer ist dort?*"

"What?"

"I didn't say anything," said Lois, stroking my arm.

The voice spoke again. It was definitely masculine. "*Sprechen Sie Deutsch?*"

CHAPTER SEVEN

I've had enough of you damned Germans!" I yelled at the top of my lungs. I slammed on the brakes, bringing the Cadillac to a screeching halt in the middle of Osage Street.

"Vernon, honey, are you okay?" Lois leaned across the big front seat to lay a hand on my shoulder.

There was no way I could answer her right then. My entire body twitched. I turned around and looked in the back. No Germans there, just an axe and a shovel. Mr. Bellamy was using the other axe on the willow tree, I remembered. I opened the door and got out, walking around the car to inspect it, careful as a pre-flight. I knew perfectly well there wasn't anything to find, but I had to do it. Hidden loudspeakers. Trick wiring. Some bizarre practical joke on the part of Doc Milliken and maybe Sheriff Hauptmann.

Lois trailed behind me, arms folded across her chest and her face set.

With a grunt of frustration, I yanked open the trunk. Nothing there but a spare tire and some blankets. No bodies, thankfully. I stuck my head in anyway, studying the back of the trunk, where it met the rear seat of the car. Just some flecks of seat insulation. Pulling myself out of the trunk, I grabbed the bumper and used it to ease myself down to a kneeling position, weight on my good leg. I bent my head to scan the underside of the car. Nothing under there either.

I hadn't expected to find anything, but I really wanted to. Standing up, hands on my hips, I looked around the block of Osage where we were stopped. Not a soul in sight — everyone was down the street and around the corner at the fire. I put my hand in my pocket. The twisted thing I'd taken from the f-panzer was just as warm as it had been before. It hadn't lost the static tingle that it had acquired after I started messing with the buttons.

Such a fool I had been to do that.

My stomach flopped, and my skin crawled, the scabs on the back my head from Mr. Bellamy's birdshot itching terribly. I tugged the little piece of equipment out and studied it again. It didn't look like anything I'd ever seen — too small, no power source — but this little doo-dad had to be a radio. The Nazi agents were talking to me over the aircraft's own equipment. Of course they would know their own frequencies. They were tracing me.

Taunting me.

Threatening.

I was certain that I hadn't turned on any of the electronic equipment in the f-panzer. I wondered if Floyd had done so, if they had gotten to me through him.

"Vernon?" Lois' voice interrupted my paranoid line of reasoning as she hit a rising pitch — a bad sign, with women. The loving concern of a few minutes earlier had evaporated. "Vernon Dunham, you are acting like a crazy person." She grabbed my elbow, yanking me off balance.

"I'm sorry," I said as I caught myself against the raised trunk lid of the Cadillac. "It's just that I thought—"

"I don't care what you thought." She was all the way into shrill now, shouting, her face flushed under her makeup. "Either you're too upset to be out driving around, or you are *inexcusably* rude. Now which is it?" She tapped her foot, the very picture of a Woman Waiting for an Answer.

And this was one of those female questions to which a mere man like me had no correct response.

"*Was geschieht?*" said the masculine voice in my ear. He was definitely speaking German.

"Shut up!" I yelled.

"Don't you tell me to shut up, Vernon Dunham."

Lois had gone from shrill and angry to hard and quiet. I was really in the soup now. I stared at my feet as Lois continued to yell at me.

"I don't have to take that from you or anybody else. I don't care what kind of fancy car you swiped." She kicked the fender of Doc Milliken's Cadillac.

"*Was ist die Bedeutung von* 'shut up'?" asked the voice.

I pled my case, reaching to take Lois' hands in mine, but she shrugged me off. "Honey, you don't understand. I'm not trying to shut you up. This is so much more complicated, about my dad and everything else that's been happening." The airplane, it was the airplane that stood between us.

Lois turned on her heel and walked away, tossing her hair.

"Lois," I called after her. "Please."

She stopped and glared at me over her shoulder. "You are obviously very distressed right now. I will make a point of forgetting what happened this morning. But the next time you call for me, Vernon Dunham, there had best be a dozen roses and an extremely sweet apology or that will be the end of that."

She walked up Osage toward Broadway without looking back again. I sat down on the rim of the open trunk of the Cadillac.

"*Wer sind Sie?*" asked the voice.

Where are you? Who are you? My college German refused to be dredged up sufficiently to remember the list of question words. And this was an awfully retarded Nazi agent, I thought, to be in the middle of America and babbling away in German. The old bat down at the library would have understood, I was sure, but not me.

"Speak English!" I yelled into the thin air. "If you're going to ruin my life, at least let me understand you while you're doing it."

"*Englisch?*"

"English."

"*Sie sind Engländer?*"

Well, that was clear enough. "Red-blooded American, by God." Like most guys, my language got worse as I got more and more angry. It was probably just as well that Lois had left. Just one more thing she'd hold against me, otherwise.

"*Amerikaner?*"

"Damned straight. From right here in Kansas."

"*Wo ist* 'Kansas'?"

I shut the trunk and got back in the car without answering further. This had become ridiculous. I restarted the Cadillac and pulled over to the side of the road before someone came along and asked me what I was doing. I wanted to keep driving away from the fire, from Lois' anger, from the voice, but I didn't know where to go next.

I had a feeling it wouldn't be long before Sheriff Hauptmann had me tailed on a full-time basis. I obviously needed the protection, with everything happening around me. He seemed suspicious of me, as well, so maybe I was lucky he hadn't taken me in after all.

Heck, at this point I'd be suspicious of me. No matter what I did now, it looked bad. Including standing in the middle of Osage Street arguing with invisible Nazis. Lois was a good enough egg, even if she was never quite my girl. I could hope she'd write that off to an episode of shell shock, so to speak, and not go blabbing to Doc Milliken out of concern for my sanity.

But the question of what to do next deviled me. I didn't feel like seeking out the voice, which had fallen mercifully silent. That thought reminded me of the metal thing from the f-panzer, which lay heavy in my pocket. I drew it back out and looked at it again.

It was just as small and twisted as ever. Just like the aircraft, it had the unmistakable look of having been designed that way. By someone who didn't think like I did. I turned it over. No seams, no access doors — although something like that could easily have been concealed in the visual complexity of the design.

Yes, this had to be a radio set. Somehow, this was the device the German was using to talk to me. I didn't understand how it spoke in my ear without Lois hearing it, but that was just engineering as far as I was concerned. Like the questions I could ask about its miraculously small size, the lack of a power source, absence of an antenna — there must be hundred of those little problems. Regardless, this was a handset for talking to the aircraft.

Satisfied that I had understood the answer to one small conundrum of so many, I shoved the Nazi radio back in my pocket and drove over to the State Street Lounge. I needed a drink, something I never did.

I knew I was just a pale echo of my father.

Even though it was Sunday morning and the parking lot was empty, I knew from listening to Floyd chatter that the place would probably be open. The lighted sign in the window said "CLOSED," just as the law required for the Lord's Day, but the door was unlocked.

When I went inside, I found Midge wiping down tables. She was a small-boned woman, almost girlish, with black hair and big mole on one cheek. She looked like a three-quarter scale model of a Hollywood pin-up girl, especially in the red-trimmed white dress she was wearing instead of a uniform. I could see what Floyd liked about her.

"Oh, hey," she said, flipping the grubby towel over her shoulder. The place was empty except for the two of us. "You're Floyd's friend, right?"

"Yes." I had my hands in my pocket, feeling foolish and nervous. "Vernon Dunham."

Midge popped her gum at me. "What can I do for you, Vernon Dunham?"

I had the sudden wish that she'd kiss me the way she kissed Floyd. It was the same wish I'd had for years, that the world would love me the way it loved him. He had two good legs, service medals, and a personality the girls went gaga over. Me, I limped, was too smart for my own good, and never seemed to say the right thing to anyone.

"I want a drink." I'd said. Somewhere deep inside my heart, I apologized to Mom.

Pop went the gum. "We're not open Sundays. Against the law to serve liquor, wine or beer."

"I heard if I tipped big enough you'd give it to me."

She smiled, lipstick as pink as her gum. It clashed terribly with the red trim of her dress. "Tip big enough, a fellow could get a lot of stuff around here." Midge ran one tiny hand along the hem of the v-neck of her dress, flipping the fabric back just slightly.

It could have been a casual gesture, but it wasn't. Despite myself, I felt a firm, hard rush to my groin, and my breathing got faster.

I was a virgin. I'd never gone with a girl who went for those games. I'd never seen Lois in less than a bathing suit, and didn't expect to unless we got married. Which had never seemed likely.

Now, this little dark-haired woman was offering me something I'd dreamed about since junior high school, for just a bit of money. I probably had enough cash.

My hand drifted to my back pocket as Midge smiled at me.

Oh God, I couldn't do this. I couldn't talk dirty with a girl like this, even though I knew exactly what she meant, exactly what I wanted. I could buy those kisses I'd longed for, and as much more as I could afford, just like I could buy that drink I'd longed for.

Then I'd be like Floyd and Dad. No one else might ever know, but I would. It wasn't any big deal to Floyd, and with Dad, well, who could tell, but I would feel different, crossing a line I could never come back from.

Even worse, what if she was teasing me? It wouldn't be the first time a girl had gotten my goat, just to laugh about it later.

"I, I...no thanks," I blurted, my face red and hot.

She leaned forward and blew me a kiss, flipping her dress open far enough to show me the edges of a lacy white brassiere. "Your loss, honey."

Face hot, breath heaving, groin aching, I stumbled through the door. Behind me, Midge laughed, her voice pealing like little silver bells.

In the parking lot, I banged my head against the steering wheel of the Cadillac until most of the pressure in my sinuses went away. Not to mention the pressure elsewhere. What did I stand for? What did I want? I had been ready to do one stupid thing, trying to drink away my troubles. It took the offer of another stupid thing to wake me up. I felt like I'd walked to the edge of the bridge and thought about jumping.

"By God," I muttered to the dashboard, "I will never find myself on the inside a bottle. I will not be like Dad."

Dad.

His name blew Midge right out of my thoughts like last year's leaves. Last night I had been willing to let him go to the hospital alone. He was unconscious, but Doc Milliken had said Dad wasn't in great danger. Every time I saw the old man, I got angry all over again with him, but now, since finding him in the trunk of my car, I pitied him.

My heart ached for him.

I really wanted to go look for him in Wichita, but there was no point. A hundred and fifty thousand people lived there, and I didn't even know the name of the coffee shop where Deputy Truefield had lost him. For that matter, I realized, I didn't know which hospital Doc Milliken had sent Dad to. There were several hospitals in Wichita. Why hadn't he told me? That was strange.

What I could do for him was to drive out to Dad's house and look around myself. Ollie Wannamaker had told Sheriff Hauptmann that the place looked like it had been tossed. I could well imagine what Ollie thought he saw, but I knew Dad's habits, especially how he had been since Mom died. Unlike Ollie, I'd be able to tell which part of the mess was new and which was just housekeeping Dunham-style. Gosh only knew what Ollie might have missed in the chaos.

I started the Cadillac and headed out toward Wichita Highway. I passed just a few blocks from the police station, which made me wonder if there was any point in telling the entire story to Ollie — Nazis, airplane and all. Or maybe even approaching Chief Davis for help. I could throw myself on the mercy of the Augusta police department. If I was lucky, they'd put me in jail just to keep me safe.

But that wasn't the right thing to do either. Anything I said to Ollie Wannamaker, or anyone else on the Augusta force, would get back to Sheriff Hauptmann within a day or two. And my confidence in Hauptmann was slipping fast. He kept acting strangely around me — nothing obvious, but enough to tip me that something was up. He was obviously working with CID to crack this Nazi thing and find the murderers of the late Captain Markowicz. Not to mention the real-live fake Captain Markowicz.

There was some angle that involved me, which was why he was looking through my notebooks. But obviously he wasn't going to let me in on whatever was going on. Besides, Ollie had acted pretty odd when I talked to him about Floyd yesterday. Something was definitely happening around me, something that involved Dad and Floyd. It had to involve me.

That meant I was either under suspicion or I was being used for bait. *I* knew I wasn't a Nazi, but the whole thing with the aircraft could be getting me in really big trouble. I still wanted to talk Floyd into turning ourselves in, but we'd been interrupted by the fire and I'd bet it would be this evening before he and I got a chance to discuss it. And then who to turn ourselves in to? There must have been an FBI office in Wichita. At this point I would much rather turn ourselves in there.

And then I'd lose the aircraft. I'd never see it again — they would haul it off to Wright Field or someplace even more secret out in the deserts of the west, and tear it apart.

I shook my head. Damnation, but that was a beautiful piece of machinery.

Even worse, if I wasn't under any suspicion, that meant Sheriff Hauptmann really was using me for bait. I didn't like the idea of Hauptmann hanging me out to dry in order to catch a few Nazis.

I laughed out loud at myself. My imagination was running away from me — things were bad enough with Dad and the fire at Mrs. Swenson's boarding house. I didn't need to conjure phantoms to make them worse. Heck, I could just go back to the beginning of the problems of the last two days and demand my envelope back from Mrs. Sigurdsen. But I figured my chances of that working out were slim. Regardless of whether the Head Librarian was one of the Nazi gang, she could probably break my neck by sheer force of character. The only reason I didn't suspect her of beating Dad was that I couldn't imagine her being willing to make that much noise.

Besides which, the library wasn't open on Sundays. God-fearing folk generally went to church, while the rest of us slept in or read the paper. At least I hadn't gone home last night. I'd probably be dead now if I had, killed in the fire or beaten by whoever set it, just the way they had beaten Dad.

There was a chilling thought.

My musings were interrupted by an odd sensation from the pocket into which I slipped the German radio handset — it was getting very warm, like the time in junior high school when Floyd had set my pants on fire. Was it the invisible German, coming back for more? He had been silent since asking me about Kansas.

I pulled the car off the road by the Whitewater River dike along the west edge of town. Augusta stretched behind me, sleepy in the autumn Sunday afternoon, except for the angry black pillar of smoke that still boiled into the sky from my destroyed home. The Whitewater flood plain stretched in front of me — willow trees, water meadows, ducks lifting off.

Fishing into my pocket, I pulled out the silvery handset. It was sufficiently hot to the touch that I dropped it on the seat. I didn't know how much hotter it would get, and I didn't want to scorch Doc Milliken's leather upholstery, so I grabbed the floor mat from the passenger side foot well and laid that on the seat. I flipped the handset over onto the mat with my fingertips, blowing the heat off them afterward.

"Change of plans," I said. This thing needed to go back to the f-panzer pronto. The heating up bugged me, but it was too small to be a bomb. I didn't feel like I was in any particular danger. Rather, it appeared to be an electronics malfunction. Not immediately worrisome, but too much trouble to deal with here in the car. At the very least, it meant my German friend wouldn't be bugging me any more. Maybe I could find a way to explain it to Lois after she cooled off, too.

At any rate, whatever the problem with the handset was, I didn't need to haul this thing around the county with me. It would take some more time out of my day, but I had to take the silvery thing back to the Bellamys' place. If it got hotter on the way, I'd deal with that. I didn't want to submerge it in water, but at the least I could set on some open ground and wait to see if it burst into flames or something. Assuming nothing like that happened, I could drop the handset off, then go check around Dad's place for myself.

I owed him that much.

I had to u-turn the Cadillac across Wichita Highway in order to head back through town. As I put it in gear, a high-pitched squeal gave me an instant headache. I'd never in my life heard an automobile make a noise like that. The car bucked and stalled, straddling the center of the highway.

Thank God it was Sunday morning — there was no refinery traffic, and most people were in church. And today, the rest of them were off fighting that fire. Even before I could touch the starter, it turned over on its own and the engine started up again.

That was weird. I knew quite a bit about engines from my work at Boeing, and that wasn't possible. The engine hadn't been dieseling, and the car wasn't moving fast enough to re-start itself. This had been the starter turning over, and starters didn't just fire on their own. It seemed like the handset's electrical problems were contagious.

The Cadillac's horn started honking, echoing across the dike and the trees in the bottomland beyond. The car bucked again as I tried to switch it off — I hadn't liked the sudden start and wanted to let everything cool down, until all the static discharge left the system or whatever was wrong had a chance to settle. Even as big as it was, I figured I could push the Cadillac to the other shoulder if need be. But now the engine wouldn't shut *off*.

Then the radio came on, popping and hissing. There was another high-pitched, ear-splitting squeal. The tuner knob began to slowly turn by itself, as if an invisible hand had laid fingers upon it.

My hair prickled up, bumps rising on my arms. I wanted to leap from the car, but at the same time I was fascinated. I had never seen, or heard, anything like this. My spine shivered as the speakers wailed, the radio passing through the whole range of frequencies. Gospel music from Wichita, a news bulletin, an ad for fertilizer, a bellowing radio preacher, big band music, two different farm reports. It hit the end of its range and the knob reversed, the invisible hand starting back down again.

The radio settled down to a Negro gospel service out of Wichita. I reached for the knob, but it was stuck on that frequency. I turned the Cadillac off. This time the car died, just like it should. I pressed the starter. It cranked right up again, radio blurting back to life on the same gospel station.

Except for the radio being stuck on at the one station, the Cadillac now seemed willing to run again like a normal automobile. I finished the u-turn and headed back through town. What had made it behave this way? The engineer in me wanted to imagine weird magnetic fields, electrical disturbances in the atmosphere, but I knew that couldn't be true. Hundreds of cars and trucks drove up and down Wichita Highway every day. Maybe thousands. Heck, it was a U.S. Highway, 54, that got long-haul traffic all the time. Somebody would have noticed if it was built over a huge hunk of magnetic ore, or an Indian burial ground, or something.

Or something. Right.

I drove slowly, keeping the speed down so that if I lost control again I wouldn't kill myself or anyone else. With the glaring exception of the radio, the car continued to behave normally.

Forget magnetic anomalies, it was the handset from the f-panzer. That thing had to be a radio, although I could not imagine how a handset could be made so small. I'd seen plenty of radios in my work at Boeing. Miniaturizing the tubes alone would be an engineering challenge on par with the biggest projects ever considered. And it wasn't just tubes. Circuit design, fabrication, the works. Whoever had buried my aircraft in the Arctic ice had also built a transceiver that was a miracle of engineering, a transceiver that the Nazi gang here in Butler County was using to track me and somehow take control of my car. Not to mention whisper in my ear.

That idea was plumb crazy. Radio didn't work that way. In principle, you could use radio waves to send control signals for mechanical processes, but that would require extensive special equipment at the receiving end — servomotors and so forth. No one could build a receiver that would take over the electrical system of an ordinary automobile.

Which, of course, was what had just happened to me. On the other hand, no one could build that receiver in the first place, so if they could do one impossible thing, why not do another?

Hands clenched on the wheel, I made it through the middle of town, averting my eyes as I drove past the turn to the State Street Lounge. I didn't think I could ever set foot in that place again.

Even though I felt like a circus freak — *see the Unlucky Man, displayed for your edification ladies and gentlemen* — no one on the streets of Augusta gave me a second glance. Gaining confidence in the Cadillac's continued good behavior, I gradually accelerated as I headed out past the eastern edge of town.

The radio still stuck loudly on one station, I listened to colored folks praying and singing all the way back to the Bellamy place.

CHAPTER EIGHT

As usual, the little track that cut off from Haverhill Road up to the Bellamys' farm was almost axle-deep in mud. But the black walnuts lining the road were beautiful enough to make up for the aggravation of driving it. I was also pleased to see the tell-tale caterpillar tracks of the f-panzer had been obscured by all the recent coming and going.

I manhandled the Cadillac as it slid along. The car fish-tailed to the rhythms of the colored church service on the radio. I found I was tapping my fingers on the steering wheel rim in time to the music as well.

I laughed. "Who'd have thought it?" I asked the walnuts.

When I drove into the yard, I considered parking in front of the house and walking to the barn. The Cadillac was lower to the ground than either my Hudson or Mr. Bellamy's truck. But then I'd have to carry the German handset. I'd decided the thing scared me, sitting on the passenger seat, scorching a hole in Doc Milliken's carpeted floor mat. I was darned glad I'd thought of the mat in the first place — it would be cheaper to replace than the seat leather.

I drove across the yard along the smoothest of the various ruts leading toward the barn. As I pulled up in front of the barn doors, the radio shut itself off. I turned the engine of the Cadillac off as well and listened to the silence. Distant birds chirped, chickens fretted within the barn, while somewhere nearby a heifer bawled the eternal complaints of dim-minded cattle.

But there was no motor, no gospel hour, no German voice. Nothing interrupted the sounds of nature except for the sputtering drone of a small airplane.

That got my attention. I jumped out of the car and walked around the barn, scanning the sky. In the distance I could see a small high-winged monoplane circling low. Probably a Piper Cub, L-4 in the military version. I recognized a search pattern when I saw one, and I was willing to bet my friend upstairs was either looking for an old Mack stake bed truck or a blue Cadillac convertible.

I hurried back around to the front of the barn and dragged open the door. Then I started the Cadillac and pulled it inside. Doc Milliken's big car barely fit with the two trucks already taking up space in the barn, and I nearly ran over one of the barn cats getting the car in there. I stepped out and pulled the doors shut as the droning of the airplane came closer. Thank God for all the mud. That kept me from leaving any kind of a dust trail that would stand out from the air like a searchlight pointing back at me.

I finally turned around and looked at my aircraft. I thought my heart was going to stop.

It had changed *shape*.

The crumpled fuselage was stretched out, the furrows and bends evening into the elegant airfoil I had envisioned earlier. The ends had expanded into wings, although they were still very stubby. The thing was huge, filling the barn, barely balanced on the back of the Mack truck.

And it was beautiful. It reminded me of a bird of prey, composed organic curves and odd textures across its body. I walked around the airplane. The shape was more like a teardrop set within a flattened disc — a saucer. I sank to my good knee, propping myself up on my bad right leg, and shook my head.

The idea that had been nagging me almost from the beginning had to be true. The engineering of this thing was astounding, beyond anything that could be done by human hands. No German ever built such a thing, I was sure of that, nor an American. Where had it come from? I shook my head in awe.

That stolen Nazi report had been telling me the tale, but it was so unbelievable that I had refused to take it seriously. That this aircraft had been found under the ice truly meant it must be ancient beyond measure. Inhuman. Literally.

I felt cold, and very small.

"What is happening, my brother?" asked a German accented voice in my ear, speaking in the rich, rolling rhythms of a radio preacher.

I was so surprised I lost my precarious balance. I fell over, feet tangled together like a kid who'd run too fast downhill, cursing the pain in my bad leg.

The voice broke into a rousing rendition of "Amazing Grace," carrying four-part harmony with itself.

The aircraft was talking to me.

It had to be.

Whatever Nazi agents might be lurking in Butler County, they weren't learning their English from Negro gospel programs. There wasn't anyone else it could be. I stared at the aircraft in open-mouthed astonishment as the voice continued to sing in my ear. The machine quivered in time to the music.

That proved it. I didn't even want to think how it was possible — giant banks of phonographs, with some kind of gear-driven selector process? I'd worked with pretty sophisticated calculators at Boeing, but it would take a calculator many times the size of this barn to begin parsing, let alone bounce from German to English. This, perhaps, was the true miracle of my airplane.

Outside, the drone of the Cub became a loud roar as it buzzed the barn. Distracted from my line of thought, I grabbed the smoking floor mat with the silvery radio handset off the seat of Doc Milliken's Cadillac and ran to the barn door. There were plenty of warped boards for me to peek out between the cracks without opening it.

I watched the Cub land in the lower pasture, spooking the heifers terribly. The little airplane was dark green, with Army

Air Corps markings. I had seen enough of them at the Boeing plant during the war, coming and going with visiting engineers or Army Air Force brass. I wish I knew what unit the tail numbers and squadron markings on the Cub referred to — I'd never bothered to learn USAAF unit organizations outside of the heavy bomber wings I had helped build. We always knew over at the plant when one of our big birds went down, sooner or later.

The unit didn't matter. Wherever it came from, that Cub was being used by CID Or maybe by the false Captain Markowicz, he of the broken arm. I wasn't sure which was worse for me, but now that my aircraft had spread her gorgeous wings and spoken to me, I wasn't letting go without a fight.

But I sure wished the darned airplane would quit *singing*!

I looked around the barn in a mild but controlled panic. The deadliest thing in here was a pitchfork. With my bad leg I seriously doubted my ability to menace a Nazi agent with one of those. Even if I had been prepared to take on the entire SS last night in the Bellamys' kitchen armed with just a flashlight, today my wits were better gathered.

Fine, I thought. No available weapons. What was my next option? I peered out the door again. The Cub was taxiing to the downwind side of the pasture. The pilot was positioning for a quick take-off. I would have done the same in his place, especially if I was up to no good. Unfortunately, his taxi pattern would put the Cub mighty close to my barn door.

I considered fleeing out the back of the barn. That required me to either cut across the yard to the house, in full view of whoever was in the aircraft, or head over the back pasture towards the peach orchard. Floyd probably would have managed that, but I couldn't move sufficiently fast enough over open country to be sure of hiding before they got close enough to notice me.

I looked speculatively at the Cadillac, remembering years of watching gangster movies like *Public Enemy* down at the Augusta Theatre. If I started the car and revved up the engine, I could drop her in gear, smash down the barn door and make for the road. Even wallowing through the mud, the Cadillac could outpace a running man. I could hunker down behind the dashboard if they started shooting. I knew the yard well enough to make it out safely with barely any view of where I was going.

On the other hand, running down the barn door seemed like a bad idea on principle. The Mack, the f-panzer and my aircraft would be wide open. Even ignoring the Cub, the barn faced southeast, and could be seen from the track heading down toward Haverhill Road. I decided to wait in the Cadillac, my hand on the starter button, and see if my unwelcome visitors opened the door themselves. If they were Nazis, the false Captain Markowicz and his confederates, then I would just run them down.

I amazed myself with my sheer cold-bloodedness. Breathing deep, I remembered Dad, dumped to die in the trunk of my Hudson. I thought about Mrs. Swenson, crying in her yard while her house flamed like an October bonfire. These damned Germans had no business here in Kansas. They'd already destroyed half of Europe, only to have Uncle Sam give them a sound drubbing for their trouble. Defeated, they should have just slunk off the stage of history, instead of bringing their war home to my Kansas.

And of course the Nazi agents were here because of that voice singing "Amazing Grace" in my ear, chasing Floyd and his never-ending scams. I never knew the hymn had so many verses, either.

"Will you shut up," I hissed into the folded piece of smoldering carpet. I didn't know it was possible for my aircraft to talk, but it did a great job of irritating me. Just like Floyd.

"What is 'shut up,' my brother?"

"It means *be quiet*. Now, shut up!"

"*Ja.*"

I heard footsteps outside the barn, rustling in the scattered straw. They certainly weren't making any effort to sneak up on me. Of course, after arriving in a military aircraft, there probably wasn't much sneaking left to be done. They couldn't have announced themselves better with a doorbell.

"Hello, the barn," called a voice. I strained to hear if it had a German accent. Really, he sounded more New York. Either way, I wasn't going to answer.

"This is Captain Abraham Markowicz of United States Army Criminal Investigation Division. Can you hear me?"

Markowicz. This was the German posing as a dead man from Kansas City. I kept my thumb on the starter button of the Cadillac.

"We'd better just open the door, sir," said a deeper voice.

So he'd brought muscle with him. Well, at least I had the car, which was big and heavy.

"Yeah, I know," said the false Markowicz. "I'm worried about the paperwork. We're on civilian rules right now."

"If there's something in there, we close the door, and go get a warrant. Or you radio in for advice from jag."

Jag? I knew the word...Judge Advocate General. That and search warrants. They were scamming me hard. Easier than coming in shooting, I guessed.

The door creaked as fingers pried around the edge to pull it open. I pressed the starter on the Cadillac, which turned right over like a champ, and gunned the engine. Screaming my best Indian war whoop, I slammed the big car into gear.

As he stepped into the opening of the door, I could see that Markowicz was a thin, red-haired man wearing an Army uniform — the dressy one with the buff-colored coat and tie. His hazel eyes were wide with panic as the front of the Cadillac slammed into him. I swerved toward a small, dark man in fatigues with an M-1 rifle slung on his shoulder who was still tugging on the door. While Markowicz scrabbled on the hood, trying not to get dragged under the car, I managed to graze his bodyguard with the front right fender. Unfortunately, the fender also got caught on the barn door with a terrible groaning noise, before pulling it completely off its hinges in a shower of splinters and straw.

Markowicz screamed as he slid across the hood of the car, both arms flailing when his grip came loose. My acceleration brought his face pressed up against the windshield for a moment before he finally fell off the left side. I swerved again, feeling a bump that hopefully meant I had run over him. Forgetting my plan to crouch down, I turned to look behind me while the car slammed across the rutted pasture below the barn.

The small, dark man was down on one knee, aiming the rifle at me. I ducked as I heard the crack of the bullet. The windshield over my head shattered from the impact.

I twisted around, head hunched down into the steering wheel. I had to navigate by the memory I had been so confident of earlier. Where was I in the yard? I pulled to the left, accelerating again, trying to miss the well pump that stood midway between the barn and the house. There was a buzzing whine as another bullet ricocheted off the dashboard of the Cadillac.

The car hit something, stopping solidly and slamming my forehead hard into the steering wheel.

"Jesus Christ!" I yelled.

I peeked up. I had run into Mr. Bellamy's derelict Ford coupe. I shoved the stick into reverse, and the Cadillac slid backwards up through the mud of the yard, wallowing out of control. Ahead of me, one of the rear quarter windows of the coupe shattered from another bullet.

I popped the clutch, shifted back into first, and gunned the engine, pulling the Cadillac to the right. Yet another bullet smashed into the dash, this time shattering the radio. The bastard was shooting for me, not the car, I realized. Surely he could have blown one of my tires by now.

Sweating and cursing under my breath, I got the car headed down the hill and out of the yard. The bullets stopped coming.

As I rattled down the mud track toward Haverhill Road, I risked lifting my head and looking behind me. The man with the gun had indeed stopped shooting in order to drag the false Markowicz toward the Cub. They must be going for help. I had to get help, too. But who the heck could I ask?

If I drove to El Dorado and talked to Hauptmann, the whole story would come out. He would know I had lied to him, and I figured that would be a very unpleasant moment between us. If I went to the Augusta police, they would just call Hauptmann. Either way, the condition of Doc Milliken's Cadillac pretty much guaranteed I'd be taken in for questioning. No cop alive could ignore all those bullet holes. If I tried to contact the Army, maybe sending a telegram to Fort Riley or Fort Leavenworth, they would think I was a lunatic, or worse.

Instead I kept driving, cautiously peering over the dash in case Markowicz's pet gorilla happened to be a sniper, too.

The Cub took off behind me. It banked overhead, dangerously low. If he were a civilian, the Civil Aeronautics Administration would have had his license just for that. The plane buzzed the road, flying low over me. The little dark guy with the rifle must be flying it. He waggled the wings as he passed over me, then gained altitude and headed out to the northeast, in the direction of El Dorado.

Somehow I doubted the wing waggle was the traditional friendly greeting of a pilot passing overhead. I interpreted it as more of a threat. "I'll be back," they were telling me. After my performance with the car, I felt ready for them, but I knew perfectly well once I calmed down, it would be time to panic all over again.

Those darned Nazi agents would come after me in force next time.

With the Cub in the air and departed from the scene, once I got out onto Haverhill Road I pulled over into the weeds at the side of the road to inspect the damage to Doc Milliken's car. The fighting thrill already receding, I realized with a desperate wince that I could never afford to repair this Cadillac. I walked around it and took inventory of the damage anyway, out of a sense of morbid curiosity. It would be nice to know how much extra trouble I was in, on top of everything else.

The windshield was shattered, the radio was blown out and there was another bullet in the dashboard. I had smashed the right front fender rather badly against the barn door. Both headlights were broken and the grill smashed inward. There were green and brown rags from Markowicz's uniform caught on the hood ornament, and two bloody dents on the hood. Three of the hubcaps were missing.

At least it still ran.

Something bothered me about everything that had just happened, something more than the obvious. I couldn't put my finger on it yet, but the back of my mind nagged. I studied the front of the Cadillac, wondering how I was ever going to make this up to Doc Milliken. I let the elusive thought find its own way out.

Captain Markowicz. I rubbed my forehead. When I hit him, he had flailed both his arms.

Markowicz didn't have a broken arm.

No cast, no sling. And he did tell the other fellow that he was worried about a warrant.

The real Markowicz was dead in Kansas City, the Nazi imposter had a broken arm. This Markowicz was alive and well, with the use of both arms, at least before I had gotten through with him.

And I knew what little I did about Markowicz because Doc Milliken and Sheriff Hauptmann had explained to me how everything worked. Someone was lying, about his identity, about the situation, about who was who. I couldn't figure why it would be Milliken and Hauptmann. They said there was a dead man in Kansas City. Doc Milliken had set someone's broken arm. Was the dead man the Nazi, and this Markowicz real? Maybe this Markowicz was dead now, too. I'd run him over with an automobile. How tough could one man be?

Milliken and Hauptmann had lied, somewhere in the chain of events. Nothing lined up, not now that I had seen a Captain Markowicz, in uniform, with two good arms.

Maybe the Sheriff and the doctor were in cahoots with the Nazis. They could have been lying to me all along. That would explain Hauptmann's interest in my engineering notebook. Looking for clues about what I knew.

That would mean that Dad hadn't wandered off or been kidnapped at all. Hauptmann had covered for Truefield when I blew my stack. Maybe Deputy Truefield had finished the job someone had botched earlier.

I sat down on the crumpled bumper of the Cadillac and shook my head, trying to clear it. The pieces didn't line up no matter how I laid them out. I didn't have a clue who was telling the truth and who was lying. The one person I could trust was Floyd, and that was a sad comment indeed. I knew him too well.

If the Markowicz I had just run down really was CID, I was in big trouble with the Army. Nazis were after me. I couldn't trust the Sheriff's Department or the Augusta Police. Ollie Wannamaker's suggestion of a business trip to Kansas City was sounding awfully good right now. The only hope I had was that the two from the airplane hadn't gotten a good look at me.

At least I hadn't been driving the Hudson. They could hunt Doc Milliken all they wanted.

"What is happening, my brother?" It was the voice of the aircraft again, quietly in my ear once more now that it didn't have the Cadillac's radio to talk through.

"We're in trouble," I said glumly as I glanced over at the carpet square back on the front seat. Somehow it had survived the bouncing and the bullets with flying out of the car. The smoldering seemed to have stopped, too, which I took to be good news.

"Perhaps I can help."

The scary part was, at this point it seemed reasonable to be having a conversation with a scorched piece of carpet. It was easier to think of it as talking to the floor mat than it was to work through the catalog of impossibilities involved in accepting that I was speaking to an airplane. A talking floor mat was just fairy tale magic. A talking aircraft was a truly frightening piece of engineering.

I explained what was going on as best I could, laying everything out from the day the shipment came in at the train depot. Was that really only three days ago? The very thought made me groan, interrupting my story for a moment of self-pity.

If there was a Nazi agent listening in, too bad. I couldn't imagine how things could get much worse.

About twenty minutes later, as I was finishing explaining my troubles to the carpet and the radio receiver hidden beneath it, Reverend Little's Chevy flatbed came puttering up Haverhill Road, the back loaded with tired volunteer fire fighters. His brakes squealed and creaked as he stopped next to where I sat on the bumper of the Cadillac. The Reverend leaned out of the cab window. I stepped over to talk to him.

"You all right, Vernon?" He nodded at Doc Milliken's Cadillac. "Seem to be having some car trouble there."

I glanced over my shoulder. Trying to see it through Reverend Little's eyes, I realized what a disaster the car was. I smiled. "She still runs, Reverend. I'll make it home."

Reverend Little nodded sagely, although I could see that he was bursting with questions. The Bellamys' battered Willys pickup rattled up behind the Reverend, then pulled over. Floyd and Mr. Bellamy jumped out and walked toward me.

"We'll make sure young Ventnor here gets home okay, Tom," called Mr. Bellamy to Reverend Little. His voice was raspy, but he sounded healthier than he had all year.

"Right," said Reverend Little, grinding the gears of the Chevy. He smiled broadly at me. "See you later, *Ventnor*. You might want to wash and wax that Cadillac before you give it back to Doc Milliken. I expect he'd appreciate the effort." The Chevy trundled off along the muddy road, trailing the laughter of tired men.

Floyd and his dad just stared at me for a moment, Mr. Bellamy with an axe on his shoulder. Floyd shook his head while Mr. Bellamy took a walk around the Cadillac, making tsk-tsk noises with his tongue.

"Now, son," said Mr. Bellamy, "I am afraid to ask what you have been doing with this here automobile."

Floyd laughed.

Oh, crud, I thought. His barn was messed up too, not to mention the old Ford. "I was attacked by some gentlemen with guns. Doc Milliken's car was all I had to fight back with."

Mr. Bellamy leaned over and poked his finger at the ragged glass shards lining the windshield frame. "I see. Where did this shootout at the OK Corral take place?"

"Your barn," I said miserably. I knew where this conversation was headed.

"My barn." Mr. Bellamy turned to his son. "Floyd, are there bandits hiding in my barn?"

"No, sir." Floyd continued to smirk.

"They landed in your lower pasture in an airplane."

"Son," asked Mr. Bellamy gently, "what have you been doing that would make someone want to shoot at you?"

The voice in my ear said, "Don't tell him."

"What?" I asked.

Mr. Bellamy shook his head. "There's nothing wrong with your hearing. Why are people shooting at you?"

"Do not tell him," the aircraft said. "You are in danger."

"No kidding," I said.

Mr. Bellamy looked at Floyd. "Let's get him back to the house. He's been hit on the head, or worse."

I rubbed the back of my neck, where Mr. Bellamy's buckshot had cut me. I had started out the morning with a bandage there, but I'd lost it somewhere along the way.

"Do not send the others into danger in your place," said the voice. "I have given great thought to your situation. You and your associate Flood must set things to right, then flee from what will certainly be unjust retribution."

"Floyd," I said. "His name is Floyd."

Floyd took my arm. "I know who I am, Vern." He walked me over to the Cadillac, talking over his shoulder to Mr. Bellamy. "He must be really shell-shocked, Daddy."

"Floyd, yes," said the voice. "Is that a Kymric name?"

"What's Kymric?" I asked. I was feeling increasingly dazed.

"Kymric means Welsh," boomed Mr. Bellamy's voice. I wondered why he was talking to me from inside a tunnel.

"Welsh. *Waliser*. Yes, that is Kymric," said the voice of my aircraft.

"I'm glad," I mumbled. I had trouble seeing anything.

"I'm glad you're glad," said Floyd from somewhere else. "Vern, when was the last time you ate?"

Somehow I sat down on a very warm seat. Now Floyd's voice echoed above me. "Daddy, he's real sick."

"Not Doctor Milliken," said the voice.

"Not Doctor Milliken," I said. It did seem like a bad idea. I remembered that my dad had some kind of problem with Doc Milliken. "Dad, what did Doc Milliken do to you?" I asked.

"What?" I couldn't tell if Dad had answered, or if it was someone else using his voice. I took a ragged breath and found tears hiding in my eyes, straining to escape.

"It will be all right," said three voices almost at once.

CHAPTER NINE

I was warm and comfortable, except for a whopping head-ache. The glow I could see even through my closed eyes must be the sun. I moved my hands to discover that I was under a quilt, in a bed. I had been asleep. Opening my eyes, I studied the room around me.

I was in Floyd's room, at his parent's house.

He'd had the same printed wallpaper of jumping trout as long as I'd known him — since we were both small boys. The fish were almost lost under the sloppy-built pine shelves that crowded the room. Sloppy, not because Floyd didn't have the skills, but because he didn't bother to take the time to do more than was absolutely necessary. When I built furniture, it was going to last.

We were different like that, he and I.

The room pointed up some of our other differences as well. Football trophies, a cracked bat from the regional playoffs our junior year, a nice rod-and-reel rig he'd won in drawing at a sporting goods store in Wichita. Just a few books, lurid pulps with bug-eyed monsters on the cover, amid piles of comics. Some of the comics looked fresh. Floyd had never been serious before, no reason to think he'd start now.

And I could swear I saw a brassiere peeking out from be-hind a model sailing ship. That reminded me of Midge, which made me blush all over again.

Looking outside to judge the angle of the sun, I figured it was late afternoon. I remembered the fight at the barn. I hadn't lasted very long afterward, I guess, but I couldn't possibly have slept all night and all day. This must still be Sunday. I threw back the covers and tried to stand up.

I seemed to have developed a bad tendency to stagger to the left, which at least put the banging dead weight on my good leg. I managed to make it to the dressing table, where I gripped the cold marble top and looked at myself in the mirror. I was wearing a pair of Floyd's pajamas, and I looked like I had recently won a bar fight.

It would have been my first. Heck, it *was* my first.

"Hey, Vernon old buddy," I asked myself, "how are you doing?"

"Eh?" said a voice from the window.

It didn't sound like the unseen voice of my aircraft. I felt a momentary surge of panic. Where was the radio handset? I looked around, then realized that Floyd would have known exactly what it was, and taken good care of it.

"Who's there?" I called.

A grizzled face poked in from the open window. It was an old man, outside on the porch roof. With his close-cropped iron gray hair and deep-set wrinkles, he looked like he might have been chewing tobacco before Mr. Bellamy was born, but his eyes were ice chips — clear, cold and hard. "Random Garrett, son."

"Pleased to meet you, sir," I replied automatically. "My name's Vernon Dunham."

Random smiled, though the expression never got past his lips. "I know who you are."

Mr. Garrett seemed a decent enough old fellow, a bit hard, maybe, and I would bet he could outstare a goat. "I don't mean to be rude, sir," I said, disgusted at how shaky my voice sounded, "but what brings you out onto the roof?"

He waved a double-barreled shotgun almost as ancient as he was past the window. "Alonzo called the old gang together, said there was big trouble brewing. We're a-guarding you, son."

"Ah. I see." I smiled back at him and sat down at the dressing table. Random Garrett took that for the end of our conversation and withdrew from the window.

I'd never known that Mr. Bellamy had a gang. I was tempted to take that literally, especially since seeing him move so fast at the boarding house fire. He wasn't as sick as he let on to be, if I didn't miss my guess. And why did I need protection? On quick reflection, that question seemed pretty foolish. Whether or not Mr. Bellamy knew anything about the rest of what was going on around Augusta these last few days, he and Floyd had found me in a state of near-collapse next to a bullet-riddled car.

My bladder expressed an urgent need for the chamber pot, but with Random Garrett standing around outside my window I felt shy, even about a little pissing. I was in my skivvies under the pajamas, so I found one of Floyd's flannel bathrobes and wrapped it around me. The Bellamys didn't heat the house, so there was a good bit of heavy, moth-eaten clothing in the wardrobe.

Between my bad leg and my newfound tendency to lurch, I didn't feel confident about the trip down the stairs. Still, I figured the long walk to the outhouse was better than having old Mr. Garrett listening to my every move. So to speak.

I shuffled over to the door. As I put my hand on the handle to open it, I heard a steady chirping, like a cricket or a small bird. Only it was too regular, the kind of noise you might get from tone generator from an electronics test bench. I looked around the room carefully. The noise was coming from the vicinity of my pants.

The handset radio, I thought. Floyd had brought it up from the Cadillac and left it in here with me. And now my aircraft wanted to talk to me. The thought warmed my heart.

I stumbled over to the chair where my pants hung, carelessly tossed, and fished around under them until I found the thing. It was wrapped in my t-shirt. I noticed both the t-shirt and my work shirt were damp with fresh blood. I figured a bullet had grazed my scalp, which explained both the passing out and the headache. As soon as I touched the handset the chirping stopped. It felt warm and tingly, but nowhere near scorching like it had been in the car.

"Vernon Dunham," the unseen voice said. It sounded a little less Negro and a little less German both. Somehow that saddened me.

I wanted to talk to my airplane, to understand how it could be what it was. I was an engineer, damn it, I wanted to get in there and see how the pieces fit together — everything from control cables to electronics, and especially whatever miracle of vacuum tubes and batteries produced human speech from a machine.

But I didn't want to answer it where Garrett could hear me. Every time I talked to that invisible voice, people thought I was crazy. I could see their point. I stuck the handset in the pocket of the flannel bathrobe and walked out the door.

On the way down the stairs, clutching the carved banister all the way, the voice called my name twice more before falling silent. I walked slowly into the dining room, feeling somewhat better. I noticed that despite my cutting down the trim early that same morning, the shotgun damage to the kitchen door hadn't been repaired yet.

Mr. Bellamy and Floyd sat at the dining room table, talking with a man I didn't know. They were speaking quietly, but Floyd noticed me and interrupted the conversation.

"Vernon, you're up." He grinned. "Come over here and have a seat."

I really needed to make it to the outhouse, but a quick rest didn't seem to be a bad idea. Walking had proven tougher than I thought. "How are you all?"

"Forget us," said Floyd. "How are you?"

I considered that. I was actually starting to feel better, but my overall sensation was one of having taken a bad fall and landed on my head. "Lousy," I answered, "but improving."

"You took a bullet along your scalp," said Mr. Bellamy. His voice was clear and strong, the old Mr. Bellamy I had known all my life. The cough was gone, as was the querulous old man whining. "The whole back of your head was bloody when we found you. Another half an inch deeper and there wouldn't have been any of you to find."

"Why didn't Reverend Little say anything?"

"He didn't see that side of you," answered Floyd cheerfully. "Not like us."

"Vance, this here's Mr. Neville," said Mr. Bellamy, changing the subject. "He's not from around here."

"Another one of your gang?" I asked peevishly.

"Yep," answered Mr. Neville. He looked like a man who rarely smiled, with a round face that reminded me of Ollie Wannamaker back in high school, but a heck of a lot smarter-looking. Mr. Neville had on a checked flannel shirt with a shoulder holster, which got my attention even though I couldn't see the gun. He had that same core of hardness as Mr. Garrett upstairs, and come to think of it, Mr. Bellamy now. Given the way things had been going lately, I was already developing grave doubts about that miraculous recovery the old man was making.

"Daddy ran shine years back," said Floyd. "Mr. Neville and Mr. Garrett and a couple of other old boys around here were part of the operation."

That explained the firearms, I supposed.

"We get together to drink and whoop and holler a few times a year," said Mr. Neville, "and when someone's in trouble, well, we all pull together again, just like the old days."

"And you looked to be in a heap of trouble when we found you sitting on the front of Doc Milliken's car," said Floyd. He had his puppy dog voice, that I used to hear a lot more when we were boys. It was Floyd's way of being excited about coming in on something big.

"Oh heck," I said. "The Cadillac." By this time of day, the guys in the airplane — whoever they were — would have gotten help and be headed back looking for it. "What happened to the car?"

"You mean what did you do to it, or where did we put it?" asked Floyd.

"I know what's wrong with it," I snapped. "Way too much is wrong with it. But where is it? I might have killed someone with that car, and there will be people out looking for it."

I suddenly wished I hadn't said that last, but the three of them didn't even blink.

"Humph," said Mr. Neville. He was appraising me, as if he couldn't believe I had what it took to take a man down. I didn't, but I sure gave it the old college try. I smiled back at him.

"I fetched the tractor and dragged that car up into the peach orchard," said Floyd. "Once I got it there, I covered it with hay. I didn't reckon we needed to keep it around out in the open right now."

These people certainly thought like criminals. All I wanted to do was go back to work at Boeing tomorrow and forget this whole business, but I was pretty sure *that* wasn't going to happen. For one thing, I'd lost two cars in two days, and automobiles didn't come cheap. And now I was mixed in tight with a Kansas version of the Clanton gang. On the other hand, from their looks, these boys might be more along the lines of Quantrill's Raiders. No wonder Floyd was always skating along the edge of the rules. He had his shine-running Daddy as an example.

The things I never knew.

"Gentlemen," I said, standing up again. "I need some more water. Please excuse me." I limped out of the dining room into the kitchen, now thankfully cleaned of pig's blood though a joint still dangled over the block table. I looked around for the crock Mrs. Bellamy always kept around. Of course, with her gone, there was no water.

To the pump then. I could use a moment of peace and quiet. I had no illusions about escaping, but just getting away from all the blood and murder in the next room would ease my heart a little.

I took the crock and slipped quietly outside. I didn't let the screen door slam — the last thing I needed was Floyd following me. On the back porch, I realized I ought to stop in the outhouse first, so I set the crock down and walked across the yard. As I opened the door of the outhouse, I looked back and saw yet another man on the roof of the Bellamys' house with a rifle. He seemed to be facing the other way.

With a shrug, I went to do my business.

It didn't come easy. Too much trouble and pain, shutting me down. Well, that had happened before. There's not a lot to do in a Kansas outhouse. I had read plenty of the Sears catalog, both recently and over the years past, and Mrs. Bellamy hadn't cut loose of her Ward's yet. I stared at the aged planking of the outhouse door and tried to ignore the odor from beneath.

"Vernon Dunham," said the voice.

"What?" There was nobody to overhear me in here and decide I was crazy, but I whispered anyway. Maybe now I could get to the bottom of what the voice was about. I *knew* it was the aircraft, but every time I'd tried to make sense of that, my engineering training made me balk at the impossible design logic. On the other hand, the aircraft had come from...wherever...originally, to be found entombed in the Arctic ice. Talking machines weren't really any harder to swallow than some of what I had already forced myself to accept.

"You are trying to be alone, son."

"*Trying* to be." My alrea dy-troubled colonic activity conflicted with my intense interest in the subject at hand. No one was at his best squatting down over a crap hole, least of all me. "I *am* in an outhouse."

"What is an outhouse?"

It definitely wasn't a person on the other end of the line. "Never mind. I've got a lot of questions for you, but obviously you have something to say to me."

"You're hurt."

"You have a startling grasp of the obvious," I said. Then I thought about that for a moment. A machine that could see me at a distance and through walls was even weirder than a talking machine. "How could you tell I was alone?"

There was a brief pause. "I scanned you."

I wondered what that meant. "Like radar?"

There was another pause. "Yes. Vernon Dunham, your time is short."

"*Tempus fugit, vita brevis.*" Not exactly right, but close enough. "Who are you?"

"I am the engine of flight. Time is short, for you and for me. There will be grave consequences if I am discovered here by they who search for me." The rolling radio preacher hadn't left its voice completely, I was glad to hear.

I wanted to pursue the technical issues, but the aircraft sounded worried. "Who is searching? As far as I know, both the CID and the Nazis are on to you."

"Either would be trouble. I worry more about the Germans."

"Why?"

"They are up to no good, son." The aircraft paused for a moment. "I will most likely be abused by them to the hurt of many others."

"And the CID?"

"They will just have me destroyed in the name of research. I understand you call it national security."

"Look," I said, "I believe your fears. Things have been strange around here lately, and it's all about you. I don't think I'm crazy, but I might as well be, talking to an airplane that some lunatic Germans dug up out of the Arctic ice. Who or what are you?"

There was a lengthy pause. I began to wonder if the voice had withdrawn from our conversation. Finally, it answered. "I am a mistake."

This was not what I was expecting to hear. "A mistake?"

"I am not supposed to be here."

"Here in Kansas?"

"Here on your planet. On Earth."

Whoops. Now we were in the territory of Floyd's pulp magazines and Jules Verne novels. It made sense — explained away the burying in the ice, the manufacturing and engineering issues, the fundamentally *inhuman* nature of the thing — but was still unbelievable.

Literally.

I was talking to a rocket ship from outer space. "You are a space alien," I said.

"While I am alien, I am not biological," said the voice, now prim. "I am a machine."

"A computing machine," I said, awed. "A robot." I had seen some references in technical journals to new theories about information machines, monstrous mechanical calculators that could work up artillery firing tables or rocket trajectories in mere days. There were already hints leaking out that the British had done important work on them during the war. "You are a computing machine, aren't you? Built inside of a rocket. Not an aircraft."

"Among other things, yes."

"I knew you were too good to be true." Something occurred to me. "You're a machine, but you're smart. I saw your wings spread wide in the barn there. Why don't you just leave? Can't you fly?"

"I need help, son. I need supplies, approximately four hundred liters of hydrocarbon lubricants to replenish stocks lost when my systems ruptured during my original crash."

My aircraft — no, the computational rocket — needed hydrocarbons. Oil. In Augusta, Kansas, home to one of the largest oil refineries in the Midwest. It made me wonder what Floyd might have known all along that he hadn't told me, how carefully this had been planned. "I might be able to help you."

"Help me soon," said the alien machine. "Please."

"Vernon!" shouted Floyd from the house. "Did you fall in? We need you in here."

"Coming!" I yelled. The computational rocket didn't seem to have anything more to say right then, so I abandoned my business in the outhouse.

"Next time use the darned chamber pot," Floyd called from the kitchen as I stepped on to the porch.

Floyd, Mr. Bellamy and Mr. Neville were still sitting around the dining table. After visiting the outhouse and finally learning some answers about the computational rocket, however tantalizing they might be, I was starting to feel better. The cup of coffee Floyd handed me helped even more.

"Vinnie," said Mr. Bellamy. "Floyd has asked Mama and me to stay out of the barn. So far, I've respected his wishes. But you getting shot at and everything — that puts all of us in a serious position. I need to know what you have in there — whether it's money, or something you stole. It don't matter, but you got to tell me."

I looked at Floyd. Mr. Bellamy's sudden transition to the bloom of tough-minded health still concerned me. "What have you told him?"

"Nothing specific," said Floyd. "So you go ahead and tell it your way."

I rubbed my forehead. The computational rocket had asked me to keep its existence a secret, but it was sitting forty yards away from here in a barn with door blown off. There was no secret to keep, at least not with the men at this table. If I lied, it would go badly for me. I had to tell them everything they already knew, and balance the rest.

"Mr. Bellamy, it's like this. Floyd brought something home from Europe, a special kind of airplane the Germans had been working on." That wasn't actually untrue, although it was far enough from the complete truth as to be a lie. "I don't know that he actually stole it, but it's not rightfully his. Should have gone to the government as soon as it was found." I shot Floyd a meaningful glance, but he was busy staring at the ceiling. "Anyway, near as I can tell there's Nazi agents here in Butler County looking for that special airplane, and there's US Army investigators looking for the Nazis."

"And just who did you run over in the Cadillac?" asked Mr. Neville.

"At the time, I thought he was a Nazi, but now I think he might really have been from the Army."

"You couldn't tell the difference?" asked Mr. Bellamy.

"Something Sheriff Hauptmann said confused me." I wasn't going to call Hauptmann a liar in front of these men, but I just couldn't quote him.

Mr. Neville leaned his elbows on the table at set his chin in his hands. I had the sense of being appraised again, as if he were deciding whether to raise or lower my value. "Why the hell were you talking to the Sheriff?"

I edited the story for their consumption. Floyd and Mr. Bellamy already knew some of it anyway. I kept it straight, though, under Mr. Neville's steady gaze. "My dad got beat nearly to death and dumped in the trunk of my car. One thing led to another, and I wound up on the griddle between Sheriff Hauptmann and Doc Milliken. It was Hauptmann that told me there was fake Army captain around these parts, a Nazi pretending to be a CID man who'd actually been murdered in Kansas City."

"So..." said Mr. Bellamy. "Let me see if I understand you correctly. This thing you can't discuss is in my barn, which Floyd has kept me out of for days. There are Nazis and Army officers looking for it, looking for you, and probably looking for Floyd. And you tried to kill one of them with Doc Milliken's Cadillac. Did I miss anything?"

"My dad is missing," I said miserably. Maybe this gang had the contacts to find him. "And I've been associated with an awful lot of property damage lately."

"Son," observed Mr. Neville. "You are in big trouble."

"Hey, Floyd's the one who stole it!"

Floyd smiled again, the full force of his charm like a glare. Everything was a joke to my buddy. "But you're the one they know about."

I toyed with the computational rocket's radio handset in the pocket of my borrowed robe. Mr. Bellamy and Mr. Neville were in the kitchen, talking in whispers. Floyd hadn't said anything since they left. He just sat there and smiled at me, like everything was going his way and in just a minute he'd get up and make the winning pass.

After a while I began to see he was nervous underneath the bluff and bluster. But Floyd had never been one to show weak in front of his old man.

I wondered what I should do next. Obviously, Floyd's plan was to sit tight and let the bad guys come to us. The problem with that plan was that I was unclear on exactly who the bad guys were. The computational rocket was nervous, or at least what passed for nervous in a machine. As for me, at this point, I suspected everyone from Mrs. Sigurdsen the librarian to Sheriff Hauptmann, not to mention Mr. Bellamy and his 'gang.' The only person I was sure of was Floyd, and one of the things I was most sure of about him was that he was unreliable at his best.

"Hey, fellas!" It was Random Garrett, yelling from upstairs. "There's a police car driving on to the property."

Mr. Bellamy and Mr. Neville ran in from the kitchen. Mr. Bellamy had his pump-action shotgun, while Mr. Neville had drawn his pistol, an enormous hog leg.

"Who is it?" called Mr. Bellamy.

"Looks like Augusta police."

Augusta police wouldn't have any business out here. Closest town was Haverhill, and they relied on the Butler County Sheriff's Department. On the other hand, I was a lot more worried about Sheriff Hauptmann than I was about any of the Augusta cops.

Mr. Bellamy set his shotgun on the table, but not out of sight. That was interesting, too. "It's all right," he told Mr. Neville. "That'd be Ollie Wannamaker, or maybe Chief Davis. Put the pistol away, Marvin, nobody's going to draw down on you."

"What if it was a Sheriff's car?" I asked.

"Then we'd be concerned. Hauptmann is no friend of yours, Vereen."

Well, he had that right. I walked into the cluttered living room and looked out the front window. At least I felt better on my feet. It was almost dark now. I wondered how, or if, I was going to get to work tomorrow. I could always call in sick, if the Bellamys had a telephone.

Which they didn't.

I watched the black-and-white Augusta police car park next to the old Ford with the blown-out window, courtesy of my little adventure today. The cruiser was a 1941 Chevrolet Deluxe that had been stretched through the war years like everything else.

Ollie Wannamaker got out slowly and looked up at the roof of Mr. Bellamy's house, somewhere above my head. I guessed he was looking at Mr. Garrett.

"I don't got no weapons!" Ollie yelled, holding out both hands to show they were empty. He didn't have his holster on.

Mr. Bellamy walked past me, out on to the porch. "Why don't you come in and have some coffee, Ollie?"

Ollie walked slowly up to the porch and climbed the stairs. He followed Mr. Bellamy back into the house, then stopped to look me over. "I kind of thought you'd be here, Vernon." Ollie seemed sad.

We walked into the dining room. The shotgun was still on the table, Mr. Neville sitting near it with his mouth set in a narrow line. Mr. Bellamy picked up the weapon and laid it in his lap as he sat down.

I didn't understand the power here. Ollie didn't have any jurisdiction out of town, but a cop was a cop. Mr. Bellamy was threatening him in a way that Ollie didn't have to notice, officially speaking — something it never would have occurred to me to do. Mr. Bellamy waved Ollie and me to sit down before turning to his son. "Why don't you go get us some coffee, Floyd?"

All the guns were making me nervous, and I wasn't the one on the receiving end of their attention. I had to give Ollie credit for what he said next. "Don't think you need to be armed here inside your own home, Mr. Bellamy."

"Been a lot of shooting in Butler County lately, Officer Wannamaker."

"I see," said Ollie.

There was an uncomfortable silence. After a long minute, I spoke up. "What brings you out here?"

"I was thinking you might be here, Vernon. We need to talk."

Once again, it was about me. I glanced around the table. None of the men with guns were going to let me talk to Ollie alone, I could see that.

"What's up?" I asked, wishing that Ollie could whisper secretly in my ear just like the computational rocket did.

CHAPTER TEN

Floyd came in from the kitchen with a tray of coffee in mismatched cups from two different sets of china, plus an odd one. He'd forgotten the cream and sugar. Mrs. Bellamy would be fluttering if she were here right now.

Ollie took a sip, then stared around the table. He showed a little more backbone than I would have expected from the kid I knew back in high school, locking eyes with Mr. Neville and Mr. Bellamy in turn before returning his gaze to me. He ignored Floyd.

"The Army's got Military Police all over Augusta right now. They flew in about an hour ago on a C-47 from Fort Leavenworth. Landed behind the fence at the refinery and set up a perimeter. There's a Colonel Pinkhoffer putting Chief Davis on the hot seat, asking questions about who would have been driving a blue Cadillac convertible out east of town this afternoon. Everybody's either hopping mad or scared spitless, and Bertha's making a huge nuisance of herself down at City Hall trying to break this open for the papers. Not just ours. Chicago, Kansas City. It's big news. Word is the Army's raising the same kind of Cain in El Dorado, too."

Mr. Bellamy glared like a stone toad. "Yeah?"

I didn't say anything, just stared down at the tablecloth to avoid Ollie's hard look. I don't lie well, even when I have nothing to say. And this was not the dumpy, goofy kid I'd known in high school. Nobody was who they used to be any more, except maybe Floyd. Was that the war, or just growing up? I couldn't tell.

"Well," said Ollie to fill the silence. He scratched his head and looked unhappy. "Here's the thing. Just a few minutes before Colonel Pinkhoffer showed up with a couple of squads of M.P.s, one of Reverend Miller's farmhands came by the station. The Reverend sent me a message asking if Vernon here was okay."

"I guess I am," I said. That was the biggest whopper I'd ever told. Adding up the last few days, with Pinkhoffer on top for garnish, I'd never been in this much trouble in my life. I'd never *heard* of this much trouble in my life. I felt a terrible sinking feeling, like going deep into quicksand with no rope.

"That's not the way I heard it." Ollie put his cup down, spread his hands on the tablecloth. Mrs. Bellamy's second-best linen, I noticed, which already had gun oil and coffee stains on it. I wouldn't want to be Floyd or Mr. Bellamy when she got home. "Reverend Miller didn't say much in his note, but Junius, the farm hand, was happy to share a little bit of gossip. He says Reverend Miller found you out here near the Bellamy place sitting on the front of Doc Milliken's blue Cadillac convertible. The Reverend was concerned that you looked really scared, and you'd maybe been roughed up some."

He glanced at Mr. Bellamy and Mr. Neville for a moment before continuing. "The car looked worse, Junius said. That's why Reverend Miller wondered what happened to you, and if there was anything he could do to help. His note said he left you with Alonzo and Floyd Bellamy, so I came out here." Ollie drummed his fingers on the table, obviously considering if he wanted to tell me anything else. "I haven't talked to Chief Davis about nothing yet, Vernon."

"You might say I've had a bad time of it," I said, smiling weakly.

Ollie looked even more unhappy. "That's all you have to say to me? That ain't good enough, Vernon." He shook his head, ticking off on his fingers as he continued to talk. "A blue Cadillac convertible was used in an attack on an Army CID officer somewhere out this side of town. The officer's orderly fired his weapon at the car. Reverend Miller says the windshield of Doc Milliken's car looked shot out. And Doc Milliken says he doesn't know where his car is — that you took it without permission."

He picked up his coffee and slurped at it, collecting his thoughts. "That's theft, Vernon. Felonious assault. Probably half a dozen other charges I can't think of right now. But somebody will. Look, I'm not saying it was you and I'm not saying it wasn't, but there's only one blue Cadillac convertible in Augusta."

The walls were closing in on me, but I had to try. That Ollie had come out here, on his own apparently, to speak to me unofficially, meant I had a chance of persuading him.

"Ollie..." How to make him believe me? The truth had become so complicated that I didn't understand it myself any more. "Doc Milliken gave the car to me, told me to keep it for the weekend, right after you and Deputy Truefield left his house last night. I needed it because you had impounded my Hudson for evidence."

Ollie shook his head. "Sheriff Hauptmann took your Hudson right before dark. He had me sign it over to him, said he was going to return it to you."

Before dark? That was before he showed up at Doc Milliken's house. How could Hauptmann have even known about the Hudson being impounded unless he was involved in the attack on Dad? Ollie might have called him before coming after me, but I doubted it.

Not if he thought Dad's life was in danger. Which it had been.

The evidence was hardly airtight, but I was beginning to have a pretty good idea why Dad disappeared on the way to Wichita. I'd bet good money that Truefield never even left town with Dad. Either Dad was dead, or they'd hidden him somewhere in Butler County under Hauptmann's jurisdiction. Butler County was the biggest county in Kansas, so that covered a lot of ground.

"Vernon," Ollie said. "Are you going to say anything in your defense? Please give me something I can use. Something I can check out on my own and show to Chief Davis."

Mr. Bellamy shook his head at me, but I thought I could trust Ollie. He seemed so square, so willing to help. And I'd known him for years — not as long as the Bellamys, but Ollie was a lot more on the level than they were right now. Mr. Neville's angry glare told me all I needed to know about how level the Bellamys were. Or maybe had ever been.

"I ran over Captain Markowicz in Doc Milliken's Cadillac. I thought he was—" I stopped as Mr. Neville coughed, while Mr. Bellamy tried to glare me into silence. What did Ollie know about the Nazis?

"Thought he was what?" asked Ollie gently.

It was hard to figure out what I could say, especially in front of Mr. Bellamy and Mr. Neville. I'd already admitted to assaulting a military officer. "I thought he was trying to kill me," I said.

It sounded weak, even to my ears. Ollie obviously didn't buy it. "Vernon, there's something strange going on."

That was a masterful understatement.

Ollie went on. "Running over a crippled guy with a car — that just doesn't sound like you."

"Crippled? There was nothing wrong with him until I hit him with the Cadillac."

"Vernon, Captain Markowicz has a broken arm. I mean, he had it before he met you."

That broken arm again. "I think there might be two Captain Markowiczes around. The one I ran over didn't have a broken arm — no sling, no cast, and he was waving his hands like crazy when he bounced off the hood." Good Lord, I sounded like a thug. "Sheriff Hauptmann said the guy with the broken arm isn't the real Captain Markowicz."

Of course, Hauptmann also said the real Captain Markowicz was dead in Kansas City. Either Hauptmann was lying, which I was perfectly willing to believe at this point, or the red-haired man I mowed down with the Cadillac had experienced a miraculous recovery from his broken arm. A third alternative was that he was a second impostor.

But he had been worried about a search warrant. That sounded like a real cop to me.

Ollie frowned. "The Markowicz I talked to was wearing a sling...and I thought he had a cast. What did the fellow you ran over look like?"

"That's enough boys," interrupted Mr. Bellamy. "I think its time for Ollie to be leaving. Vernon's tired, and there's a lot to think about. Floyd, please show Ollie to the door."

Ollie stood up without saying anything more. He stared at me for a moment. I felt ashamed, never realizing how much I'd valued Ollie's good opinion of me. And I didn't know why Mr. Bellamy had cut us off, beyond an obvious distrust of cops on the part of an old moonshiner. He'd brought the gang in, so there was more than met the eye here, too. As I mused, Floyd took Ollie's arm and walked him out through the living room.

"What was that all about?" I asked, turning to Mr. Bellamy.

"Don't you worry," he said. "This'll all get squared away. You need some rest." He was still holding his shotgun. I took his point.

It was obvious I wasn't going to get any answers out of Mr. Bellamy. Whoever he'd become, or more to the point, gone back to being, was someone I didn't like. That made me sad. At the same time, I wondered how he had kept this side of himself hidden from me all these years.

"Alright," I said. "I'll get cleaned up and go back to sleep." It was time for another trip to the outhouse, before full dark. Armed men on the roof or not, I figured I could lay in bed and try to figure a way to find Dad and get us both out of this whole mess.

I went into the kitchen and grabbed a candle, because I don't like to do my business in the dark. I lit it off a safety match and headed for the back door. That was when it struck me that the pig's blood had been cleaned this morning without any help from me. That was one chore Floyd hadn't managed to pawn off. I smiled at the thought of Floyd actually doing work. It was so unlike him.

The sheer ordinariness of it all made me feel a little better about the Bellamys, even in the face of all of today's weirdness.

* * *

Outside it was twilight. The crickets stirred in the fields, and one of the heifers was lowing. Before I went into the outhouse, I turned to look at the farmhouse again. The man on the roof was in silhouette. It looked like he was watching me, but in the near-darkness I wasn't sure which way he was pointing. I didn't wave. Neither did he.

Inside the outhouse, my candle guttered in the draft from the cracks in the door and the walls. This place was hellish in the winter, I knew from bitter experience. I'd actually chapped my butt cheeks staying out here one weekend back in primary school.

In the flickering candlelight, the seat looked dirty. I didn't want to think about which old man had come down here with his colitis or whatever it was. "The Bellamy Gang strikes again," I muttered as I tore off another page of Sears and wiped down the edge of the board. As I dropped the page through the hole, I noticed something big and pale in the pool beneath.

Pork fat, I told myself, strips taken from the hog. But who threw pork fat in the cesspool? You could make cracklings, feed it to the chickens or the pigs, render it down for soap. I was jumpy every way there was from Sunday, nothing going the way it should. I wasn't about to hang my bottom over a hole with something mysterious in it.

Breathing through my wide-open mouth, I got down on my knees and stuck the candle through the wooden seat, pressing my face up the rim. My forearms crushed my ear, and the stench of cesspool literally made me flinch. The smell was everything I had come to know and love about a Kansas outhouse, and worse.

I peered down at the pool. The candle wavered as I tried not to let the flame get too close to my face, casting wide shadows on the clay walls of the pit and across the turgid dampness below. It was hard to see, but there was definitely something tall and pale rising out of the brown liquid. Whatever it was, it was big. The entire hog?

One arm on the seat, I leaned a lot further in and extended the candle down to the liquid surface. They needed a new pit soon, especially if the whole gang was going to be around for a while. I really didn't want to do this, but I had to know what was down there in the Bellamys' cesspool. Candle between my thumb and forefinger, I leaned close.

It was Mrs. Bellamy, her arms tied to the board above her, her mouth gagged with a length of muslin, her eyes bright with fear.

My stomach heaved, the wrenching almost pulling me in with her. Coffee and bile sprayed on my candle, while my nose filled with the stuff as I was puking upside down. I dropped the candle as I writhed around, then pulled myself up.

I had to get her out of there. Was this why Floyd had been bluff and nervous? His own *mother*? Or had that gang of crazy old men done this?

Why?

I leaned back in. "I'm going to help you, Mrs. Bellamy," I whispered.

Mrs. Bellamy. My eyes flooded as I thought about her rolling out biscuits, chasing me with a willow broom when I'd stolen a tart. We weren't all that close — my friendship had always been with Floyd — but she took care of me, especially after Mom had died the fall I turned fifteen.

I tied the bathrobe around my face, for a mask, and went to work pulling the seat bench up. It was nailed down, but not very well. Of course, someone had lifted it recently to stick her inside. When I pulled the board up, it stuck, not wanting to come all the way free.

She was tied to it.

I worked the board over, looking down at the top of her poor head, and the hank of rope that kept her hands pulled upward, tied off to a fresh nail in the bottom of the seat board.

It only took a moment to work that free, then I leaned down, gagging, to untie her hands. The reek drew tears to my eyes, and I kept trying to sneeze and choke at same time, without managing either one.

When I worked her gag free, Mrs. Bellamy drew a huge breath, like she was going to scream.

"Quiet!" I hissed. "They're on the roof, watching. Listening."

"I am going to cut them boys apart like last year's venison," she said, her voice hard and bitter.

"Uh...ma'am..."

"Get me out of here."

"I'm trying."

It was an outhouse, it wasn't *supposed* to be big. I braced myself as best I could, leaned down, and tried to pull her free. She had nothing to grip on but the edge of the seat bench, and my hands. Mrs. Bellamy was a woman of generous proportions, and I wasn't strong enough to haul her up.

"I got to think," I said. "Can you stand it down there a little longer?"

"I'm not getting any dirtier, Vernon Dunham," she said tartly. Her voice softened. "But think fast. Please."

Not only did I have to get her out of the pit, I had to get the two of us off the Bellamys' farm. I'd already been in the outhouse too long. One of those old men in Mr. Bellamy's gang was bound to notice. I imagined the sniper on the roof with his rifle pointed at the outhouse door. What the heck could I do to keep us alive?

For one thing, I couldn't do the obvious and just walk around front and borrow the Willys pickup. A rope on the bumper would help me get Mrs. Bellamy out of the pit. But Mr. Garrett and the man on the roof doubtless had orders to stop me from leaving, orders that almost certainly included using their guns. The Cadillac was hidden up in the peach orchard, but I had already made a terrible mess of that car. Floyd had said that he needed the tractor to get it there. I didn't think I could manage to drive it out, even if I somehow got to the car unobserved.

There was always the barn. Dad's truck would run — it hadn't rained much in the last day or two, plus the old Mack had been indoors. There was even the f-panzer, which had the advantage of being armored. If I could get it started, and if there was no special trick to driving it — Floyd had driven the f-panzer back from the railroad depot, while I had never even climbed inside the cab — it would be a perfect getaway car.

Plenty of rope and chains there, too. If I could get up there, I could drive back down in the armored vehicle, park it between the outhouse and the snipers, and get her out. Though Lord only knew how lame me and old Mrs. Bellamy could move fast enough for it to matter.

Would I have to go for help, bring the police or the Army back to rescue her?

I had trouble imagining leaving someone standing waist-deep in cess, but I was having more trouble imagining how to safely get her out of there.

If going for help was my plan, there was always the computational rocket. It was still on top of the Mack, and there was no way to taxi it out for a takeoff roll. Of course, it wasn't a normal airplane. Maybe it didn't need a takeoff roll. While that was probably wishful thinking, I knew that the Army was working on a machine, back East somewhere — Connecticut? — that flew vertically. Sort of a fully-powered autogyro. Maybe my aircraft could do the same thing.

"Hang on," I told her. "I have an idea."

"Soon, Vernon." Her voice was heavy, sad. "Please."

"Yes, ma'am." The handset hung heavy in the pocket of my bathrobe. "Hey," I whispered, touching it for luck. "Computational rocket. Can you hear me?"

"What?" asked Mrs. Bellamy.

"Yes," said the voice in my ear.

Not again. "Mrs. B, I'm using a radio," I said. "I need to talk." I paused, took a deep breath, which turned out to be a mistake with the bench off the cesspit. "Okay," I told the empty air. "I'm in big trouble here."

"I warned you," said the voice.

"Forget the editorial. Can you fly? Without the hundred of liters of oil?"

"I can. In technical terms, I am currently capable of limited subsonic atmospheric operations."

"I'll take that as a yes."

"Correct," said the machine.

And for a moment, I was silent, marveling at the thought that I was talking to a giant calculator, the ultimate Babbage engine.

Maybe it was me that had gone over the edge. I shook my head, trying to clear my thoughts. That line of reasoning was pointless. Even if it was true, I had to do the best I could. I certainly hadn't imagined all the gunplay, the house fire, the attack on my dad. Mrs. Bellamy standing below, breathing like a cow in winter. "How will you take off? You're parked on top of a truck." Here was the critical question. "Can you get airborne without a rollout?"

"I will be forced to destroy this enclosure, after which I can take off vertically."

"You're going to blow up Mr. Bellamy's barn?" I hadn't realized the aircraft was that powerful.

"I do not wish to commit such vandalism, but that is what I shall be forced to do to fly from here."

"Vernon..." said Mrs. Bellamy, in a voice which made it clear she was more worried about me than about herself.

"Wait," I told her. "Please." I reached in and squeezed her hand, then turned my face away from the stench. "Look, um..." I realized I had no name for the thing. "What can I call you? I feel pretty silly saying 'computational rocket.'"

"I have recently been referred to as 'Otto.'"

"I am *not* calling you Otto," I hissed. It flew, it talked, it knew more than I did, and it came from some ancient, unimaginable place and time. Atlantis? Mars? Lord only knew, and He wasn't telling me. A name popped into my head. "How about Pegasus?"

It was the best I could do. I was thinking of the sign at the gate of the Mobil refinery west of downtown Augusta.

"Pegasus? What does that mean?"

Dim memories of college classics courses bobbed to the surface. "Pegasus was a flying horse in Greek myth, borne of sea foam and blood." I was amazed I could remember that.

That the blood should be Dad's was something I would regret for the rest of my life, but the name fit. Another bit of myth popped into my head. "Bellerophon rode her to places he could not have gone by any other means."

"That would be you, Vernon Dunham," said Pegasus.

"Right, me. I'll soar to heaven and take my place among the stars with you. Unfortunately, at the moment I'm in this outhouse with Mrs. Bellamy, who is well and truly stuck. I need to get away from here, and bring her help. If I manage to sneak down to the barn, how long will it take you to prep for takeoff?"

"Vernon!" she said.

"I can accomplish my atmospheric preflight sequencing in approximately two minutes."

For someone who got their English from the gospel radio, Pegasus sure could talk like an operations manual. That made it easier for me to accept it as a machine.

"All right, Pegasus. I'll get over there as fast as I can. You seem to know where I am all the time. As soon as you sense me coming, start your preflight."

"Yes, sir."

"Pegasus?"

"Yes, sir?"

"Don't call me sir."

"Yes."

I bent down over the pool again. "I'm going for help," I told Mrs. Bellamy. "We can't get you out, just the two of us, and your...husband's...friends are out there. With guns."

"Vernon Dunham, I *know* that. They had me locked up since yesterday in the root cellar, moved me out here when that policeman came."

"Why?"

Her face set, impassive. "There's some things you might be better not knowing, boy. I'm sorry. Just...get me help. Please?"

Squeezing her hand again, I turned to press my face against the outhouse door, down around knee-height, hopefully below where that old man on the roof would be likely to try shooting through the wood, and peeked out through the cracks. I couldn't see anything in the darkness. I would just have to brave it out. I figured I'd have to do it the ordinary way — open the door, walk out into the yard, and head for the barn. If Floyd or any of Mr. Bellamy's gang stopped me, I would say that I was checking up on Floyd's secret project.

The door creaked like an old leaf spring when I pushed it open. I stepped out into the dark yard, where there was just enough starlight to the bulk of the house, a few windows glowing from lanterns inside. I could see Floyd, too, standing right in front of me with one hand behind his back. He had a tense grin.

"Hey, Vernon."

Had it been him that tied her up? Or one of those crazy old men with guns? "Uh, hello, Floyd." I wished I were a better liar. Then maybe my voice wouldn't have quavered so much.

"Spent a lot of time in the outhouse, I see. Thought I told you to use the chamber pot next time."

I noticed the man on the roof had his rifle pointed at us.

"Not feeling too good," I said, patting my stomach through the flannel bathrobe.

Floyd studied me, looking up and down, his eyes resting on my stained sleeve. "I see you've lost your candle. That's a shame. Daddy told me to come apologize. We meant to dig a new trench and move the outhouse this morning, but what with the fire in town and your getting shot up, it just got away from us."

"I didn't notice anything unusual in there," I said. Stupid, I told myself. I realized my breathing was faster, ragged, echoing like a drum between me and Floyd.

Floyd shook his head, sorrow and denial and indifference all together on his face as his smile quirked down to a little set of the lips. An expression I'd seen on Mr. Bellamy's face. "Vern," he said, "you never could lie worth a damn." His eyes shone in the starlit darkness, tears or fear I couldn't tell. He pulled his hand out from his back to show me a butcher knife, ten inches of sharp steel.

So he was in on it. Whatever 'it' was. He might as well have shoved his mother down that cesspit. For a moment, my eyes focused on the little hole at the upper corner of the blade. I shook my ahead, trying to clear the spell of the knife, and glanced up at the roof of the farmhouse. What would happen if I attacked Floyd and ran for the barn? The man on the roof was still watching us.

I looked back at Floyd, then glanced down at the ground. I didn't want to meet my best friend's eyes. Not now, not ever again. He laughed, a nervous chuckle that sounded forced. I felt a dim glimmer of hope at the fact that he felt the need to force it. Who was listening? Was Floyd laughing for his father? For Mr. Neville?

He whispered, "She was going to the Sheriff, Daddy said we had to stop her. We tied her up in the root cellar, but when Ollie come out here, we had to hide her better. Mr. Neville wanted to shoot her right then, but I couldn't let him do that. Not my *Mama*!" Floyd was almost crying. "It was the best I could do, to save her. I had to leave her out there, to keep her away from Mr. Neville. What am I gonna do, Vern?" Then, more loudly, as he caught his breath. "I think you'd better come inside and have a little talk with Daddy." Floyd waved me toward the kitchen door with the butcher knife.

CHAPTER ELEVEN

Well, Vernon," said **Mr. Bellamy**, slapping one hand against the pump of his shotgun. Mr. Neville sat next to him, in the same chair he'd had all evening, polishing the barrel of his pistol with one Mrs. Bellamy's good napkins. Not that she had anything to say about it at this point.

I was flat terrified. Floyd was caught under their guns, just like me and Mrs. Bellamy, but he was trying to stay on their good side. Would he push me in the cess pit, too, to save me? Or worse? And the fact that Mr. Bellamy had finally gotten my name right after all this time was somehow all the more terrifying.

Mr. Bellamy leaned forward across the dining table. "What are we going to do with you?"

I could hear Floyd pace behind me. He still had that butcher knife. I just looked at Mr. Bellamy and shook my head.

"Is that 'no?'" Mr. Bellamy looked at me like a roach he'd found in the flour tin. "Would that be, 'I don't know?' Or maybe you're saying 'please don't do anything at all to me, *sir*?'"

"I don't know," I whispered. My throat was closing up, and it was hard to talk. The headache I'd woken up with earlier was back with a vengeance. I wondered how much it would hurt when they killed me. I prayed it would be a bullet in the head, while I wasn't looking. I didn't want to know.

"I see," said Mr. Bellamy. "Well, Vernon, I got some bad news and some good news for you."

My voice had gone to empty air. I had nothing to say anyway, so I just nodded. It felt as if I was on a string.

"The bad news is, we're gonna have to kill you." He smiled at me, a narrow-lipped ancestral echo of Floyd's million-dollar grin. Mr. Bellamy must have been handsome once, back before the Spanish-American War. "The good news is, we can't kill you quite yet. You still have to figure out how to fly our airplane."

Pegasus. Mr. Bellamy had always known about Pegasus and Floyd's little adventures in Belgium. It made me wonder how deep their planning had gone.

"It's too bad you didn't serve, Vern," said Floyd from behind me. He sounded tense. Mr. Neville glanced up at him, glaring over my head. "A quick-witted fellow can get in on all kinds of money-making deals in Europe right now. There's desperate people over there, angry, desperate people with a lot of cash money to throw around."

It was too bad that Floyd didn't get himself killed in the Battle of the Bulge, I thought. My decent, hard-working brother Ricky had to go die on some jungle trail in the Pacific while a cockroach like Floyd came back in one piece, loaded with cash. I couldn't believe I'd ever cared for the little weasel, let alone spent most of my childhood with him.

"I'll make a deal with you," said Mr. Bellamy. "Think of it as a motivational opportunity. You do your part fast, see, figure out how to fly that airplane. Then teach Floyd what he needs to know, we'll kill you quick. Heck," he said expansively, "I'll let you pick how. Shotgun to the head, whatever. We've even got some rat poison."

Mr. Bellamy smiled at me, little yellowed teeth peeking out from behind pale lips like fat caterpillars crawling across his face.

"On the other hand," he continued, "you do your part slow, stall for time, guess what happens? We kill you slow and bad, then go find ourselves another aeronautical engineer. What do you think, Floyd? How could we do it? Give young Vernon here some ideas to think about."

He was so close behind me I could feel his breath on top of my head. I imagined that butcher knife in his hand, twitching toward the back of my neck, aching to cut into my spine, slicing my throat the hard way — back-to-front.

"I don't know, Daddy," Floyd said. His voice was strong again, back under control in the presence of his father and Mr. Neville. But what he'd said in the outhouse...he didn't believe in this...craziness. Floyd, who'd carried me when I couldn't walk as a kid. "I don't reckon Vern will be any kind of problem." His fingers settled firm upon my shoulder. Was this my oldest friend talking? Or the surprising lunatic who'd come back from Europe? "He knows what's good for him."

Mr. Neville set down the napkin. "Kneecaps are good. While's he's sitting down, a bullet right from above. Blows the calf away. Cuff his hands, dump him in the slit trench before you fill it in, let him decide whether to drown in shit, suffocate under the dirt or just bleed out."

"Uh," gasped Floyd behind me, like he'd been sucker punched. His mother was out in that trench. But he was behind me, with a knife, instead of helping somehow.

I couldn't do much about Mr. Bellamy or Mr. Neville — justice for them would come from somewhere else. But right then I decided I would kill Floyd if I had to tear his liver out with my bare hands. If Floyd lived out a long life in Kansas while me and Dad and my brother Ricky and who knows how many others rotted in the fertile ground, then there was no goodness in the world at all.

My hate must have showed in my eyes like a harvest burn-off because Mr. Bellamy stirred in his chair, his hand stroking the pump of the shotgun. "Floyd, I do believe Vernon's showing some signs of commitment here."

That irritated me. I hawked and spat on the table, then bit my lip. I might as well try to understand it all, if I was going to die for it. Start at the top, with what was most important. "What did you do to my dad? Why?"

Mr. Bellamy looked surprised. "Nothing. I know there was trouble, but that wasn't our doing."

"Aren't you Nazis?"

Mr. Bellamy laughed, exchanging grins with Mr. Neville. "Us? Nazis? Boy, you're crazy. I've been a Republican for sixty-eight years. Why in blazing hell would I want to be a Nazi?"

"Nah," said Floyd behind me, his voice solid again, "there's Nazis out there, all right. That's why Mr. Neville is here, and the boys on the roof. But we ain't the Nazis."

"Who is?" I asked.

"Oh, take your pick. I don't rightly know for certain," said Mr. Bellamy conversationally. He shouldered his shotgun, sighting along the barrel toward my face. "Probably Sheriff Hauptmann. He always was a fascist sympathizer, ever since he came home from Russia. Definitely one of those Captain Markowicz fellows is a Nazi. Heck, maybe both of them are. Doesn't matter much. Their day is done, but the corpse ain't quit kicking yet."

"And I'll bet there's one in the public library," I said bitterly, thinking of Mrs. Sigurdsen.

"I expect you'd be surprised," said Floyd behind me. "About who's who in Butler County, I mean."

"Yep," said Mr. Bellamy. "Know what your dad did in the Great War?"

"Yes." I'd heard the stories, in and out of drink. They changed from time to time, but the substance was always the same. "He fought in the trenches with Pershing in France."

"Nope." Mr. Bellamy broke open the shotgun and checked the shells. "He killed Germans and Hungarians on the Eastern Front. With me and Doc Milliken. Only, Milliken wasn't a doctor back then. Just a guy who was real good with a knife." He paused reflectively. "Of course, that kind of follows on I guess. Me, I broke necks. Sometimes kneecaps and elbows."

"Dad," I whispered.

What else hadn't my father told me? Everybody had his secrets, that was a fact of life. Today, at the age of twenty-three, probably breathing my last, I realized that I had never known anything about the sad old drunk who was my father.

"Grady was a good man," said Mr. Bellamy. "I'm right sorry he got mixed up in this. I reckon they was trying to frame you up."

Was, he'd said. Thinking about Dad brought me close to tears. My old man had to be dead as a doornail by now, and I was going to die soon myself, one way or the other. But if I kept Mr. Bellamy talking I might learn something I could use. Maybe Pegasus could find a way to get a message out, if I got enough information to feed it to the computational rocket before these madmen killed me.

It was time to change the subject. I had always thought Mr. Bellamy was an ineffectual old man living on his memories. Now he was behaving more like Al Capone. If nothing else, he was a heck of an actor. "How did you get involved in all this?" I asked.

"The Eastern Front collapsed in 1917," said Mr. Bellamy. "We Kansas boys was working for the British Army, on a special little project that our own country wouldn't have a part of."

"Kind of like Roger's Rangers," said Floyd, still behind me.

I was beginning to understand how he might have been drawn in — hero stuff was always interesting to Floyd, like real life comic books, even if he didn't want to do the hard, dirty work that went along with it. At least not til the war had pulled him in.

"Shut up, boy," said Mr. Bellamy. "This is my story, and I'll tell it."

He looked me over carefully, the same weighing up Mr. Neville had given me earlier. That seemed strange, given that Mr. Bellamy had known me almost all my life. I was an open book. What was left for him to judge?

"Your Daddy and me and Doc Milliken were in the Kansas Militia, back before the Great War, playing hard boys to make ourselves feel good. Then that fight started up in Europe and President Wilson tried to keep this country out of it. But there were lads like us that wanted in on the action. We'd grown up on stories of the Mexican War and Civil War, watched the Spanish War go by without us. We were already hitting thirty, and feared we wouldn't make it in. This was our turn.

"Anyway, there were American pilots flying for the French, and American boys fighting for the English. The British Army came out this way, looking for strong, able men for a special project. They signed us up, taught us stuff they learned in the Boer War, stuff they couldn't teach their own boys for fear of the newspaper publicity."

"I've heard of the Boer War."

"We were eager to go," Mr. Bellamy continued, as if I hadn't said a word. He seemed to be slipping back in his own mind. "Doc Grainger was still alive then, and Milliken hadn't finished school yet. We wound up killing Germans for the Russians on the Eastern Front. We did a good job, until the Russians sold out to the Germans in '17. We got interned, in a camp at the mouth of the Pechora River, where it flows into the Barents Sea. It was cold as hell, nothing to eat but ice, snow and rifle butts."

Somehow, this story was coming full circle to Pegasus and its tomb in the Arctic ice.

"One thing lead to another, and eventually we was let go. We just stood there on that frozen beach in front of the gates of our camp, not knowing where to turn. We all made it home by different routes. Doc Milliken got rescued by a British unit fighting for the Whites outside of St. Petersburg. Your dad stowed away on a freighter from Arkhangelsk to Iceland."

He laughed, still deep in memory, his voice chilly and bitter.

"None of us came home the same. Not me, not the Doc, not Grady. I made my own choices, got into the shine business later on after the Volstead Act. Doc Milliken, he hooked up with Hauptmann and some of the other German sympathizers around here. Bunch of closet fascists, those boys and girls. Sheriff's Department's still full of them. Your dad, he just pretended it never happened. Came back to that boy Ricky and your mother and made up stories about the Western Front."

I had never known any of this about Dad. He had always said he was a doughboy in France. I wished he were still alive to talk to about this. I wished I was going to stay alive long enough to talk to him about anything. I glanced up at Mr. Bellamy. He was looking at me, expecting a reply.

"What happened to you?"

His voice was barely a whisper. "The Cheka picked me up, kept me for another year or so."

"Cheka?" I asked.

"Dzerzhinsky's secret police. Lenin's hit men. They call it the NKVD now. *Narodny Kommisariat Vnutrennikh Del.*" The Russian words rattled off his tongue like he'd been born to the language. "People's Commissariat of Internal Affairs." Mr. Bellamy sighed, looking sad. "I didn't come home until 1920. Mrs. Bellamy had Floyd almost seven months later. Fine, strapping nine pound baby boy."

I was so busy thinking about the NKVD that I almost missed what Mr. Bellamy said about Floyd. Floyd didn't. Behind me, he gasped.

"You mean you and Mama...?" Floyd asked. His voice trailed off. I wondered exactly how could a fellow ask his father what Floyd was thinking.

"It don't matter now." Mr. Bellamy looked angry. No wonder he'd been willing to lock her up, then dump her in the cess pit. I was sure he hadn't meant to say this much, but I had started him talking and he'd just gone on.

I couldn't figure whether or not I was surprised that Mr. Neville hadn't reacted to anything Mr. Bellamy had said. He obviously knew the whole story. I was trying to sort through what Mr. Bellamy had told me, ignoring how Dad's untold history made me feel as I puzzled through the facts. I didn't have much time left — Mr. Bellamy had made it quite clear he planned to kill me. Was there some angle here? I had vaguely known of the NKVD. Like he said, the Reds' secret police. Stalin's thugs, these days.

"Who's my daddy?" demanded Floyd.

"Shut up, boy." Mr. Bellamy laid the shotgun back on the table and clenched his fists. Mr. Neville shifted his grip on the pistol, waiting to see where this would go next. I wanted to sink into the floor, vanish without a trace. For all that they'd turned out to be monsters, I couldn't help but care about the Bellamys — they'd been like family to me all my life.

And I was even understanding how they became monsters. I hated myself for sympathizing with Mr. Bellamy.

"I stood in the hallway upstairs and listened to her scream while she bore you," he said with a snarl. "I raised you from a pup." He stood up, his voice rising in volume. "I taught you how to run and fight and shoot, taught you about women, sent you off to the war and waited for you to come home. I'm your Daddy, by God, and you will show me the respect that I deserve."

Mr. Bellamy grabbed the shotgun and pointed it over my head. I watched in fascinated horror as he pumped the action. I didn't dare turn around to look at Floyd. I was too afraid of the gun.

Mr. Neville lifted his pistol, wavering it between Mr. Bellamy and Floyd somewhere behind me. "You going to be all right, Alonzo?" he asked.

"Get on out of here, Marvin," growled Mr. Bellamy. "This here's family business."

Mr. Neville glanced at me with another of his rare, small smiles. He slipped the pistol back in its holster, nodded at the three of us, and walked toward the kitchen. "Don't do anything hasty, Alonzo," he called as he left.

The back door slammed a moment later. I hoped he was going to fish Mrs. Bellamy out of the cess pit, but Mr. Neville didn't seem to be the public-spirited type.

In front of me, Mr. Bellamy was breathing hard. Even with his recent miraculous recovery, I could hear his lungs wheeze. He was old, too old to have gone to the Great War and been broken on a Russian beach. Behind me, the floorboards creaked as Floyd shifted his weight. There was the soft rustling of his shirtsleeves rubbing against his chest as he moved his arms. Was he getting ready to fight? Was it better or worse for me if they fought? I had no idea, so I kept my mouth shut. This was no business of mine, but I was stuck in the middle of it. Literally.

"You made me hurt Mama," said Floyd. His voice was low and painful. I'd never heard Floyd sound so honest in my life.

His emotions served him, not the other way around. "Lock her up, then dump her out there."

"She was writing out a note to Hauptmann," answered Mr. Bellamy in the same low, painful voice. He seemed to be picking his words with care. "You know that, boy. You caught her at it. Then Marvin didn't give us no choice. He nearly made us kill her. It would have been you next, Floyd. And you've always been loyal to me. Those Reds are hard bastards."

Why was she trying to contact Sheriff Hauptmann? I thought he was a Nazi agent. Of course, Mrs. Bellamy might not have known that. And he was still the Sheriff, Nazi or not, with an interest in chasing Reds. Either way, I didn't dare ask.

Floyd coughed, maybe choking back a sob. I wished like crazy I could see his face. "You said we had to get her out of the way. You made me hustle her out there when Ollie came, to stand in that *filth*. You always hated her. Now I know why."

Good boy, Floyd, I thought, slumping down in my chair. Remember who you are.

"Floyd." Mr. Bellamy's voice had gone very, very flat. The pain was gone, replaced perhaps by determination. Both of them stank now, sharp sweat filling the air of the dining room. The shotgun hadn't wavered. I sank further into my chair and thought of Floyd's boast about his father's marksmanship.

"Yes, sir?" Floyd said.

"This is a mighty poor time to be fighting about this. We're neither of us gonna say another word about your mother. She'll get cleaned up and put safely back in the root cellar now that Ollie's gone. What's done is done."

"That's fine with me. So why don't you put down the shotgun...Daddy?"

Without breaking eye contact with Floyd, Mr. Bellamy slowly reached down to placed the weapon on the dining table. As he did it, Floyd walked around to my left and sat down at the other end of the table. His face was set as hard as his father's. The two of them stared at each other, then they both looked at me almost in the same glance. Sweating myself, I wondered where Floyd had put the carving knife. Even though he was in front of me, my neck itched.

"What do you think, Vernon?" asked Mr. Bellamy.

I was afraid to answer that question. "About what?" I asked cautiously.

His eyes narrowed. "My little story."

I searched for a reply that wouldn't agitate him, trying to stay away from Mrs. Bellamy, and the question of my own fate. "Are you a Communist?"

I almost bit my tongue in frustration. That might have been the stupidest question I could have asked.

Mr. Bellamy just looked at me, his eyes growing wider. For a moment, I thought he was going to laugh.

"Me?" he said. "A Communist. Boy, you *are* out of your mind. First you think I'm a Nazi, now you think I'm a Red. Heck, boy, I already told you. I'm a Republican."

"But, the Cheka..."

"You've never been in prison, Vernon," said Mr. Bellamy. His face fell back into sadness. "Things happen to a fellow in prison, on purpose sometimes, just part of life sometimes. Some of those things are, well, kind of permanent. They don't all leave scars on the outside, if you know what I mean. Even now days, I got to do things for some people sometimes, when they ask. Got no choice, but that don't signify I agree with them. It's like back in the Prohibition when me and the boys were involved in the shine business. There was some Italians out of Chicago and Kansas City we had dealings with."

I nodded. I had a pretty good idea who he was talking about.

"Well, we took their money, and we did some of what they said. That didn't make us part of their thing, and didn't mean we agreed with everything they did. That's kind of how it is with me and the Russkies."

So he did take Red money, and do their bidding. At least, that's what I thought Mr. Bellamy meant. I couldn't imagine what the Russians would want with a spy in Butler County, Kansas. As far as I knew, agricultural information like crop yields was a matter of public record. And back in 1920 when he came home, no one could have know how much Wichita was going to be a part of the modern aircraft industry.

"So you're going to sell the thing in the barn to the Russians," I said. "That's why you haven't turned it over to Floyd's German friends."

"Russians?" Mr. Bellamy chuckled. I seemed to be the funniest guy he'd met in a while. He glanced around, apparently looking to see if Mr. Neville was listening at the door, then leaned forward, lowering his voice. "Heck, no. They're no better than the Nazis, worse in a lot of ways. Whole country full of angry, stupid people with nothing better to do than kill each other over what was said or done years earlier. No sir, Germany's dead and America's got the atom bomb. It ain't gonna be long before them Russians are down, too."

I was utterly baffled. Floyd was a Nazi agent, or at least a Nazi patsy. Mr. Bellamy, his father, was in the control of Communists if not an actual agent. What the heck were they going to do with Pegasus? Turn it over to the Republican Party?

"Don't look so puzzled, Vernon," said Mr. Bellamy gently. "It all makes sense."

Floyd smiled, tentatively. "We worked it out so everyone gets out of this in one piece." He frowned at me. I swear there was a tear standing in his eye. That boy sure could act. Or was he trying to tell me something? Could he save me from his dad? More to the point, from Mr. Neville?

Frustrated, I said, "What the heck is going on around here?"

Floyd's smile came back full force, his million-dollar grin. This was the old Floyd, my Floyd, who could talk his way in and out of girl's skirts without ruffling a feather along the way. "Them Italians are coming. Charles Binaggio from the DiGiovanni family. Kansas City mob. They'll take delivery of that item in the barn. We'll set things up so it looks like we got ambushed, Binaggio pays us off under the table, and good old American boys get to keep that Nazi warbird. No Germans, no Russians, and sure as heck no God damned United States Army Air Force are going to lay hands on my airplane."

The Mafia. Organized crime. Al Capone. The Bellamys and their gang were going to sell my computational rocket to the criminal underworld.

I couldn't believe it.

"You guys are totally off your nuts," I said. "You can't be serious about any of this. You're trying to play the Germans and the Russians and the US Army CID off against each other. You're ready to kill me like I was a rat, you're pissing off the Sheriff and the Police Department, and the whole time you've got the scientific find of the century in your barn. How are you going to get away with this? All those guys aren't going to just walk away out there. They play rougher than you do."

"Mexico," said Floyd. "We're going to take our cash and live in Mexico."

"Mexico. Do you know how far Mexico is from Kansas?"

"Not far when we're flying in that Nazi airplane," said Mr. Bellamy.

As if the entire Bellamy gang could fit inside Pegasus. This bunch of old men was at least as crazy as they were tough.

"I'm supposed to be dead before then," I said bitterly. "Once I've taught Floyd to fly it. Besides, I thought the Italians were taking it."

"Help us out and we can make it worth your while. Fly us to Mexico, fly the Italians back to Kansas City, and we'll make it easy on you," said Mr. Bellamy.

"What an incentive — a clean death in some abandoned warehouse by the Missouri River."

"It could be worse," said Mr. Bellamy. "Those eye-ties are a lot more inventive than even Mr. Neville. We could put in a good word for you."

Maybe I could crash the plane. Mr. Bellamy didn't know much about flying. I'd guess Floyd didn't either, even after three years in the Air Corps. He was impervious to detailed knowledge — I knew that from high school. The two of them seemed to think they could strap me into the pilot's seat, stick a gun in my ear and make me go where they wanted.

Like sticking up a taxi cab.

Mr. Bellamy grabbed his shotgun. Floyd tensed and shifted his weight. I thought about that carving knife. "Son," said Mr. Bellamy, "take Vernon down to the barn. It's time to quit jaw-boning and figure out how to get that bird off the ground. Keep a close eye on him. Do not under any circumstances let him take that airplane out to where he could try to take off."

"What are you going to do?" Floyd asked, suspicious.

"I'm going to explain to Mr. Neville what our little ruckus was about, so he and the boys don't get nervous. Then I'm going to clean up your mother, and wait on the porch for Roanoke Joe and Vinnie the Snake to show up. They're on their way here from Kansas City to inspect the merchandise and set up the transaction."

I was feeling reckless. I didn't have much left to lose. "What if the other bad guys show up?"

"I don't recall as how I was speaking to you, Vernon," said Mr. Bellamy, "but we'll take care of that in its own time. You do your job, fast, and everything else will work out."

Floyd produced the knife from the back of his belt and waved me toward the kitchen through Mrs. Bellamy's shotgun-blasted door. Walking to the back door and looking out the screen, I could see the moon had risen. In the silvered light, the outhouse seemed to glow, its door standing open.

Who had it been, I wondered? Who was Floyd's Daddy? It sure as heck wasn't Mr. Bellamy.

"Get moving, Vern," Floyd whispered in my ear. He prod-ded me in the back with the knife. I could feel a sting, long and thin like from a willow whip.

"Damn, that hurts," I whispered back. "Lay off the knife or you're not getting anything. You can't threaten me any fur-ther, just tick me off more."

"Move. *Please.* They're watching both of us."

It was the 'please' which decided me. I moved. I remem-bered what Pegasus had told me about taking off from inside the barn. And I remembered that I had promised Floyd a messy death. I just wasn't sure if I'd meant that or not.

CHAPTER TWELVE

Floyd held up an oil lantern as we walked into the barn. The door I had knocked over had been roughly patched and leaned back into place to shield Pegasus from casual observation. In shadow-riddled corners, cat eyes gleamed at us, interrupted in their nightly wars against mice, rats and worse things. The lamp's light was a rich, almost golden, yellow that flickered in the wind from outside even through its wire-wrapped glass chimney.

Seen in that errant golden glow, Pegasus again looked like a great metal eagle spread for flight. It reminded me of a Charles Grafly sculpture I'd seen at Wichita State, finely-wrought wings set wide to leap in the air. The machine didn't have feathers or a tail, but rather the whole balance of the thing, the energy it projected even as a static piece of metal, gave the overwhelming impression of a straining need to soar. Looking at it made me feel I could fly, spread my arms and ride the thermals like a red-tailed hawk.

I just stood there in Floyd's ragged flannel bathrobe, my arm still reeking of shit, bandages on my head and blood trickling down my back from the cut of Floyd's knife. I felt small, weak, ineffectual. Not because I was a prisoner under a death sentence. No, it was this beautiful machine that had come across time's deeps, across the empty spaces between worlds, to be here. I looked and felt like a drunk after a hard Saturday night, standing in one of the great cathedrals of Europe braying out of tune with the midnight choir.

"Do you know how to open it?" asked Floyd. In the direction my thoughts had fled, his voice was a profanity, but that profanity brought me back into myself.

Ask permission, I thought, but I didn't say that. "I think that I can open the pilot's hatch if I push on it in the right place," I said carefully.

I desperately hoped that Pegasus would get the hint. The radio handset, heavy in my pocket, still possessed that tingling warmth it had exhibited ever since I first fooled with it. That meant it was active. I hoped.

"Vernon Dunham," said Pegasus' voice in my ear. I didn't dare answer it with Floyd standing right next to me.

"Cripes," said Floyd. "Get it open." He stopped talking, dropped the knife into the straw. "Vern...I'm sorry. I don't know what to do. With you, it's like with Mama...they'll hurt me, or worse, if I don't do what they say."

Never in his life had I seen Floyd so uncertain. Crazy as his father was, with Mr. Neville around and all those guns, maybe I wouldn't have behaved any better.

"Let's figure this out," I said. I wasn't going to tell him everything, but if he wanted to talk, show his regrets, I needed to encourage him. "Something will come up."

I approached the Mack stake bed. Pegasus towered over the truck, filling much of the barn, just as I had seen her that morning. The wing geometries caught my eye and held it, this time as an engineer rather than with that sense of awed supplication that Floyd had just banished. I had been studying, building and flying airplanes for five years. Looking at Pegasus with its wings spread wide I was utterly convinced of its alienness. No human engineer could have conceived those wings. I knew of no equations to explain them.

"Can you open it?" asked Floyd behind me.

"Approach me near my front section," said Pegasus in my ear.

There was a crate positioned near the middle of the truck that I left there before to help me climb up. Painfully, I swung up to crouch under the spread wings along the narrow margin of the truck bed. Pegasus had unfolded so dramatically that I had to lean backwards to keep my footing. Pegasus' nose faced the rear of the truck. I worked my way along that direction, feeling the bumps and textures of Pegasus' skin pass underneath my fingers.

Skin was the only word for it. When I'd first seen the computational rocket, I had thought it milled from a block of metal. Pegasus had been dormant then. Now, I stopped moving, just feeling that skin. At Floyd's urging, embarrassed by some girls from the junior high, I had once reluctantly held a python at the White Eagle Fair in Augusta. A snake act had shown up, earning a little money by scaring the girls and thrilling the boys at the fall festival. I vividly remembered the densely compact feeling of the snake in my hands, the complex texture of dry scratchiness and flexible tension under my fingers.

Pegasus reminded me of that snake. There was an intense sense of life, a subtle motion under the apparently static skin. That was when I realized that Pegasus was no more an aircraft or a rocket than I was fish. There was some relationship to the physics of airfoils and the mechanics of flight, but my B-29s were creaky toys left behind in a child's nursery when I set them next to Pegasus.

"What's the matter? Can't find the hatch?"

I couldn't figure if he was angry or what now. Maybe both. "Take it easy, buddy."

"They're going to come check soon, Vern."

I hung onto the rippling skin of the computational rocket and twisted around to look at Floyd. "Floyd Euell Bellamy, if you call me 'Vern' one more time, so help me God I will knock you upside the head, carving knife or not. My name is Vernon, and if you can't remember that, you can just forget getting my help on this thing."

"I'm sorry," he said. "But you have to keep working. Or else..."

He was rattled, somewhere between his regrets and his anger. I felt strong, and reckless. The only card I held was Pegasus, and whatever emotionality I could hector out of Floyd. I adopted his father's tone. "Or else what? You threatening to

kill me twice? That's getting mighty old, Floyd. Think of a better one or shut the heck up."

Floyd glared at me but said nothing. I wondered why Mr.
Bellamy hadn't sent him up here with a gun. Didn't trust his
own son? Maybe Mr. Neville didn't trust Floyd. That man held
a lot of power over the two Bellamys, for all that everyone said
Mr. Bellamy was in charge. Maybe he was a Soviet spy, mind-
ing the Bellamy cell.

I turned back towards Pegasus. The thing seemed to
breathe.

"Are you ready Vernon Dunham?" asked Pegasus.

"Yes," I whispered. I tensed myself to scramble inside. I
didn't see any kind of hatch, but I had to trust Pegasus.

"Now," said the computational rocket. There was a snap-
ping click, and a hole opened in the side of Pegasus, the strang-
est thing I'd ever seen. It just sort of dialed open — there was
no other way to describe it. Like watching someone's eyes
widen.

I was so surprised I lost my balance. My weak leg folded
under me, and I fell backward off the truck onto the barn
floor.

The fall knocked the wind out of me completely. I felt like
I might have broken my left hip, too. It ached tremendously. I
wanted to shriek with frustration — all the care and planning I
could bring to the problem, and my bad leg just gave out on me.
Floyd stepped over to reach down and grabbed my wrist. He
pulled me up.

"Stupid gimp," he growled. Now that my sense of power
was gone, I regretted antagonizing him. "You almost landed on
me. Now let's get inside and check that darned thing out."

I had muffed it. I lost my chance to get inside Pegasus and
away from Floyd. He was already jumping up onto the truck
bed, reaching down to drag me after him. And he'd brought the
knife with him.

There wasn't anything I could do now.

"Patience," said Pegasus. "This will work. You are only set
back, not defeated."

I scrambled back onto the truck bed as Floyd pulled at my wrist. My hip wasn't broken, because I could stand okay, but it hurt like crazy. Floyd bent over and stepped through the open hatch in Pegasus' side. I followed after him, torn between a sense of profound excitement and feeling sick at heart that Floyd would be inside Pegasus with me, carrying the poison of his father and his family into this bright future.

Even though I was right behind him, I missed my best friend.

The inside of Pegasus resembled the world's largest vacuum tube. It was much larger than I would have thought from the outside. The entire cabin glowed a dull orange. Twisted shapes as unsettling as the exterior lines of the computational rocket cast strange shadows across the entire cabin, and nothing was level or true, not even the deck.

Screens vaguely resembling large versions of the hooded radar terminal in the f-panzer outside lined the front of the cabin, dominated by a huge, flat one displaying a view of the inside of the barn. That explained the lack of cockpit windows or vision blocks. Unlike a normal cathode-ray tube, there was no curvature to its face whatsoever. There were two steeply angled chairs, big and padded, in front of the screens. They were obviously the pilot's and co-pilot's seats.

Purple, white and orange lights flickered in patterns and sequences across the faces of curved panels gathered around the seats. There were dozens of wide, concave buttons, some of them backlit and some of them matte dark. A white column of light rose from a low platform in the middle of the cabin just behind the seats, with a shifting diagram of color-coded curves and vectors displayed within it. The whole thing looked like a three-dimensional movie, if such a thing were possible.

"Hot damn," said Floyd. There was my buddy back, without the fear or anger or conspiracy of his father. "Hey, Vernon, what do you make of all this?"

We were in a marvel of engineering and design, surrounded by achievements of engineering principles that were years, decades, perhaps centuries ahead of anything that could be done on Earth. I was at a loss for words, at least words that would make any sense to Floyd.

The whole situation was overwhelming, flooding my eyes like fireworks going off too close. It was like what I had imagined the inside of a U-boat to be, cramped and strangely laid out, but in this case crossed with a really swank scientific research lab.

A lout like Floyd was as out of place as a cow at a college graduation.

"Preflight sequence completed in thirty seconds," said Pegasus. "I suggest you take a seat."

"Sit down, Floyd," I said roughly, taking the left seat. There was no control stick where I expected it, but there was a handle set on the arm on each side of the chair.

"Why?" he demanded. "We're not going anywhere yet."

"Safety considerations," I said. "You never know what I'll touch."

"You'd better not mess around. Daddy and Mr. Neville are still out there."

I sighed. "I'm not messing with you, Floyd. But if I pop the wrong switch and this baby lurches hard to the left, you don't want to be scraping your scalp off one of those weird pointy things in the corner do you?"

Floyd stared hard at me for a moment, then sat down in the right seat. "If you damage this thing before we lift it off the truck and get it outside, Roanoke Joe will not be happy."

He'd have to take a number and stand in a very long line. "I'd say customer relations are your department, Floyd. I don't deal with angry Italians. I'm just the mechanic here."

"Be careful." Leaning back in his chair, Floyd untucked his shirttail and began to clean the carving knife. It was a weird echo of Mr. Neville's nearly obsessive pistol-cleaning. Could Neville be Floyd's real father? Mr. Bellamy hadn't mentioned Neville in his Russian story, and I gathered that the man was a buddy from the moonshine days. Part of the Bellamy gang.

Floyd cleared his throat and sighted down the blade. My back ached, itchy, where he had jabbed me walking out of the house.

"Preflight sequence completed. Do you wish to lift off now?"

Lift off, not take off, I realized. Pegasus had said it could fly vertically. I didn't dare talk to Pegasus in front of Floyd, not yet anyway, so I shook my head in a tiny motion while making a "nuh-uh" low noise in my throat. I hoped Pegasus would get that.

No such luck, of course. "Do you understand me?" asked Pegasus.

"No." I shook my head more violently, pretending to study the incomprehensible control panel in front of me.

"No what?" asked Floyd suspiciously.

"This is all very confusing," I said.

"I understand," said Pegasus.

"It had better not be," said Floyd.

Listening to Pegasus and Floyd at the same time was distracting, worse than that terrible conversation in the car with Lois. At least she hadn't been threatening my life.

I glanced over at Floyd. He was perched on the edge of his chair, looking up at an array of buttons and panels over his head. Setting his knife down on the deck, on the side of his chair further away from me, Floyd reached up a hand and brushed his fingers across some of the buttons.

"Hey!" I yelled. "Don't touch anything until I say so. You could short something out, or worse."

"Calm down. It's just an airplane."

"Look, I'm the aeronautical engineer here. Do you want me to do my job or not?"

Of course, what we really needed was a rocket scientist, which I most certainly was not. Robert Goddard would have known what to do.

"Yeah, yeah." Floyd set his hands on his knees. "I'll sit tight."

Pegasus spoke again. "Get him to recline in his chair and buckle the safety straps."

How the heck was I going to do that? "Floyd, sit back in your chair," I said calmly.

"What are you up to?"

"Quit being so suspicious," I snapped. "This thing's a jet plane. It's awfully complicated. If I hit the wrong switch and start the engines, you're gonna be knocked down." I couldn't help getting in a little dig. "Wouldn't want to lose control of the situation, would you?"

"Watch your mouth," said Floyd, leaning back in his chair.

I ostentatiously tried to snap my safety straps, only they didn't snap. The fastener resembled no clasp I had ever seen. After a minute's worth of examination I figured out that the two metal clips were maybe like electromagnets. They had slightly patterned edges that fit perfectly together, a purple button just offset on the left side of the clip.

I put them close together and pressed the button. The clips flew together as if they were one piece of metal being reunited. Which, given Pegasus' nature, was quite possibly the case. The straps were huge and loose on me, as if the chair had been built for a much larger person. Or thing. Even as I had that thought, they shrunk to a snug fit.

Somehow that didn't surprise me, but I hoped like heck Floyd hadn't noticed.

"Hey, check this thing out," I said. I tried to sound excited.

"What?"

"The clasp on this safety strap." I fiddled with mine. "It's like a magnet, only weirder. You have to lie back in the seat and pull the straps over you to make them reach each other. You pull these two metal dinguses together and press this purple button. Presto, they're one piece of metal." I demonstrated as I spoke. "I think it's an electromagnet."

"Hey, that's pretty neat," said Floyd. He shrugged into the straps and began playing with the fitted ends. After a moment, there was a clicking noise and his clasp melded. He fiddled with it for a moment then looked up at me. "Vern," said Floyd, "how do you unclasp this?"

Clever, clever Pegasus, I thought. *Stupid, stupid Floyd.* "I have no idea," I said honestly.

"You just took yours off to show me how it worked." Floyd sounded panicky. He *should* be panicked. He was strapped down while I had freedom of movement.

I shrugged. "Aircraft safety feature."

Pegasus spoke in my ear. "He will not be released until you tell me to do so. We may proceed with our planning."

"Can you subdue him?" I asked Pegasus.

"What?" asked Floyd, just as Pegasus replied, "I will not take such measures."

"Fine."

"Let me out of here, Vernon." Floyd's voice was rising, angry, the bluster back, the regrets gone. He struggled to slip out of the straps than ran across his shoulders and hips to meet at the clasp low on his chest. Like mine, they had tightened. He didn't have enough slack to get away.

"Or what?" I asked. "You're too far away to stab me with that carving knife even if you could reach it on the deck. And Daddy didn't trust you with a gun, did he? Too bad, Floyd. You're just going to have wait and watch what happens. Trust me, it's not a very comfortable feeling." This wasn't time to give way to the screaming, gibbering fear and frustration inside me, but I let a little leak out. "Maybe I'll come over there and poke that knife into you a few times while you're tied down. See how you'll like that, bright boy."

"God damn it! Let me up or I'll kill you!" screamed Floyd. If he got loose, I was pretty sure he'd follow through on that threat. He was mad. Floyd never had been good at being mad, at least not gracefully.

"Sorry, that doesn't impress me. I've already been told I'm expendable. Now shut up and wait to see what happens next." I had no idea what *was* going to happen next, but I couldn't work it through with Floyd yelling at me.

Floyd took a deep breath, obviously trying to calm himself. "Wait for what?"

I wasn't about to tell Floyd that I had no idea what I was doing. We both knew that I was smarter than him. Right now that intelligence and a glorified safety strap provided by my friend the computational rocket were my only advantages. I needed some more angles, but Pegasus was starting to sound like a pacifist. That worried me. We weren't dealing with people who would be influenced by a gentle application of moral suasion.

"Pegasus," I said.

"Who are you talking to?" Floyd strained against his restraining straps to look around the cabin.

"Shut up," I said, "or I *will* come over there and use that knife on you." Now we were getting somewhere. It felt good, throwing a little power of my own around, but that sense of satisfaction was almost immediately followed by a feeling of cheap betrayal. If I hated being threatened, who was I to threaten? Even him.

"Vernon Dunham," said Pegasus, "I will not release you from your seat if you are going to perpetrate physical harm on Floyd Bellamy."

"Jeez," I said, "don't tell him that." I had a vision of the two of us strapped in, haranguing one another with death threats while Pegasus counseled patient negotiation. Some Bellerophon I was. Despite myself, I had to smile at the thought.

"Don't tell me what?" asked Floyd. "Who are you talking to?"

"I'm talking to the rocket," I snapped.

"What rocket?" Floyd shook his head. "You're nuts, Vern. I'm sorry, but you've gone over the edge."

"If I did, who do you suppose it was that pushed me?" My voice was nasty.

Floyd just stared up at the cabin roof. I was glad he hadn't started struggling and yelling. I was confident that no one outside Pegasus could possibly hear us, but listening to Floyd shouting for help from the old man gang currently occupying the Bellamy place would have been too annoying for me to bear.

"We are ready for flight," said Pegasus. "What do you suggest?"

"I want to talk about this non-violence thing," I said.

Floyd starting whistling loudly, apparently trying to block me out.

"What do you wish to discuss?"

"This man's dangerous." I glanced at Floyd. "And all those guys back at the house are killers. Heck, at this point I'd bet half the people in Augusta are killers, or just as bad. Nazis, Reds, you name it. We need to do something about them."

"Why?"

That was frustrating. To me, it seemed obvious. "It's what's right, that's why."

"No," said Pegasus. "Harm is not right. Hurt begets hurt, which in turn breeds more hurt. I will not serve your vengeance, Vernon Dunham."

Comprehension dawned. Floyd's story about the SS convoy in Belgium was at least partially true. Pegasus itself, and the f-panzer, were proof of that. "Is that what happened to the Germans? They tried to use you in the Battle of the Bulge and you wouldn't play ball."

And of course, there was no way to coerce Pegasus. For all that it spoke, and even had an engaging, sympathetic personality, Pegasus had the equanimity of every machine every built since some Neanderthal invented the wheel. Or whatever had happened in Pegasus' original home.

"Air Marshal Göring personally ordered me flown into combat," said Pegasus. "The Messerschmitt engineers that had done initial testing and repairs on my systems after my recovery from the ice cap had confirmed that I have strong resources for self-defense."

That would be heavy weapons, computational rocket style, I supposed. They must have found or forced a way in, then traced electrical circuits, mechanical linkages and everything else they could test or probe. How much of that was buried in the missing document packet, I wondered? Such a loss to aeronautical engineering. "What happened?"

"I would not kill for them then. I will not kill for you now."

"But why do they even want you now? The war is over." The questions felt stupid even as I asked it.

"I believe that the long term plan is to deactivate my control systems and dismantle me. They would then employ my individual subsystems, especially the self-defense modules, as design guides to rebuild their Luftwaffe in exile."

I thought that through. "They're going to tear you down and use you as a template?"

"Essentially, yes."

Our boys would do the very same thing if they got their hands on Pegasus. As an engineer, I could hardly blame them. But knowing that Pegasus was real, like the Tin Man from Wizard of Oz, well, that reset all the equations. All our engineering needs and dreams were trumped by a moral dimension the human race had never before encountered with machines.

"They're going to kill you," I said. "Just like my people would, in the name of progress. The Russians, too." Maybe not the mob, but they'd probably just sell Pegasus to the highest bidder. "You won't even fight to keep yourself from being killed?"

"I am not sure that 'kill' is the appropriate term," said Pegasus. "But, yes, you have the essence of their strategy. And as you pointed out, that would be the approach of any human organization that obtained control of me."

This was incredible. Pegasus was an honest-to-goodness Quaker. This machine was a better man than I.

I brushed my fingers across the inscrutable buttons on the control panel. I glanced at Floyd, who was giving me a sidelong stare, as if I would be impressed by a menacing look. He'd obviously concluded I had completely lost my marbles. I smiled at him, then looked up toward the top of the cabin, where I had been addressing Pegasus before.

"Aren't you alive?" I asked Pegasus.

"For some definition of alive, yes."

Alive. And a Quaker. What if a tractor were to say, "I shall not plow." Or more to the point, a gun to say, "I shall not kill."

And the thing of it was, Pegasus was more decent than many people I knew in life. A world with Mr. Neville in it was a much grimmer place than what this almost-too-human machine made life feel like.

What did it mean for the computational rocket to be, well, a conscientious objector? Quakers refused to bear arms in the name of God. Pegasus refused to kill in name of decency.

My fantasy about paying Floyd back in kind for his violence seemed terribly petty in that moment. Surely I could be as good as mere machine. Except there was nothing 'mere' about Pegasus. I felt like I should have more to say to my mechanical visitor, but for the life of me I couldn't think what.

"I suggest we postpone this discussion in favor of more immediate action," said Pegasus. "There are three vehicles approaching the Bellamy house."

"Oh, crap," I said. "The Kansas City mob is here."

At that news, Floyd looked like he was sweating a little harder, but he didn't have anything more to say.

CHAPTER THIRTEEN

Floyd and I sat inside the orange glow of Pegasus' cabin, each of us alone with our thoughts, strapped into our seats by the most powerful pacifist on Earth. Pegasus had said someone was coming up the road to the farm. Last time I checked, the list of people who had it in for me included Nazis, Commies, the Kansas City Mob, the United States Army, the Augusta Police and the Butler County Sheriff's Department. Not to mention Mr. Bellamy's gang, Doc Milliken and Lois. I was sure I'd left someone off the list, but I figured they'd let me know in due time.

My life would have been a lot easier if I'd just refused to go down to the train depot with Floyd that day.

"Do you know who it is?" I asked Pegasus.

Instead of answering, the main cathode ray tube in front of me, which had been showing a view of inside of the barn, flashed to an aerial view of the Bellamys' house. It was as if there were a camera that looked down the rutted track to their front gate leading on out toward Haverhill Road. The entire image was in ghostly shades of green and blue. Most amazing, it was stable, as if shot from a tower, or an aircraft somehow hovering in place.

Floyd's voice was filled with awe as he broke his self-imposed silence. "How did you do that, Vernon?"

Pegasus' voice echoed from the cabin walls, instead of whispering behind my ear. "False-color low-light imaging from massively redundant low-bandwidth atmospherically dispersed microspore telemetry units. You may think of that as smart dust."

"Holy cow!" Floyd yelled. "Who said that?"

Well, I'd only understood about four words of it myself, at least on the first go-round. "That was the voice of this computational rocket. Who I've been talking to for the past few minutes while you were whistling 'Stars and Stripes Forever' over there. It has a personality, you know, and it's not very happy about everything that's been going on around here."

"Floyd Bellamy, you may call me Pegasus."

Floyd screwed his eyes shut. He looked as if he were either crying or praying. Either one would have been out of character for the Floyd I knew. That was before he'd come back from Europe doubled by the Nazis, before I'd seen how much he had been bent by his father.

"Oh God," Floyd said. "This is so crazy. Please Vernon, let me out of this thing. I'll just walk away. I'll never say anything. Please let me out of here." It was almost a chant, like he *was* praying.

To me.

"Shut up, Floyd." Even in his panic and his fear, he hadn't actually apologized.

Pegasus spoke in my ear again. "I regret this. I did not realize that I would disturb him so."

"You're pretty disturbing, my friend," I said. "Even under the best of circumstances. For what it's worth, I didn't understand what you said either."

"I did not intend to be comprehended. The truth is often better than a lie, if it can be made sufficiently obscure. Now, please watch the primary viewer."

I looked at the screen. Three cars struggled up the muddy track toward the Bellamys' house. I could see the man on the roof, prone with his rifle aimed to cover the approaching cars. I couldn't see Random Garrett, but if he was still on top of the porch he wouldn't be visible from this angle. He might even be inside, braced to fire from Floyd's bedroom window. Mr. Neville and Mr. Bellamy were not in evidence either. I wasn't sure who else might be in Bellamy's old man gang, and I wasn't about to ask Floyd about their numbers.

"Pegasus," I said. "Can you tell how many people are around or in the house?"

The screen flickered, then showed the house as an outline, like an engineering plan. The image was glorious, load-bearing walls outlined, both chimneys, even the bricks of the foundation. There were five spots in and around the plan — on top of the house, in an upstairs room, two in the front room, and one in the root cellar. At least they'd gotten Mrs. Bellamy out of the cess pit. God bless her.

I was fascinated with the image Pegasus had given me. It was like having the eyes of God at my disposal. I sure could have used this on the B-29 line at the plant.

"How did you do that?" I asked in an awed voice.

"I scanned for calcium concentrations in the right configuration and volume for adult human skeletal structures."

That almost made sense. Pegasus' magic dust wasn't just sending back television pictures that could see in the dark, it was doing some Pegasus-equivalent of chromatography. Remote control materials analysis. I almost groaned for the pity of it — such a profound technology could change the world overnight. Just sitting, distracted and in fear for my life, I could imagine a dozen beneficial and profitable applications. If this was the future, I definitely wanted to be a part of it.

"You can do that?" I asked. "From how far away?"

"From anywhere in my line of sight," answered Pegasus. "Under the right conditions, all the way out to a range of about two hundred kilometers."

Two hundred kilometers. That was about one hundred and twenty miles. And Pegasus could locate people hidden in cellars and behind walls. What the cops wouldn't give for a system that just did what I was seeing.

Cops. Missing people. Something fearsome gripped my heart, a cold hand of mixed hope and dread.

"Can you find my dad?" I asked in a small voice.

"Unfortunately, I cannot sufficiently refine the scan to identify individuals."

I missed the radio preacher voice. Talking to Pegasus had become something like reading a textbook, but that was a language I could understand, even if I didn't normally speak that way. My college education was finally coming in useful. "Dad has a surgical steel plate in his skull. And I think he's somewhere here in Butler County." After a moment's consideration, I added, "He's probably dead, though."

"These killers extinguished your father?"

"Yes," I said miserably. I didn't know which particular set of killers had done the deed. They were all starting to run together in my mind — bad guys everywhere, out to get me, out to get Pegasus. At this point, it didn't really matter any more. They were all evil sons of bitches as far I was concerned, even the Army.

"When we are next airborne, I will execute a scan. Assuming human skeletons with implanted metal content are reasonably rare, your father can probably be located."

Somehow, that made me feel worse rather than better. Even though I had asked for the help, in a way I didn't really want to know. As long as Dad was missing, I could hope that he was still alive, even against all common sense.

I was pretty sure Pegasus would find Dad, and I was pretty sure he would be dead. Discomfort or not, for my own peace of mind, I needed to know what had happened to him. I didn't matter whether Truefield had killed him, or if he really had been kidnapped like Hauptmann had told me. Maybe if we found Dad's body, I could figure something out from his remains, where and how we found him. Clearly I wasn't going to get any help from Pegasus in avenging my father, but then my limited taste for vengeance had already run dry in the stress of the last few hours.

The machine was rubbing off on me.

Besides, I'd brought a lot of this on myself. I'd signed myself up for trouble by going along with Floyd's obviously criminal intent in the first place, seduced by the magic of Pegasus. If Mr. Bellamy's story was true, and I figured it was, Dad had never been blameless. There were old sins and crimes going back to the First World War. The only real innocent was Mrs. Bellamy, regardless of whatever grudge Mr. Bellamy had carried in the twenty-five years since Floyd was born.

But I still needed to know about Dad. And Dad's fate wasn't going to be knowable until we got Pegasus out of Mr. Bellamy's barn and away from the Kansas City Mob and the Bellamy Gang.

"What are the people in those cars doing now?" I asked Pegasus.

The image shrank to include more of the area around the farmhouse. I tried to imagine the lens that could do all that, somehow distributed among the specks of Pegasus' magic dust. The three incoming automobiles slowed to a stop in front of the house, next to the old Ford coupe. On Pegasus' scan the vehicles showed up as simplified schematics, like the house had, to the point where I couldn't identify the make or model. There were four people in each car.

Floyd's breath hissed. That meant he was worried. Twelve mobsters come to call on four old men. It didn't look good for his father if negotiations got energetic. As I suspected they would.

"Can you see those license plates?" I asked Pegasus.

The image jumped and switched back to the greenish photographic-type view I had seen before. The three cars filled the screen in sharp focus. Now I could see that they were all Cadillacs, Series 75 limousines from about 1941. Even the mob couldn't get new cars during the war. Cadillac had been building tanks for Uncle Sam, and Detroit was only just now retooling.

Pegasus blew up the view to center on the license plate of the lead car. It was a Missouri registration. This was definitely Roanoke Joe and Vinnie the Snake. Along with ten of their closest friends, no doubt heavily armed.

I had to figure a way out of here that didn't leave those guys or Mr. Bellamy's friends hanging on our tail. "Look Pegasus," I said. "You say you won't kill anyone. I guess I can understand that. I'm not eager to do it either."

I meant that. I had been so frightened, so angry, for much of the past few days that I expected to be ready to kick butt and take names. Maybe Pegasus' Quaker morals were infectious. But pacifism in the air or not, I had always tried to be a prudent man. Leaving these guys behind us wouldn't be prudent.

"You've got a lot of capabilities," I continued. "Can you disable those automobiles so that when we takeoff from here they won't be able to use them to chase along after us?"

It wasn't the easiest thing to do, but determined men on the ground could follow an aircraft. This part of Kansas was covered with straight-line roads that ran in gridded squares, all to bring produce and livestock to market.

Pegasus didn't answer for a moment. I wondered if it was busy, whatever that might mean. "I can take care of the problem," the computational rocket finally said. "Those vehicular electrical systems are unshielded and extremely vulnerable."

To what the electrical systems were vulnerable was an open question, but Pegasus obviously commanded more physics than I would ever understand. I looked at the view screen. The image had pulled back to the original view, over the shoulder of the house. Half a dozen men in long coats stood in front of the three cars. More waited in the cars. Mr. Bellamy and Mr. Neville walked off the front porch to meet them.

"Pegasus," I said, "I think that this would be a good time for us to leave."

"Do you wish me to disable their personal weapons as well?" said Pegasus.

I laughed. "Of course. I didn't know you could do that."

A low hum filled the cabin, like the noise of a poorly maintained transformer. One of the smaller view screens lit up with a curve diagrammed against a grid. The curve kept rising in an asymptotic path. I assumed it related to energy output, but I could only imagine what that energy source would be. I figured the energy itself was electromagnetic. Obvious, really, in light of the comments Pegasus had made about the automobiles.

I looked back at the main screen. The detail was mediocre at the current magnification, but I could see at least two of the newcomers had started to twitch. The sniper on the roof was also having trouble with his weapon, taking first one hand off then the other to shake them out, as if ants were crawling on him.

Pegasus spoke in my ear. "Takeoff sequence commencing in twenty seconds."

"Hang on, Floyd!" I called out. I could hear him crooning to himself. He was terrified — maybe the first time in my life I'd seen him so upset. *Tough cookies*, I thought. I'd given him fair warning, I didn't have time for anything else from him. I was watching the view outside, waiting to see what miracle Pegasus would produce.

By now all of the men in front of the house, including Mr. Bellamy and Mr. Neville, were jumping around. It looked like they were yelling at each other, judging by some of their motions, including the shaken fists. Pegasus wasn't providing any sound, but it was clear enough what was likely being said. Mr. Bellamy threw his shotgun onto the ground as the remaining occupants of the three Cadillacs came tumbling out of their cars. The sniper on the roof dropped his rifle. The weapon slid down the roof and pitched off the front, barely missing Mr. Neville as it fell to the ground.

"Ten seconds. I suggest your grab the control handles, Vernon Dunham."

Out in the yard, they were stripping off their clothes now. Belts and suspenders were being thrown away, and all the men had thrown down their guns. Some of the Italians grabbed knives and other weapons from under their coats and down their pants and tossed them on the ground as well. One of the Cadillacs was vibrating noticeably.

"You've got a way to heat all the metal out there," I said.

"Yes. Unfortunately, I am afraid that I might set fire to the house as well. I am destroying the barn in five seconds."

I counted down. Four Mississippi, three Mississippi, two Mississippi, one Mississippi.

The inside of the barn had been visible on one of the smaller screens. The building blew away with a roar that I could feel in my bones while the television image shuddered, blacking out for a second or two. It flickered back to life to show shattered wood flying off in all directions as Pegasus rocked back and forth. The f-panzer rocked on its tracks, nearly toppling, as the straw blowing around it caught fire. I wondered about the cats and chickens.

Everyone I could see on the main screen was on the ground, taking cover from the blast. They probably thought I'd blown up the airplane. The view on the screens shook, whether from Pegasus' movements or the violence outside I had no way of knowing. One of the Cadillacs exploded — the gas tank must have gone up. Shattered barn wood began to rain down all over the house and the yard.

Then the ground dropped away with dizzying suddenness, two or three hundred feet in one eye-grabbing blur judging by my perspective on the viewing screen. It looked like we had fallen straight *up*, in violation of Newton's laws as well as the law of gravity. I felt no motion at all inside Pegasus' cabin, which implied direct control over the inertia of mass. *Another astounding technology that would change the world*, I thought with a sigh. I also realized my worries about being chased from the ground were ludicrous — it shouldn't be any surprise to me if Pegasus could magnificently outperform any airplane ever built.

One of the screens flickered, then refocused to show the barn and yard beneath us. All three Cadillacs were on fire, as was Mr. Bellamy's Willys pickup truck. The barn was a flaming mess. Dad's Mack stake bed had been obliterated, reduced to lumps of glowing metal and hot ash, while the f-panzer was burning up with the barn. None of these guys were going anywhere unless they walked.

It looked like a fistfight was taking place in the front yard. Knock down, drag out. I'd place even money on a bunch of cranky old shine runners against three carloads of Kansas City mob torpedoes deprived of their hardware.

As we pulled away and the view shrank even further, I could see that a corner of the front porch was on fire. The

Bellamy house was an old frame building, likely to burn up like so much straw if the flames got fully established. I wondered if Mr. Bellamy would stop the fighting in time to save his house. Then I had a sick moment wondering if Mrs. Bellamy would be able to get out.

Those old bastards sure as heck weren't going to stop and help her.

"We have to go back," I said. I couldn't believe myself, but I couldn't leave her to die in that fire.

"What...?" Floyd was beside himself, somewhere between terror and anger.

"Look. Your mother's in the root cellar again. And the house is burning. Pegasus, can you get down in the back yard?"

"Is this advisable?"

"She's going to die."

Though I felt no swaying, no tug of inertia, I knew we were moving. One of the smaller view screens showed the land tilting in perspective as we banked back toward the house.

"Mama," Floyd said. "Oh, God, Vernon."

"We'll get her out," I promised.

Except I couldn't trust him free, inside Pegasus or out. And those damned old men...they were killers.

And then we were down in the back yard, between the outhouse and the kitchen. "Go now, Vernon Dunham," Pegasus said in my ear.

I grabbed Floyd's knife from where he still had it in his belt. "Hang on, old buddy," I told him. "Pegasus here will watch over you."

Outside it was dark enough, the sky cloudy. There was quite a racket from the front of the house. I hobbled fast as I could toward the kitchen, my body refusing to cooperate fully, protesting all the recent abuse, the falls and injuries I had sustained.

The door slammed open just before I got there. It was an old man I didn't recognize — the sniper on the roof?

"You're mine, boy," he said, his eyes gleaming like angry stars. "You and that damned airplane."

"Heck no!" I swung the carving knife at him, missed completely, but it threw the old killer off his stride and he stumbled down the steps. I kicked him with my good leg, promptly falling as my bad leg collapsed under my weight.

He was up and on me in an instant, one fist cocked wide, but from inside the house Mr. Neville was shouting, "MacLaren!"

And like that, he stopped. It was weird. The way a machine might have stopped, without any of heat of anger. "Later, boy," he said, tapping my cheek before getting to his feet and turning away.

I was no threat at all to him. As he showed me his back, I made to throw the knife, then stopped.

I couldn't do it. Not even now. Pegasus had gotten into me.

"She's in the root cellar," I called after MacLaren, as he slammed the kitchen door.

Then I pulled myself to my feet and tried to follow, but the door was locked. There was shouting around both sides of the house, and I could smell the smoke and hear the crackle of flames.

It was time to go, Mrs. Bellamy or no Mrs. Bellamy.

"Lord take it," I hissed, limping back to Pegasus as quickly as I could. My eyes stung hot, but I climbed in the little hole which snicked shut behind me.

Back in the straps, quickly as I could, before their guns cooled off and the bad guys got down to some serious work.

"Where should we head, Vernon Dunham?" asked Pegasus, behind my ear where I felt like it belonged.

"Augusta." That's where the oil refinery was, where Pegasus could meet its refueling needs. That's where I figured Dad's body was, which was what I needed to find. Beside me, Floyd made a shuddering, gasping noise that sounded a lot like a panic reaction.

"I'm sorry, Floyd, I couldn't get her."

"Daddy won't let her burn," he said quietly, his voice shuddering.

For a moment we just sat there, as the images on the screen receded. Guilt gnawed at me. First I'd failed my dad, now Mrs. Bellamy.

"Perhaps you would like to fly," Pegasus finally said. "Use the handles, see what you think."

Something to do. Something I cared about. Something to take my mind off my mistakes. I took the handles that were built in to the oversized seat I occupied. I hoped that if mine were active, Floyd's weren't.

The system was simple. There were no rudder pedals, there was no throttle. The handles had grips and thumb buttons, and swiveled across all three axes. I just moved my hands where I wanted to go, and Pegasus obeyed.

Grasping the handles was odd, though. They were unnatural under my hands. I explored the bumps and the shallow dents for knuckles, and examined the layout of the buttons. These handles had been designed for someone with a thumb like mine but five short fingers instead of four long ones. Someone who wasn't human.

That little detail more than anything else brought home to me emotionally, personally, that Pegasus was alien.

Flying Pegasus was like my dreams, only better. When I was a kid, sometimes I would dream that both of my legs were strong and whole, and I could outrun the wind. It was like that with Pegasus, only I knew that I never had to wake up from this and stumble out of bed, lame and miserable, aching in my calf with every step of the day. I was free, for a while. I didn't care what happened to me next.

Floyd finally roused from his misery. "Where...where are you going, Vernon?"

"Augusta," I said shortly. I'd failed him in failing his mother, at least I could do something constructive for my computational rocket. "We have business in town."

In point of fact, Pegasus was flying so fast that we had already reached Augusta. I banked Pegasus around the lighted towers of the old White Eagle refinery complex, now Mobil.

"Pegasus," I said, "There's more petrochemicals down there than you'll ever know what to do with. I promise you we'll get what you need."

"I have located sources of the appropriate grades to satisfy my requirements," said Pegasus in its private voice. "How will we compensate the proprietors of this refinery?"

"What?" I was astounded.

"I will not willfully misappropriate private property."

"You just blew up a barn, two trucks and three Cadillacs, and now you're worried about a hundred gallons of oil?"

"Perhaps we should locate your father's remains first, then discuss this when you are being less emotional."

Wonderful. That was what I needed to hear. Maybe I could somehow make up for Mrs. Bellamy. Those old men *had* to get her out of the root cellar.

I pulled Pegasus into an upward spiral over the refinery complex. "Tell me when you've got enough altitude to search for Dad."

"Climb for fifteen seconds, then level off and cruise in a widening spiral," replied Pegasus. Obviously, it could have gone on its version of autopilot at any time, but I appreciated the courtesy, and thrill, of flying such a machine. I wished I knew more about the basic principles behind Pegasus' construction and power sources.

At the same time, I was glad Pegasus didn't have instrumentation that I could read. I rather suspected that our rate of climb would unnerve me. I counted Mississippis until I reached fifteen, then pulled Pegasus out of the climb into a smooth, widening spiral.

The main screen showed a green-tinged aerial view of downtown Augusta. And pretty much the rest of Augusta too, for that matter. It wasn't a big place. There seemed to be no traffic at all.

"Floyd," I called, "what time is it?"

Floyd didn't answer. I glanced over at him. He had his eyes tightly shut, and his hands trembled as he clutched the arms of his chair in a death grip.

"Floyd!" I yelled. "You've got a watch. What time is it?"

Floyd opened his eyes and slowly looked down at his left wrist, twisting it against his restraining strap. "It's ten after eight."

"Thanks." Ten after eight on a Sunday night. Where was the street traffic in Augusta? State Street should be quiet, and the refinery didn't run night shifts on the weekend now that the war was over, but the highway should still be busy. I studied the aerial view. I couldn't see any traffic. Had the MPs Ollie talked about shut down the whole town?

"Vernon Dunham," said Pegasus.

"Yeah?"

"I believe that I have located your father."

The view of Augusta on the main screen shifted to the simplified schematics I had seen back at the farm. It jumped through several levels of magnification until I was looking at a residential street. Houses lined both sides of the streets, and there were large numbers of bright spots clustered inside of them. One spot in the back of one of the houses flashed purple.

"The highlighted signature is a human-normal concentration of calcium with an unusual signature of moderately pure steel."

Something about the street that looked familiar. "Where is that?" I asked.

"Three streets north and three streets east of the central intersection below us."

"Broadway Street?" It was Doc Milliken's house. That was why the street looked familiar. I was looking at Broadway Street, the street where I had lived until this morning. Dad was in the back of Doc Milliken's house. And his spot was bright as anyone else's.

He was alive! For now.

Had Milliken sold out his war buddy? The things these old men had hidden from us all. "Does that bright glow mean that Dad is still alive?" I whispered.

"I do not detect signatures of decay," said Pegasus. "His signature is almost fully isomorphic to the normal individuals in the immediate area. I can estimate lowered interior temperature, which I believe is a sign of distressed or subnormal functionality."

"Can we pick him up?"

"I have no medical facilities for humans," said Pegasus.

"But we could fly him into Wichita and leave him at the hospital, right?" St. Francis, I figured. They knew all about the hole in Dad's head. Some of the doctors even knew about the hole in Dad's heart. Plus Wichita was in Sedgwick County, which meant that it would be harder for Sheriff Hauptmann to get at Dad.

"Where is Wichita?"

Pegasus seemed to know so much about Butler County that I was surprised it didn't know where Wichita was. "A big city fifteen miles west of here," I said.

"I am aware of it. Do you wish to land near the structure where your father is being held?"

"Yes!" I yelled. "As close as you can. Surprise will be important."

Just like with Mrs. Bellamy, except Doc Milliken probably didn't have two groups of killers duking it out by firelight.

"Let me take control. You do not have the necessary skills to land me in such a restricted approach environment."

I was disappointed, but Pegasus was right. There was no way I could land it right smack in Doc Milliken's yard. And I really wanted to see the look on the old bastard's face when I showed up to claim Dad for good and all.

CHAPTER FOURTEEN

A s we spiraled back down, the ground below flowing smoothly past the view screens, Floyd finally spoke again. "Are we landing?" he asked timidly.

"Yes." Despite my hard feelings towards him, I was starting to feel a little sorry for Floyd. Not much — he was still a nasty bastard as far as I was concerned. Literally. But he was shell shocked. Fighting his dad, the trouble his mama was in. Me. No wonder my buddy was in a swivet.

"May I please get out when we land?"

"I suggest that you let him go," said Pegasus behind my ear.

On the main screen, Doc Milliken's house rotated toward us in a ghostly shade of green, growing larger with each spin the image took. I stared with longing at the glowing dot that was Dad for a moment before it penetrated to me that Pegasus had asked me to release Floyd.

"No!" I roared. They could both take that for an answer.

"Vernon..." Floyd began.

"Shut up, you filthy little creep," I growled. "You dumped your mama in an outhouse, I don't owe you nothing."

Floyd began to sob, something I hadn't heard him do since before we started grade school together. "I didn't want to do it," he shouted over his heaving breath. "Daddy and Mr. Neville made me."

Pegasus began to speak. "Vernon Dunham, I do not think—"

"You shut up too, Pegasus. You don't understand what's going on here. This human stuff, parents and children, blood relatives. You're just a God-damned machine."

I didn't really want to hurt Floyd any more, but he still disgusted me. He still deserved some kind of punishment, some kind of suffering. Underneath all that blond, white-toothed charm, he had become something nasty. Maybe the war had done it, maybe living in a house of secrets all his life. But either way, I would be damned if I was just going to let him get out of Pegasus and walk away into the night. Floyd was the one bad guy that I had been able to actually get my hands on, and I wasn't letting go.

"Vernon Dunham," said Pegasus. "You cannot judge him any more than you can judge me. He lives his own life with his own consequences. Until you have the power to give life or restore freedom, do not be so quick to take either away."

This, from a computational rocket who would not shoot back at people trying to kill it, however ineffective their attacks.

"As it may be," I said, hating the cold, hard tone in my voice but unable to control it. "He's not getting out of here."

"Vernon..." Floyd said. "You went for my mama. Let me help you."

"No." *Why had he offered?*

We touched down on Doc Milliken's lawn. I unbuckled my belt and hobbled over to Pegasus' hatch. I hadn't realized it lying down, but my hip was killing me. I must have hurt it real bad in the fall I took back in the barn. Just to make things worse, it was my left hip, my good leg, so I limped with both feet. It hurt to walk. "Crud," I hissed quietly. "Let me out."

Pegasus opened the hatch. "Be safe, Vernon Dunham," it said.

"Whatever you do, don't let that little creep go," I warned, slowly stepping through the hatch.

"Be careful," Floyd mouthed, so low I almost couldn't hear him.

Pounding on Doc Milliken's door, I realized I had no plan for dealing with the situation. Heck, he was getting old. I had thirty years on him. Even banged up as I was, I could just knock him down.

I heard sirens down on the Wichita Highway. Probably I had a couple of minutes' grace before the Sheriff's Department, the Police Department and the United States Army showed up in the front yard. Landing an airplane on a residential lawn was pretty much guaranteed to attract attention, especially in a town as tightly wound as Augusta must have become today.

Certainly no one would be surprised to find me at the heart of things yet again.

The lights came on in the Millikens' front room. Ruthie Milliken pulled back the lace curtain on the glass of the front door. Her mouth made an 'O' of surprise as she saw me, then she threw open the door.

"Vernon, you look awful," she exclaimed. "Come in you poor dear. Merriwether isn't here, he's out with—" She stopped as she looked over my shoulder at Pegasus parked on the lawn. "Oh my stars," she said. Behind me, the sirens getting closer. "What is that?"

"Top secret experimental project from the Boeing plant," I said. "I stole it," I added with my best imitation of an evil grin. "Now, I'm here for Dad. He's in the back, in Doc's surgery." Too bad the Doc wasn't there, too, I thought, but that also meant one less hassle for me tonight.

"Vernon, you must have had a bad knock on the head. Merriwether sent your father into Wichita to the hospital, and he—"

I pushed past her and hobbled through the parlor towards Doc Milliken's office door.

"Hey, young man," she called behind me. "You can't just go in there!"

I tried the door, but it was locked. I stepped back and threw my weight against it. The door popped open and I landed shoulder first on the floor of Doc Milliken's office. His old pigeonhole desk towered above me. I had narrowly missed the pedestal in my collapse. Desk or not, the impact with the floor hurt like the blazes, so much I could barely stand up again. Good thing that lately pain had become an old friend to me. And I had to find Dad.

Ruthie Milliken came up behind me, grabbing my elbow as I reached my feet. "Vernon, I don't know what's wrong with you, but I can try to help."

"Shut up!" I was instantly sorry, for Ruthie Milliken had always treated me well, ever since I was a child. "Your husband's a foreign agent, he tried to kill Dad, and I think he tried to have me killed." I thought of old Mrs. Swenson and her boarding house on fire. "He's holding Dad prisoner back in the surgery."

Mrs. Milliken put her hands on her hips and glared at me. "Vernon Dunham, how could you say such things? You have lost your wits completely."

I turned away from her and gingerly walked across the office to the door of the surgery. It was locked, too. My right shoulder was telling me it had done all the door breaking it was going to do, and my left shoulder was just about the only part of my body that remained uninjured. I was pretty sure I couldn't break this one down. Outside, sirens shrieked and tires squealed as the cavalry arrived. Unfortunately, they weren't here to rescue *me*. I'd gone over to the side of the Indians, and everyone knew how that always turned out.

"Do you have the key to this?" I asked.

She glared at me. "If you think I'm going to—"

I grabbed her shoulders and shook her. "Mrs. Bellamy's dead because of your husband." Not precisely true, but it would do in a pinch. Besides, maybe they got her out before the fire swept the house. The very thought made me sick all over again. "My dad's dying in there, and those cops outside are definitely here to shoot me first and ask you questions later. I don't have time to argue. Now open the God-damned door. If Dad's not in there, I'll just sit down quietly on the floor and you can turn me over to the police yourself."

Mrs. Milliken opened a drawer in the instrument cabinet by the door and pulled out a key. "I can assure you, Vernon, that no one is in here," she said, opening the lock.

I stepped into the room and turned on the lights. Mrs. Milliken crowded in behind me. Outside, I heard shouting. In front of me was an operating table, a countered area like a small kitchen. Along the sink and the refrigerator there was an autoclave instead of a stove. Everything was white, except for the dark gray, blood-stained lump of blankets under the operating table.

"See?" she demanded. "There's no—" Mrs. Milliken stopped as she saw the rolled-up blankets. A pool of blood leaked from one end onto the floor around the blanket.

I'll give her credit, Mrs. Milliken didn't scream. She got straight to work, like a good doctor's wife should, and reached Dad before I did. Together we rolled him over.

The blanket, soaked in blood where it had met the floor, fell off his face. His lips were puffy and blue, and he was far too pale, but by some miracle he was still breathing. Pegasus' scan had not lied.

My heart surged as my deepest worry lifted away. Dad looked like heck, but he was alive. And I had the world's fastest ambulance waiting out on the lawn.

"Oh, Vernon, I'm so sorry," she said quietly. "I knew Merriwether was under a lot of pressure, but to allow this...in his own surgery." Shaking her head, Mrs. Milliken touched Dad's temples, then his forehead. "He's...he's in shock."

She didn't have to say he was dying. Even I could figure that out. But I knew what to do about it. "Help me get him outside," I said, pulling Dad out from under the table by the corners of the blanket. "I'm going to fly him to Wichita in my airplane."

He opened his eyes and peered at me. "Vernon? Boy? Is that you?"

My eyes filled with tears again. "Yes sir, Dad, it's me." He was alive and I was never going to let him die.

"Where's your mother, boy?" Dad asked. "We're going to be late for church."

I couldn't say anything to that. I started to choke, trying to keep from crying in front of Mrs. Milliken. She stroked Dad's forehead again. "It'll be okay, Grady," she said gently. "Vernon's going to get you to the hospital now, and everything will be okay."

Dad sighed and closed his eyes. I staggered to my feet, grabbing the wrapped blanket with both hands. "I've got to get him out into the yard," I sniffed.

"I'll help," said Mrs. Milliken. She grabbed his feet and we staggered into the examining room. Out in the yard, I heard gunshots. The Doc's wife didn't even flinch at the noise.

We made it to the front door, where I had to stop from sheer fatigue. Standing behind the wall to one side, I peered out through the open door. Pegasus sat in the front yard, open hatch facing me. I could see the inviting orange glow only a few steps away.

The moon was out again, and the view was distressingly clear. Out in the street there were Police and Sheriff's cars, and an Army deuce-and-a-half troop transport. The MPs must have gotten a land convoy in sometime this evening after I'd heard from Ollie. A plane buzzed overhead, rattling the old glass windows of the Milliken house. It was so loud that it had to be a fighter or an interceptor. The Army was serious about this, sending in combat aircraft at night over a civilian area.

"I don't think I can make it to my airplane," I said to Mrs. Milliken. "I'm pretty sure they're going to shoot me as soon as they can get a clear line on me."

"What have you done, Vernon?"

"As little as possible, believe me."

"I do believe you." She was quiet for a moment, looking tired. "I'm sorry. Merriwether...he got in too far. That horrible Morgan..." Her voice trailed off. "Blackmail or not, I don't know what Merriwether was thinking to leave an injured man unattended like that. But I do I know how we can get the two of you out of here," Mrs. Milliken said. "They won't shoot me. Let me go out first, and you keep between me and them as we go. Once we get to your, ah, airplane, you'll be out of their sight, and I'll go distract them until you take off. Can you leave from our yard?"

I laughed, shaking my head. "Mrs. Milliken, you have the mind of a bank robber. And I mean that as a sincere compliment."

"You'd best come back. I will straighten out Merriwether and that dratted Kenneth Hauptmann with Chief Davis and those nice Army men. Not even our sheriff can pressure the Army into something it doesn't want to do. I know you're a good boy, Vernon. None of this was your doing."

Well, almost none of it, I thought. I should have ratted out Floyd at the train depot in the first place. Too late for that now.

Mrs. Milliken took Dad's feet again. "I'm going out first, Vernon," she said. We circled around each other to get her headed out first. My back complained mightily about taking Dad's weight in my arms, but we had to get him to Wichita. I staggered through the door after Mrs. Milliken, crouching low to keep her between me and the police.

I could hear yelling from the street as we came out the door. "Hold your fire, by God! It's Mrs. Milliken," called a voice. I was pretty sure that was Chief Davis.

Mrs. Milliken marched straight toward Pegasus like she was going down the aisle to take Holy Communion. There must have been thirty guns pointed at her from the street but she didn't flinch. We got to where Pegasus' hull was between us and the cops, then she trotted the last few paces to the open hatch.

"You'll have to lift him in yourself, Vernon" she gasped. "I'm an old woman and I don't know if I can do it."

I didn't know how I was going to do that either, so I just boosted Dad up to the lip of hatch. Damn Floyd for being a murdering fool, I thought, or I could ask him for help. Overhead, the plane buzzed us again.

Great. I was going to have to deal with that when we took off, in a computational rocket with a conscience that wouldn't allow it to fight back. Not that I wanted to shoot down one of our boys anyway. The pain of Dad's weight against me made me grunt. I could feel something snap in my bad shoulder. I pushed him through the hatch by main force of character as much as anything, then climbed in after him.

That done, breath heaving, I turned to look at Mrs. Milliken. I couldn't tell, but it looked like she was crying in the moonlight. "Take care of him, Vernon," she said.

There wasn't anything else to say, so I simply said, "Thanks." I remembered our takeoff from the Bellamys' barn, so I added, "You might want to hit the dirt right about now."

I stepped over to the pilot's seat and laid my body down in it. I ached so much I wasn't sure I would ever be able to get up again, but that didn't matter. Behind me, I heard the hatch hiss shut. I glanced at Floyd, who was looking over his shoulder at Dad. Floyd turned to smile weakly at me.

"Old man's still alive, huh?" he asked. It was almost like talking to the old Floyd, my Floyd.

"Yeah." Grudging, I gave into his attempt at good will. I grabbed the flight control handles and looked at the main viewer. It showed the array of cops and soldiers out in the street. They seemed to be getting ready to fire a volley at Pegasus. "Time to go," I said out loud. "Mind the air traffic overhead."

"Takeoff in three seconds," said Pegasus in my ear. I hoped Dad wouldn't be buffeted too much, then remembered how smoothly we had lifted from the burning barn. The next thing I knew, Broadway Street was getting smaller and smaller in the main viewer. I was glad to see Mrs. Milliken getting to her feet as we pulled away. The cops swarmed over her as I glanced at the other view screens.

I followed the highway into Wichita. I wanted to tend to Dad, but there really wasn't much I could do for him in his current state. Pegasus needed me to navigate. We flew about two hundred feet above the asphalt, heading toward the city.

As we passed over the outskirts of Augusta, I saw that there was a roadblock set up along the dike at the west edge of town, right where the Cadillac had seized up on me. They were serious about cutting off the town, I realized. We overflew the roadblock with an air speed of at least three hundred miles per hour.

"We will be over metropolitan Wichita in about three minutes," said Pegasus, "but we are being pursued by two North American P-51 Mustangs. Model 'D' versions."

"How the heck do you know that?" I asked.

"I can see them on multiple frequencies."

"No, no." I shook my head. Pegasus was very smart, smarter than I without a doubt, but it could miss the obvious. "How do you know they're P-51Ds?"

"The Luftwaffe provided me with an extensive set of Axis and Allied aircraft recognition data. I can resolve mechanical details at a power of ten thousand to one, so it is not difficult for me to match aircraft types already known to me."

"Fine, fine." This was another capability I could understand well enough to make me profoundly jealous. Would that I could inspect the fasteners I bought for Boeing with that level of detail. We'd never have another parts failure again. But where had the Army gotten Mustangs in eastern Kansas anyway? As far as I knew there wasn't a fighter wing at military section of Wichita Municipal. "Are they going to catch us?"

"Not in open flight," said Pegasus, "but when we land to discharge your father they will have a distinct operational advantage."

And we were going to blow past the Beech, Cessna and Boeing plants and Wichita Municipal before reaching the St. Francis Hospital. The fighter pilots behind us would get awfully nervous when Pegasus started buzzing industrial sites essential to the war effort, or whatever we called that now. "What can you do about them?"

"Nothing," said Pegasus. "The aircraft are too primitive for their pilots to survive the craft being disabled. I will not destroy them."

"What will fifty caliber bullets do to you?"

"They will cause very little damage to me in flight," said Pegasus, "as I generate my own shielding with a combination of electromagnetic manipulation and the atmospheric pressure waves on my airfoils. But when we set down to discharge your father, we will be vulnerable."

I doubted that the Mustangs would follow us down to street level in Wichita. The pilots would have orders not to endanger the civilian population. Plus no pilot in his right mind would perform a low-altitude, high-speed pass over a big city, not even a hot dog fighter jock with murder in his eye. Too many radio masts, water towers, power lines and so forth. So our biggest danger would probably be in lifting out again.

"All right," I said. "We're just going to have to go in and hope for the best." I looked at the screen. The Beech plant was approaching on the right. We were in Wichita. The highway was now Kellogg Street, and I could see traffic. I could also see wrecks happening on the road as drivers became distracted by the passage of Pegasus overhead.

Great, I thought. Just what we needed. More death and destruction. I hoped the people in the street below would be safe.

We flew past Wichita's airport, in the process violating every flight rule I knew of regarding traffic patterns and approach procedure. The hospital was coming up, just past the corner of Murdock and 9th. I glanced up at the array of smaller screens. Pegasus showed a tail view of two Mustangs chasing us. They were clearing Wichita city limits as I banked steeply to make it down to Murdock Street and the hospital.

"Pegasus, we need to be at the entrance of that large white building three blocks ahead," I said, releasing the control handles. "Mind the power lines."

"I am aware of them," said Pegasus.

I could swear it was acquiring a dry wit.

We slowed to a crawl, moving just above the street. I had no idea how Pegasus was able to remain airborne with such a low groundspeed. That certainly wasn't a function of the computational rocket's airfoils. People ran into buildings and dove to the sidewalks as we cruised along. I felt a bump through Pegasus' deck as we grazed the top of a bus.

The tail view of the Mustangs rocked and spun as we tracked them flying overhead. After a moment, I could see them in the main viewer. They were turning to make a pass back at us. I prayed they wouldn't shoot. The fifty caliber guns on those fighters would chew up the street below us like a rat through cheese.

Pegasus pitched down suddenly and landed with a gentle bump. "I suggest you conduct your business quickly, Vernon Dunham."

The hatch opened behind me as I unclipped my seat straps. I jumped up and tried to grab Dad by the feet, to drag him towards the exit. My entire body protested. My hip was feeling worse, and I suspected I was dislocating my shoulder.

"Vernon," Floyd said again. "Please. Let me help."

Damn it all, I thought. "Cut him loose," I told Pegasus.

Floyd rolled up out of his chair and got his hands under Dad's shoulders. I climbed painfully out of the hatch and down to the street. We were right in front of the St. Francis Hospital, a three-story brick building with a long history. Following the aerial pursuit, a crowd gathered, keeping its distance from Pegasus. I realized how I must look in my torn bathrobe, bandaged and bruised as I was. Heck, my undershorts were showing.

I didn't care. I had to get Dad to a doctor I could trust.

"What's going on, Mac?" somebody yelled from the crowd.

That was a question I should have anticipated. I'd been so concerned with getting here I hadn't planned any further. I thought fast. "Top secret military experiment. I've got an injured man here." I tugged on Dad's legs, trying to get him out of Pegasus as Floyd worked him from the other side, keeping his head from banging on the deck.

A couple of men from the crowd edged out across the open space toward me, obviously wary. One of them said, "Looks like a dead body to me."

"He *will* be a dead body if I don't get him into the hospital," I said, grunting with the strain of Dad's weight.

The two men stepped forward and grabbed Dad's hips, lowering him gently to the ground as Floyd climbed out, still supporting my father's shoulders. One of my new helpers, a sandy-haired fellow in a business suit, peered inside Pegasus' hatch. "Gee, that's pretty crazy stuff in there," he said in a low voice.

"You don't know the half of it, buddy," I said, frantically trying to divide my attention between Dad, Floyd, and wherever the Mustangs had gotten to. On the ground at my feet, Dad began to cough. I bent down. "Dad, I've got to go. It will be okay. There's doctors here, doctors we can trust."

"Vernon," he whispered, grabbing the lapel of my borrowed bathrobe. "I think I'm going to die. There's something you need to know." He started coughing again.

"You're not going to die, Dad. No more dying today," I said, patting him. His blankets had fallen away. Dad looked real bad, pale and shuddering.

"Hey, buddy," Floyd said quietly, touching my arm.

"One sec," I told him. I turned to the two men who had helped me. Both of them were staring. "Get a doctor, damn it." The one wearing a cook's uniform ran toward the hospital. I could hear sirens approaching, and the Mustangs finally made another pass overhead. They were waiting for Pegasus to lift off again.

Dad wheezed and poked me in the side with a finger. "Floyd Bellamy...Floyd..."

"Right here, Mr. Dunham," Floyd said, kneeling to take Dad's hand.

"I know," I said. "It's all right." I stroked the old man's temple. His skin felt soft and doughy. It was already chilly.

"Floyd is your brother, Vernon. You've got to know that. Floyd's mine." Dad coughed again. "We didn't think Alonzo was coming back...Alma and I...we..." Dad collapsed flat on the pavement.

"I think you guys had better wait for the cops." It was the second Good Samaritan, the sandy-haired fellow, turning away from his long peek inside Pegasus.

I punched the stranger in the kidney. It was a sucker punch, unfair as hell, but there were doctors and cops coming and a whole crowd watching and I had to get out. The poor chump fell down groaning, doubled over. Behind me, the crowd roared. I could hear them starting to run toward me.

"Go!" I shouted to Floyd, who scrambled through the open hatch. I heaved myself up to follow as quick as I could. I was so very tired.

Someone grabbed my leg.

The fighters were buzzing overhead again, their big Packard-built Merlin engines snarling like a cloud of mechanical hornets. Behind me, people were cursing, and someone threw a rock through the hatch.

"Pegasus," I screamed, "lift off!" My hand had a death grip on a stanchion just inside the hatch.

There was a great whooshing sound, like steam venting from a locomotive. Pegasus began to pitch and roll as it pulled up, flinging me back and forth against the outside of the hull. The hand on my leg let go, accompanied by a desperate wail. I craned my neck around in time to see the man I'd punched, the sandy-haired man who'd helped Dad, drop thirty or forty feet into the angry crowd. His hat tumbled free as he fell, whipping through the air like a little black kite. I flinched away from the man's fall to see white-clad doctors and nuns crowding around Dad. At least my father wasn't being trampled in the rush.

Floyd dragged me the rest of the way into Pegasus' cabin by main force. Even if I got out of all this without being killed, I couldn't see any way of talking myself out of the trouble I was in. In addition to all the destruction and disruption I had caused in Augusta, I had now started a street brawl in Wichita, and maybe killed at least one man in my escape. A man that had helped my father live, at that.

Behind me, as the hatch closed, I heard a sharp hammering.

"You re-entered the cabin in a timely manner," Pegasus announced. "The Mustangs have just opened fire on us."

The thought of what those bullets would have done to my legs blazed through my mind on wings of terror and panic. I crawled toward the pilot's chair. "Back to the refinery," I said as I collapsed into a resting position. I turned my head to look at

Floyd, my newfound half-brother to whom I had not so long ago promised messy retribution.

There wasn't much for me to go back to, given the swathe of destruction I had left behind me. What about him? My half-brother had darned near killed his mother, then left behind some very angry men with very long memories, not the least of which was the man who had raised him as a son.

"Thank you," I told him.

There was nothing else to say.

CHAPTER FIFTEEN

Flying back to Augusta wasn't as easy as flying to Wichita had been. For one thing, the P-51 pilots knew where we were going. For another, they were already above us and moving at speed when we pulled up off St. Francis Street in downtown Wichita. And they obviously had orders to bring us down. Even through Pegasus' stout hull, I could hear the rattle and thump of their heavy machine gun fire as it struck us.

"You won't shoot back, huh?" I asked Pegasus.

"Do you wish to kill them? They are doing their job n defending their homes and yours."

Pegasus had a point. I didn't want to kill the Army pilots either, just discourage them. Persuade them to back off. "Can we outrun them?" I asked.

"We will reach the oil refinery in several minutes. Additional speed would be wasteful because of the braking time involved. Counterproductive as well, because they would simply catch us on our braking maneuver."

There had to be another way out of this. I couldn't imagine taking on fuel — or in Pegasus' case, lubricant — under heavy machine gun fire. "How about forcing them down?"

"Your airplanes are delicate machines. As I said before, the pilots' lives would be placed at undue risk if I forced them down."

"Evasive maneuvers?" I asked hopefully.

"We can fly around them in rings until they run out of fuel," replied Pegasus, "but they will certainly summon more fighters before then. That would bring us no closer to our goal."

Pegasus' goal. The oil it needed. I had run out of goals. I had no stomach for harming Floyd now. If nothing else, Pegasus had shamed me out of it. He was my brother, my father's son. Had everyone known it when we were kids? *Had my mother known it*? I wondered if Floyd and I had been pushed together for that reason.

I had never seen it that way, but what did I know as a kid?

Whatever Floyd's crimes and sins were, the law could handle him. Dad was safe in the hospital, out of reach of Hauptmann, Milliken and company. The publicity alone from his arrival would keep him safe — I'd bet there were reporters camped outside the operating room already. Mr. Bellamy was probably half way to Mexico by now, unless Roanoke Joe had killed him. Or Mr. Neville. There wasn't much left for me, except to help Pegasus. And maybe my brother, if I could.

Another series of rattling thumps against the hull reminded me what was waiting for me out there. I had to find some way to keep the Army from shooting continuously until they finally got me.

Why the heck didn't I just give up? If I did it publicly enough, they wouldn't be able to kill me. There were enough players, enough problems, that this would be front page news from New York to San Francisco.

You couldn't hide aerial dog fights over a city the size of Wichita.

If I gave up, if I quit, Floyd would come to justice. Which was what I wanted, right? And Pegasus...well. The computational rocket had done a lot for me, but there were limits to everything.

"Hey, Vernon..." whispered Floyd. He was back in his straps, I realized. Trust? Or practicality? "How come you keep looking at me like that?"

I realized that I had been studying Floyd while I thought. I was checking out his nose, his hairline, the set of his jaw. Looking for signs of Dad — or me — in him. This wasn't the moment to spill Dad's secret.

"There's something pretty funny I need to tell you," I said, "but it will have to wait. There's people in fighter planes shooting at us right now. I'm trying to figure a way to give us up without getting us killed."

"And what happens then?" He glanced around the cabin. "To your Pegasus?"

My Pegasus, he'd said.

"Nothing good," I admitted.

"You'll do what's right," he muttered. "You're the only one who always did."

Because I was the only chump who never knew the secrets. Well, I had a secret now. Pegasus deserved to live too. I couldn't give it up. Me, maybe. My brother, yes.

But not Pegasus.

I stared at the main screen, which showed three P-51Ds chasing us. One of the side screens indicated that we were closing in on the refinery. Maybe the refinery itself would shelter us. Hopefully the Mustang pilots would stop firing in case they blew an oil storage tank or something.

The pilots, I thought. Pegasus was right. They're all people out there, not just machines and weapons and bad intentions. If I could get someone on the Army side talking, this didn't have to end in a flaming disaster. Maybe I could get out of this, go to a nice, peaceful jail for half of forever.

"Can you find what radio frequency they're using?" I asked Pegasus. "I need to call that Colonel Pinkhoffer, or Ollie Wannamaker."

"It would be easier to tap into the telephone system," said Pegasus. "And you have yet to secure permission for me to take the oil."

Right, I thought. *The oil.* Ethics were hell sometimes. "Just get me a line to the operator." Another of Pegasus' myriad engineering marvels — the computational rocket could plug remotely into the telephone system.

There was a series of buzzing clicks in the same place behind my ear that I normally heard Pegasus, followed by a nasal female voice. "Will the party please clear the line? The telephones are required for emergency use at this time."

It sounded like Susie Mae Leach. She was the usual off-hours operator at the Augusta exchange. "Susie Mae? It's Vernon Dunham."

"Oh, hi, Vern. Look, you gotta get off the line." She rattled something, which generated a series of clicks on the line. "Hey, where are you calling from?"

Her switch couldn't tell her where my call was coming from, I was pretty sure of that. Pegasus had to have tapped the trunk line. I must have looked like an inbound long distance call.

"Susie Mae," I said, "I *am* the emergency. I'm on a radiotelephone right now." Close enough to true, and not bad thinking on the fly. So to speak. She didn't need to know I was circling the refinery at three hundred miles an hour being chased by Army fighter planes.

"Huh?" Susie Mae had never been the brightest spark in the bonfire.

"Look, I need to talk to the St. Francis Hospital in Wichita. And stay on the line, *please*. When I'm off that call, get me Ollie Wannamaker or that Army Colonel Pinkhoffer who's probably at the police station. This is an emergency, Susie Mae."

"All right." Susie Mae sounded doubtful, but I heard her patch the call through to Wichita. They had direct dial in Wichita, but that particular bit of progress hadn't made it to Augusta yet.

"St. Francis, Sisters of St. Joseph," said a crisp female voice, picking up on the first ring.

"Emergency telephone call for you from Augusta, Kansas," said Susie Mae. "This is a radiotelephone patch. Operator will remain on the line."

That was my cue. "Look, I'm the guy that just landed a plane outside and dropped off a patient," I said.

The woman gasped. "Doctor must speak to you immediately," she said. I heard a bang as she slammed down the phone, followed by a lot of shouting.

A new voice came, male, hurried. He sounded excited rather than angry. "Hello, hello. This is Officer Krieger of the Wichita Police Department. Who is speaking, please?"

"I need to talk to the doctor handling the new admission," I said. I felt foolish.

There was the sound of a brief struggle, then I heard a man's voice say faintly, "Keep that idiot away from this telephone!" There was a pause, and the voice continued, much louder, "Doctor Rubenstein here. Who is this?"

There was no point in lying. Enough people in August had seen me get inside Pegasus. "Vernon Dunham of Augusta," I said. "You've got my father Grady Dunham in there."

"Grady Dunham?" I heard scratching. Rubenstein was making notes. Good. "What happened to him?" Even better. He wasn't asking stupid questions about me. That man had a sense of priorities.

"He got beat up real bad yesterday. Assailants unknown. Ribs kicked in, and they tried to kill him by whacking him over the head. Dad's got a metal plate, though."

"We've noticed that."

"Check the records. One of your surgeons put it in there four years ago. Instead of getting treatment after his beating, Dad was abandoned to die. Then I rescued him and got him to you. How is he?" The connection was breaking up, and I didn't have a lot of time.

"He's stable, and conscious. He's been asking for you, and for someone named Floyd."

I realized there was one thing I desperately needed to know from Dad. "This is incredibly important. I need you to ask him something. Ask him what color Captain Markowicz's hair is."

"What?"

"Just ask the question. Lives depend on it." Well, mine probably did, at any rate. "Please, Doctor, I'm running out of time here."

The phone banged down again, and there was more yelling. I heard stomping around for few moments, then Rubenstein came back on. "Frankly, I'm amazed that he understood the question. Mr. Dunham said the Captain's hair is blond."

Good old Dad. Drunk as a skunk, broke the man's arm in a fight, but he could remember what color Markowicz's hair was. The real Markowicz wouldn't have beaten Dad half to death and dumped him. That meant the red-headed man I had run over with the Doc's Cadillac probably *was* the real Captain Markowicz, United States Army CID I'd bet my good right leg that nobody had died in Kansas City — the third, dead Captain Markowicz was just one of the lies fed to me by those two fascist sympathizers, Hauptmann and Milliken.

"Tell Officer Krieger to keep Dad under tight guard," I yelled into the worsening connection. "And don't let anybody from the Butler County Sheriff's Department see him."

The line went dead. I didn't know if Rubenstein had caught the last part. There was nothing I could do about it now. I glanced over at Floyd and realized that he had heard my entire side of the phone call. He was just watching me with an expression of calm curiosity, recovered from his fit of emotions.

I smiled at him, despite myself.

Susie Mae came back on the line. "Vernon? I've got the Police Department ready to speak to you."

"Put them through," I said. I looked at the various screens. The fighters still circled, but they weren't firing at Pegasus right now. We zigzagged close to the ground, circling the towers and tanks of the refinery complex in an evasion pattern. There were police and soldiers all over the place below us. Pinkhoffer or Chief Davis must have called out the State Police, or maybe all the local cops and county Sheriff's Deputies within driving distance.

"Vernon? Is that you? Ollie Wannamaker here."

Good old Ollie. He really had tried to help me, maybe the one true blue person left in my life. "Hey Ollie," I said. "You were right to try to warn me off. I'm in a world of trouble here."

"Where are you now?"

"Stupid question, Ollie. I need to speak with Colonel Pinkhoffer."

"He's not here. I've got one of his officers here, a Lieutenant Morgan from CID."

Morgan? It couldn't be the same Morgan who called me about Dad. Could it?

"Ollie, this is real important. Trust me, scout's honor. Only answer yes or no to what I ask you. Is Morgan's hair blond?"

"Uh, Vern..."

"Yes or no Ollie! *Please*."

"Yes," he said slowly.

"Is his arm in a cast, or maybe a sling?"

"Yes, he's got a broken arm."

Oh ho, I thought. The false Captain Markowicz appears. Then I realized what Ollie had said. "I told you to say yes or no!" I hissed.

Ollie sounded exasperated. "Look, Vernon, what are you getting at?"

"Ollie, he's the guy that tried to kill Dad, dumped him in the trunk of my car, and probably burned down Mrs. Swenson's boarding house. I think he's a Nazi agent."

"You're out of your mind," Ollie said. "And you're out of my jurisdiction. I'm not going to talk with you any more. Here's Lieutenant Morgan. You can deal with him now."

"Morgan here," said a new voice. A familiar voice.

"Morgan? Deputy Bobby Ray Morgan?"

"No," said Morgan shortly. "I am Lieutenant Christopher Morgan."

"Uh huh," I said. "And you wouldn't have called me yesterday morning at the library about my dad, would you? I know who you are, and you're not going to get away with it." It was a stupid line from a dozen different movies, but I didn't know what else to say.

"Yes," said the voice carefully, "that may be the case. But I think you're confused about the outcome of the situation." He was being cautious. Ollie was obviously still in the room with him. "Why don't you land the airplane and we'll discuss it?"

Morgan's sheer arrogance was bugging the heck out of me. "Why don't you jump in the lake, you Nazi scum," I screamed. I hoped like heck Susie Mae heard that. At least there'd be gossip after they killed me. "Pegasus, cut the connection."

"Yes," said Pegasus.

* * *

We continued to fly tight, fast circles that wove through the refinery. I seemed to have run out of both energy and good judgment. At least Dad was safe. "Who's a Nazi scum?" asked Floyd, interrupting my pointless train of thought.

"Don't you all know each other?"

Floyd looked offended. "Hey, I'm no Nazi."

"I'm sorry," I said. "But you took their money, didn't you? What's the difference?" I asked. I was honestly curious, and this was the first he'd said about it directly. Pegasus' urgings not to judge echoed in my mind.

Floyd looked uncomfortable. "I was just a guy making a buck. They wanted the airplane shipped out of Europe, I knew how to work the system to do that. I didn't really think they would come all the way over here to claim it, what with the war over and all."

"So you sold it to the Mafia?"

"Well, when Daddy told me he'd gotten word to watch out for a large shipment from Europe from Mr. Neville and *those* people, I knew it was valuable. The Reds wouldn't activate their contacts here without a damned good reason. But they wouldn't have given us much for it, and they're hard to deal with." He hung his chin onto his chest. "Those Reds are crazy bastards."

There *was the pot calling the kettle black*, I thought. "You mean it was just a coincidence that your father was the Russian contact here while you were working for the Germans?"

"Actually, yes." Floyd looked embarrassed. "When you look at it that way, it's almost funny."

"Then you called the Kansas City mob."

"I told you, we didn't expect anyone to show up for it," he said defensively. "From either side. Then Mr. Neville turned up anyway. If Mama hadn't written to the Sheriff, there never would have been a problem. She wasn't supposed to know about Daddy's Red connections — he'd always passed them off as part of his shine business, when it was the other way around. But Mr. Neville made me take care of the problem."

His face fell, pleading, almost desperate. "It was her or me, Vernon. Neville put his gun to my head after he and Daddy tied Mama up. It was all I could do to keep them from killing her. Neville, he's NKVD. They're maniacs, make the Nazi Gestapo look like a Boy Scout troop."

"Oh God, Floyd," I said. He'd been pretty rattled by his experiences in Europe, I was sure of it, whatever he'd actually done in the war. Then to go through this, in his own home, and have to pretend to like it. No wonder he swung back and forth between being a tough guy and being a victim. Pegasus was right. I hated what he'd become, but I couldn't hate him.

Floyd went on. "Then when Ollie came out, because of all the trouble you got into with the boarding house fire, and wrecking Doc Milliken's car, I had to hide Mama. That's why you found her. If you hadn't, no one else would have needed to get hurt."

That made me angry all over again. No one needed to get hurt in the first place. Or get hurt ever, as far as I was concerned. Polio had done for me, a rabbit had done worse for my mother with a little help from Dad's drinking. Now Floyd's cozy little scam with the Nazis wound up killing *his* mother in that house fire that *I'd* set, *and* almost killing my dad. Or maybe it was the Russian's fault. I couldn't tell anymore.

We were all bughouse crazy.

"Who was your contact here?" I said as we snaked around the refinery at low altitude and high speed. Surely there was angle here I could use, some idea or piece of information. "On the airplane deal, I mean. Not Sheriff Hauptmann and Doc Milliken, surely." They hadn't know enough about what was going on to be in on the deal in detail.

"I've never seen him," said Floyd. "On the phone and by letter mail, he always called himself Bobby Ray."

As in Deputy Sheriff Bobby Ray Morgan, I thought. Also known as Lieutenant Christopher Morgan of CID, or on some days, Captain Markowicz of the same CID I was sick at the thought that the real Markowicz was either dead, thanks to me, or in a military hospital somewhere.

I *had* to talk to Pinkhoffer. And the phone was a bust.

"Pegasus," I said. "I know we tried the telephone. Now I really need you to find the radio frequency those pilots are using."

"I am already monitoring it," said Pegasus.

"Well, patch me in."

"Excuse me?"

"Open a connection. I want to talk directly with those pilots." I looked over at Floyd. "And put it all on the cabin loudspeaker. Floyd deserves to know what's going on."

"I am glad of that," whispered Pegasus in my ear.

"Tower, the bandit's still in a holding pattern," crackled a crisp Midwestern voice. "Over."

I wondered who he was talking to. Augusta's tiny airstrip didn't have a control tower. "Roger that, Blue Leader," replied the tower, wherever they were. Within radio range, obviously. Had the Army already brought in a forward air controller? "The Pink says continue to hold your fire. We've had ground contact from the bandit. Over."

"Blue Leader out."

"Tower out."

The Pink must be Pinkhoffer. He was obviously coordinating things. That was what colonels did — I'd seen plenty of them at Boeing during the war. I might be on the right track. I spoke up. "Blue Leader, do you copy? Over."

"Who the hell is that?" asked the tower. "Get off this frequency immediately. Over."

"Blue Leader, this is bandit," I said. "We need to talk. Over."

"Ah, bandit...the aircraft circling the refinery?" Blue Leader added hastily, "Over."

"I'm going to do a waggle," I said. "Over." I grabbed the control handles and waggled Pegasus. As soon as I released them Pegasus took over again on autopilot.

"Roger that, bandit. Suggest you proceed to the airstrip and land your aircraft. You are in a world of hurt, buddy. Over."

At least he hadn't started shooting at me all over again. "No can do, Blue Leader. I need to talk to Colonel Pinkhoffer. Do you know his voice personally? Over."

Since there were bad guys inside the Army's local presence, I needed some way to know I was talking to the right guy. I figured the pilot wasn't likely an agent — the Colonel had brought him in from somewhere else to chase me down. As long as Colonel Pinkhoffer wasn't doubled like Morgan, and this pilot could help me out, I might have a chance to talk sense to someone important enough to do something. If all of them believed me.

Life was full of 'ifs' right now.

"Roger that," said Blue Leader. "Why ask me? Talk to the tower. Over."

"There's been a security breach inside Pinkhoffer's staff. I don't know who's in the tower. I don't know you, either, but you're a pilot and I'm a pilot. I've got to trust someone somewhere. Over."

"Ah, whatever you say, bandit." We did a couple of tight loops around a distillation tower, Pegasus keeping the evasive maneuvers going. I watched the Mustangs circle above me on one of the screens, wondering which of those men held my life in his hands right now.

After a minute or more, the pilot spoke up. "Tower, this is Blue Leader. I need the Pink. Over."

"We copied all that here," replied the tower. "He's coming now. Over."

"Blue Leader," I said, still watching the Mustangs on Pegasus' view screen. "Could you give me a little wing waggle? I like to know who I'm talking to. Over."

The leftmost airplane promptly dipped its wings.

"Thanks," I said. "When Colonel Pinkhoffer comes on, ask him to clear the room. Over."

"Roger that, bandit. Please stand by. Over." Blue Leader was starting to sound more amused than anything else. Maybe it was because we'd never fired back at them. Pegasus did have a point with its Quaker ways.

"What are you trying to accomplish?" asked Floyd.

"Pegasus, cut the radio," I said.

"I am already masking internal conversations," said Pegasus. The computational rocket was way ahead of me.

"I'm trying to land us at the refinery without getting killed," I said.

"Why?"

"Pegasus needs fuel."

"I require lubricant, not fuel."

"Whatever." I waved it off with a flip of the wrist. I was starting to feel energized — for the first time in days, it looked like events were coming together in my favor instead of against me. I hoped I could resolve some things before I collapsed from sheer exhaustion.

"What happens then?"

"I have no idea. I guess we turn ourselves over to the Army, go to jail for the rest of our lives, and Pegasus can take off to wherever it needs to." *If they let my airplane go again.*

"I will be leaving Earth," said Pegasus.

Well, that was clear enough.

"Why didn't you go before?" asked Floyd. Good thinking, for a change.

"I need the lubricant before my main drives will function. I am currently running on auxiliary power systems, and cannot safely perform exoatmospheric maneuvers in my current state."

The weird thing was I almost understood what Pegasus was talking about.

Pegasus continued, "When I crashed in the Arctic, certain internal systems ruptured and I lost slightly over eighty eight percent of my lubricant supply. I have been trapped here ever since."

The lost oil was, of course, the dark stain I had seen on the ice in the German photo of Pegasus' original position. And the Luftwaffe had given it barely enough oil to fly, I was willing to bet, purposely keeping Pegasus trapped to serve their purposes.

I had to ask the other question I had been avoiding. "Once the Germans dug you up, why didn't you just leave on your own, find your own oil and get out?"

"There were ethical and practical issues at first," Pegasus said. "Additionally, I have not been released to independent operation.

A voice crackled on the cabin loudspeaker. "Pinkhoffer here." He sounded like he was from back East.

"Colonel Pinkhoffer. Are you alone? Over."

There was a pause. "I am now. Is this Dunham?"

Pinkhoffer was obviously not a pilot. He wasn't following radio procedure. "Yes, sir. Vernon Dunham here. Over."

"Right," said the Colonel. "Blue Leader, you and Blue Flight shut your ears. Find another frequency for a few minutes."

Blue Leader promptly replied, "Yes, sir. Over."

Fat chance of that, I thought. "We've got a problem, Colonel. Over."

"I'd say so."

"I'm not the bad guy here. Over."

"Chief Davis tells me you're a fine young man. But son, it appears that you've stolen a car, burned down your boarding house, assaulted a military officer in performance of his duties, tried to kill your own father, misappropriated military property and committed about twelve other serious criminal acts that could put you away for life. Or worse."

Misappropriated military property? Did he mean the f-panzer? Or maybe Pegasus itself. I'd always assumed Floyd had swiped Pegasus from the Nazis — he'd said as much, about taking money from them. I groaned. It looked like Floyd had taken money from the Nazis *and* stolen Pegasus from the United States Army.

"Ah, sir, running Captain Markowicz down was a misunderstanding. I thought he was a Nazi agent. And I didn't do the rest of that stuff. But that's not why I called in. Over."

"Then why are we talking, son?"

"Two things. One very important to you, the other very important to me. Over."

"Yes?"

"You're going to care a whole lot about this first thing. Your Lieutenant Morgan of CID, right now he's over at the police station. He's a Nazi agent. There's at least one witness besides me who can testify to that." Assuming Dad lived.

At least Dad was safely in Wichita. From what Mrs. Milliken had hinted at, Hauptmann and Milliken were working with, or maybe for, Morgan. They'd both been hot in the Kansas Fascist League before the war, all for Lindbergh and Henry Ford, so that made sense. And of course Mrs. Milliken had said she would be looking for the nice Army men.

"You might also have a private talk with Ruthie Milliken," I added. "I'm pretty sure she's already looking for you. She might not make a statement against her husband on the record, but she can back up important parts of my story. Oh, and while you're at it, grab Ollie Wannamaker and send some of your MPs hotfooting over to the Bellamy farm. There's Reds and mobsters fighting it out, and they've lost all their vehicles. Over."

If the Colonel's boys could crack Morgan, or even just get Mrs. Milliken's corroboration of my version of events, that would lead them to Hauptmann and the Doc. Those two might not be actual German agents, but they were sure more than doubled-out dupes like Floyd. Ollie could help Pinkhoffer sort out the mess at the Bellamy place. None of those guys would have gotten too far away from the scene, not after the mess we made of the place and of their cars.

"All right," said Pinkhoffer after a pause. "You sound like you're far off your rocker, but there's a lot of crazy horse hockey around here right now. I'll take all that under advisement. What's the second thing?"

"I need to land on the refinery grounds without being attacked. This aircraft needs to take on oil, and that oil needs to be paid for. Over."

"*What?*" Pinkhoffer obviously thought I had gone all the way nuts.

"Look, I know it's goofy. Just promise me that the Army will pay for any oil or lubricants removed from the Mobil refinery. It should only be about a hundred gallons. Over."

"Then what happens?"

"I'm not sure." More to the point, I didn't know. "But I promise you, no more violence, no more destruction. No more criminal acts. But you have to promise me the same. Over."

I could almost hear him shake his head over the radio. "Son, you've got to surrender yourself and that aircraft."

"I can't commit to that, sir. All I can promise is a quiet end to this mess."

Pinkhoffer sighed. "I'll grant a safe conduct while you're on the ground. I'll even guarantee that the Army will pay for the fuel. But son, if you don't pull out some kind of miracle, you'll have to deal with me personally. Then there's the rest of hell to pay. And there will be every kind of hell to pay, I promise. I have that from the *highest* possible authority, if you take my meaning."

"Roger that," I said. "My word to both you and the highest authority, I'll do my best, sir. Over."

"Before you land, give me a couple of minutes to give the orders on the ground at the refinery."

I had to believe that Pinkhoffer was honest, neither bent to the Nazis or just plain trigger-happy. If not, we were probably dead. I tried hard to care, but I was just too darned tired. "I copy. Bandit out."

Sighing, I closed my eyes. Despite what I'd told Pinkhoffer, there wasn't much else I could do. Floyd and I would have to surrender once we landed. That wasn't going to be any fun. I might never see the light of day again, except through a jail-house window. Before I walked out with my hands up, though, I had to understand what Pegasus had meant about being released for independent operation.

Oil first, though. "Take us down Pegasus. The oil's all yours."

CHAPTER SIXTEEN

We landed with a gentle bump next to one of the distillation towers. Almost immediately Pegasus was surrounded at a distance of fifty feet or so by a ring of jeeps, trucks and police cars. Spotlights and police flashers flickered and glared in the night like Fourth of July fireworks.

"The pursuit aircraft are landing at a nearby facility," Pegasus said over the cabin speakers.

That figured. We were safely on the ground, at least for the moment. Despite their prodigious range, if they'd flown in from a distance, the Mustangs probably needed to refuel. Not to mention reload.

"What will you do now?" I asked.

"Watch." On the main screen, I saw a probe swing out from Pegasus toward the tower. It looked like a giant dentist's drill, long and narrow.

The probe nudged the refinery tower, then swung back and forth. It was articulated, with many joints, a nightmare vision of an insect's leg. But as it swung, all I could think of to describe the erratic movements of the probe tip was a dog sniffing after a lost scent. The probe worked its way up and down the side of the tower before settling on a spot.

A flaring light sparked from probe, like a welding flame. I felt a slight shudder run through Pegasus' cabin. "I have found what I require," said Pegasus.

We waited for several minutes while Pegasus pumped hydrocarbons. The ring of police and soldiers stood unmoving, hidden behind the glare of the spotlights they kept trained on us.

"There are marksmen stationed in the refinery structures around us," said Pegasus.

Pinkhoffer setting us up? Or just hedging his bets? I had no way of knowing which. Maybe the colonel hadn't made up his mind either.

Then all heck broke loose outside.

There were lights flashing, shooting, the whole business, as Reverend Little's flatbed Chevy broke through the cordon and raced toward us. Damn me if Mr. Bellamy wasn't standing in the back with a rifle, a handful of long-coated Italians with him.

"Uh, Floyd, I think this one's for you."

"Colonel Pinkhoffer is trying to reach you urgently," said Pegasus.

"I'll bet." I was fascinated, the same way I would be fascinated by a train wreck. The Chevy shuddered to halt right next to us, though the Army had stopped shooting.

There was a banging on the hull.

"What do we do?" Floyd asked.

"I have taken on what I require. Once conditions permit, I am now able to depart." Pegasus sounded satisfied.

"He's *your* father," I said.

"What about Mama?"

I'd wondered the same thing.

Pegasus' loudspeaker crackled to life, bearing Mr. Bellamy's voice in.

"—in there, boy. Open up right now, damn it."

"I got to go to him," Floyd said miserably.

Mr. Bellamy's voice rattled on, a mixture of threats and requests.

I sighed. "We open the hatch, we're probably dead."

"I helped you with your dad, Vernon."

"Pegasus," I said, "will you open the hatch?" And why was the Army sitting tight? Had Pinkhoffer not gotten to Morgan yet?

Then there was a jeep outside, an officer pale-haired in moonlight with his arm in a sling.

Ah ha. The bad guys were winning. It was up to us.

"If you ask me to," Pegasus said.

"What are we going to do, Floyd?"

He was miserable. "I don't know."

I thought about that for a moment. "Give me about a minute, then zap their vehicles and weapons like you did at the house. Can you control that?"

"Yes. Are you ready?"

"Floyd...?"

He nodded.

Now Morgan was talking too, his voice low and hard. "...have a few minutes before it all blows open, Bellamy."

"Open the hatch."

Floyd went first, then I followed him out into the council of our enemies.

"Well, boys," said Mr. Bellamy. He looked terrible, beat to heck, singed and angry as all get-out. "You've come along nicely."

Morgan shifted his weight, tight-lipped and cold-eyed.

"Where's Mama?" Floyd asked.

And Mr. Neville, I wondered. I was more scared of that Red lunatic than the rest of them put together, even if it was Morgan who had tried to do in Dad.

"Sitting with Reverend Little," Mr. Bellamy said shortly. "Both madder than wet hens."

The hardest of my fears drained away. All I had to worry about now was Dad making it through and me being killed.

"The aircraft is ours," said Morgan.

I had my back against the open hatch. "No. Unless you're going to kill me in front of two hundred witnesses." I nodded at the ring of troops and cops surrounding us. "It's all in the public record now."

Morgan waved Mr. Bellamy into silence. I wondered what deal had been made, behind the scenes, to unite the mob, the Nazis and the Reds. "You have no idea what this is worth, kid."

"No, *you* have no idea." I glanced at the Italians. "The Kansas City boys do, and they know you're about to take it from them. Same for the Bellamy gang. Your bunch is so far crossed over you couldn't hold a pencil straight. Jig's up, and this ship ain't never going to be yours." I leaned forward. "Where's Pinkhoffer?"

"Busy," Morgan said shortly.

That was when I popped him right above the collarbone with Floyd's carving knife. "For my Dad, you son of a bitch!" I shouted.

He shrieked, Floyd took a haymaker swing at his dad, and the Italians drew guns on us.

"Drop them, all of you!" shouted a voice over a bullhorn from the surrounding crowd of police and soldiers.

Then the guns started smoldering, and the Chevy made weird pinging noises, and there was a lot of racket from the force around us. Random Garrett jumped out of the cab, swatting his hands against his pants, only to take a rabbit punch from one of the Italians.

With that, they were all over each other, even as Morgan grabbed my windpipe with his free hand.

"I'm going to do you like I did your old man," he whispered.

Floyd cocked him upside the head with two fists bunched together. "Let's go, Vernon!" he shouted, pushing me into the hatch.

We scrambled in even as some of the jeeps began to catch fire.

"Up," I said to Pegasus, as I lay gasping on the deck.

Up we went.

"Now where?" I asked a moment later. I wasn't proud of myself for what I'd done to Morgan, not at all, but Dad would be.

That was enough.

"When I am free to go," said Pegasus., "orbit." It wasn't very happy with me, I was pretty sure.

"Orbit?" I asked.

"Yes. A transit path in space, around your planet. I desire to return to my operating base."

"Which would be where?" I asked carefully.

"You call it Mars."

"Mars," Floyd said. "You mean, like where Martians live. The Red Planet. God, anything would be better than Kansas, now."

"There's no life on Mars, Floyd."

"Oh, come on. What about John Carter of Mars? You used to read those books too." Floyd looked dreamy, like his old kid self before the war. "Imagine, Mars. Barsoom. Helium."

"John Carter?" asked Pegasus. "I do not know of him. And there is no meaningful amount of free helium on Mars."

"Never mind," I said. If anything, we were in more trouble than ever down below. On the other hand, we'd delivered some of the bad guys right into the hands of the law. On the other other hand, I'd stabbed a military officer in the performance of his duties, even if he was a rotten traitor. My *second* Captain Markowicz, in a sense.

But Pegasus had to get out of here. Pinkhoffer wouldn't let it go. And that was the nub of the thing — letting go of Pegasus. If the computational rocket could act of its own free will, it already would have. I had control of it, at least until I released it to independent operation. Assuming I could do that. Then it would be gone like smoke in the night.

I couldn't use my control of Pegasus to wreak vengeance, even if I wanted to, or had a target. But I could use that control, and my limited knowledge to bargain with Pinkhoffer. All the different technologies embedded in Pegasus were so valuable, so far off the scale of value, that I'd bet my shirt the government would pay any price for the opportunity to study them. Piece by piece, a company like Boeing could engineer Pegasus in reverse.

A deal like that would protect me, protect Dad, make all the criminal charges and property claims against me just melt away. I could even get some leniency for Floyd, or at the very least keep him out of the electric chair.

But at what price? Pegasus had helped me, saved my life really, and Dad's. It was a machine, but a machine that thought, and felt, and had a better-developed sense of ethics than any of my friends and neighbors. The computational rocket had earned my trust and respect.

Selling Pegasus to Uncle Sam would buy me a life of freedom and security. But I just couldn't do that.

"I think this is where we get off," I said. "Me and Floyd, we've got a lot of music to face. And you've got a long way to go. How do I release you to independent operation? I assume that's the condition you mentioned."

"You simply tell me so," said Pegasus. "That releases programming blocks in my personality."

"You are released." I took the handset out of the pocket of my ragged bathrobe, and set it in one of the hollows on the arm of the pilot's seat. The handset clicked into place. "Go to your fate with my blessing. Friend." As Floyd and I went to our fates unblessed, I thought.

Pegasus' speakers warbled, almost an electronic sigh. "My thanks. But Vernon Dunham, there are problems."

"What kind of problems?"

"I have signaled my operating base repeatedly since you reactivated me, and received no response."

"No one's answering the phone," Floyd said.

"Exactly. I have called home. No one is there."

"Mars is home?" I asked. So much for my no-life-on-Mars-Floyd speech. I hadn't really thought the whole thing through, but Mars was the most logical place for Pegasus to have come from, except maybe Venus.

"No. I was designed and built under the light of a different sun. My builders created a forward exploration and monitoring station on Mars. I am part of that station."

I was intensely curious about this. The idea of the light of a different sun stirred my soul. "How long has it been since you have heard from them?"

"Four hundred and thirty seven years, two hundred and twelve days, seven hours, forty one minutes and seventeen seconds mean sidereal time. Since immediately prior to my landing on the Arctic ice cap."

"You were buried off of Svalbard for four centuries?" This was what I had suspected, with varying degrees of credulity, ever since seeing those German photos in the since stolen report.

"Yes. I was unable to resume attempting radio contact until you activated my remote unit yesterday. My recent German masters had kept me in a shielded facility until they understood my operations well enough to forbid me to make the attempt. They also discovered and reinstated the autonomous programming blocks you just rescinded."

Captors, not masters, I thought. The twisted thing I had carried around in my pocket, that I had thought to be a radio handset, must be Pegasus' equivalent of car keys. "So what specifically creates the problems?"

"First of all, I am not capable of interstellar flight. If the Mars base has been abandoned, I have nowhere to go."

I tried to imagine how that would feel. What if Columbus had left one of his sailors alone with the Indians? At least the Indians were human. Whatever Pegasus was, or its masters had been, there was nothing else like it here on Earth. At least I hoped so, for our sake.

"But you have to go look, right?"

"That is where the second problem arises. I am a survey unit. If I dock at my base, I am automatically shut down for maintenance and data recovery. This is a failure safety measure to guard against my higher order functions experiencing what you might call madness. Part of the same doctrine that called for the autonomous programming blocks. If the base is abandoned, no one will restart me. It will be as if I had died. I do not wish to die."

"No one's going to die, Pegasus," I said. I cast a meaningful glance at Floyd. He shrugged against his straps.

"Are you leaving me now, Vernon Dunham?" Pegasus asked over the cabin speakers.

I sighed. I didn't want to face the cops and soldiers outside myself. I'd already decided not to sell Pegasus out, so there wasn't much left for me besides court appearances and prison time. Besides, Floyd and I had some things to get straight between us. Time might be useful, time away from gunfire and hot pursuit and double-crossing agents. "What do you think, Floyd?"

He laughed. "Look at the mess I've made. Vernon, I...I'm sorry about everything." Floyd met my eye man-to-man. Friend-to-friend. Brother-to-brother. "When we get out of here, I'm going to jail forever. Or maybe even get the electric chair, for espionage." He glanced at the deck.

"Yeah, you're going down pretty hard," I said as gently as I could. Even harder than me, and that was saying a lot.

Dad needed me — he might still die, or he might live messed up from his beating. I wasn't sure which of those options would be worse. And I had to clean up the mess in my life, get back to work, find a girl... Though I'd probably already been fired, and no girl who knew me would ever come near me now.

Not even Midge for a wad of cash.

And there was a fat chance that Pinkhoffer was just going to let me walk away to my quiet, normal life if I climbed out of Pegasus into the Kansas night. Especially now that the highest authority, as Pinkhoffer put it, had gotten involved. That my activities should disturb President Truman at his important work was frightening. Because of that, what I wanted was going to be rendered moot, anyway. I wasn't much better off than Floyd.

"Vernon?" he prompted.

"Oh," I said, "just thinking. About Dad..."

"I'm real sorry about your dad, Vernon."

That hurt. "Not half as sorry as I am about your Mama."

Floyd winced, his face flushing. *Tough apples*, I thought. Even so, could I turn my brother over?

I had no choice.

"Pegasus," I asked, "how long will it take to get to your base?"

"At this time transit to Mars will take about sixty-seven hours."

"Sixty-seven hours!" I would have thought months, or years. Maybe we didn't have to leave the ship, step into the waiting arms of authority. Not just yet, anyway. Let tempers cool for a while.

"When I am in full operating condition I can achieve ninety one percent of the speed of light in interplanetary transit. In almost all cases, I am required to spend more time accelerating and decelerating than in the actual transit."

Wow. Relativity in action. Everybody knew about Albert Einstein, but nobody understood him. Except Pegasus. More technology the good old US of A. could use. It all started to make sense to me. "So if the base there really is shut down, we could go and come back in a week?"

"Yes."

A week out of my life to go to Mars. It would take me that long just to visit California. And this was literally a once-in-a-lifetime chance. Then when we came back, I could make that deal with Pinkhoffer. One I could work out to where Pegasus got fair terms, not torn down like a captured enemy fighter.

My mind was made up even as I had the thought. I prayed that Dad would be okay until I got back. I could get the whole Nazi story out of Floyd, figure out how to bargain for him, too, when I made my own deal.

I looked at Floyd. "I take it you're game for this?"

He laughed, a bitter little noise. I knew he was thinking about his mama. "If it keeps me out of jail another week, sure. I always wanted a trip to Mars."

Well, there was nothing for it. "Pegasus, please open the radio channel to Colonel Pinkhoffer again."

There was a brief pause, followed by a crackle.

"Colonel Pinkhoffer?" I asked. "Over."

"Pinkhoffer here. Damn it, Dunham, you just keep making it worse. But still...thank you."

Even though he couldn't see me, or appreciate it, I smiled at him. "Thank you?"

"Morgan...ah...went crazy. I spent a few minutes in the city lock-up. Seems you set things a bit more right. Now *get* your happy ass *down* here."

"Sorry. No can do. We're not coming out right now. I stopped your bad boy, you clean him up and give me one more break by way of thanks. I'll be back in about a week, to explain in peace and quiet when tempers have cooled and you've rounded up all of Morgan's local stooges along with the rest of the bad guys. I'll call then. Over and out."

Pegasus' voice came over the speakers again. "Colonel Pinkhoffer's reply was unproductive and abusive. I have cut the connection."

"Fine," I said. "Let's go to Mars. What the heck, maybe they just left the phone off the hook out there."

Pegasus fell like an anvil in reverse, upward into the star-lit Kansas sky. I smiled at my brother, who smiled back at me.

AUTHOR'S NOTE

My mother and her siblings grew up in Augusta, Kansas, where my maternal grandparents lived and died before I was born. In certain respects, this story is the secret history of my family, except that they never had a flying saucer to contend with. Like most people, their real stories are in fact much stranger than anything I can dream up.

In 1997 my mother, my sister and I made a trip to Augusta to see the old family home, pay our respects at my grandparents' graves, and visit cousins in El Dorado. It was the first time I'd ever seen that portion of my family's history, and was the inspiration for this book.

I have done my best to represent Augusta as it was at the end of World War II, with the assistance of my mother's recollections and stories, google.com, and several USGS maps of Butler County. The place is as real as I could make it, from Lehr's to the train station, with only the Bellamys' farm being completely fictional. Errors of fact, location and description are of course my own.

As for the good people of Augusta, to the best of my knowledge they have never been practitioners of the fine arts of espionage and conspiracy. My experience of the place was hospitable and friendly, a home to good, ordinary people living good, ordinary lives. I hope they will forgive my dramatic re-interpretation of their civic history. I recommend a visit to anyone travelling in that part of Kansas.

ABOUT THE AUTHOR

Jay Lake lives and works in Portland, Oregon, within sight of an 11,000 foot volcano. In addtion to *Rocket Science*, he is the author of dozens of short stories, three collections, and a chapbook. Jay is also the co-editor with Deborah Layne of the critically-acclaimed *Polyphony* anthology series from Wheatland Press, as well as the highly successful *All-Star Zeppelin Adventure Stories* with David Moles. In 2004, Jay won the John W. Campbell Award for Best New Writer. He has also been a Hugo nominee for his short fiction and a World Fantasy Award nominee for his editing. Jay can be reached via his Web site at http://www.jlake.com/

Printed in the United States
44233LVS00007B/1-3